BOUND BY A PROMISE

Garet Cambridge was the most compelling man Kathryn Summers had ever met. Tall, dark, commanding...and now blinded by a twist of fate. Kathryn knew that if he discovered the truth behind the accident that took his sight, she'd lose him forever. But she was bound by a promise...and bound by love.

PASSION FLOWER

A working vacation at a Texas ranch was just what successful interior designer Jennifer King needed—until she met the brooding, dark-eyed owner of the Circle C! Everett Culhane thought they were worlds apart, but when he branded her lips with his, Jennifer knew she'd have to make this headstrong cowboy her own!

Dear Reader:

Back by popular demand! Diana Palmer has long been a favorite of Silhouette readers, and it is with great pleasure that we bring back these impossible-to-find classics.

After the Music, *Dream's End*, *Bound by a Promise*, *Passion Flower*, *To Have and to Hold* and *The Cowboy and the Lady* are some of the first books Diana Palmer ever wrote, and we've been inundated by your many requests for these stories. All of us at Silhouette Books are thrilled to put together books four, five and six of Diana Palmer Duets—each volume holds two full novels.

Earlier this year we published the first three volumes of Diana Palmer Duets, containing *Sweet Enemy*, *Love on Trial*, *Storm Over the Lake*, *To Love and Cherish*, *If Winter Comes* and *Now and Forever*, to universal acclaim and sell-out crowds. Don't miss this chance of a lifetime to add to your collection.

The twelve novels contained in the six "Duets" show all the humor, intensity, emotion and special innocence that have made Diana Palmer such a beloved name at Silhouette Books. I'd like to say to Diana's present, past and future fans—sit back, relax and enjoy!

Best wishes,

Isabel Swift
Editorial Manager

DIANA PALMER DUETS

BOOK FIVE

BOUND BY A PROMISE
PASSION FLOWER

Silhouette Books®

Published by Silhouette Books New York

America's Publisher of Contemporary Romance

SILHOUETTE BOOKS
300 E. 42nd St., New York, N.Y. 10017

Silhouette Books edition published August 1990.

DIANA PALMER DUETS
© 1990 HARLEQUIN ENTERPRISES LIMITED

BOUND BY A PROMISE © 1979 Diana Palmer
First published as a MacFadden Romance by Kim Publishing
Corporation.

PASSION FLOWER © 1984 Diana Palmer
First published as a Silhouette Romance.

ISBN: 0-373-48226-4

Contents

A Note from Diana Palmer

Dear Readers:

This fifth book of Diana Palmer Duets features one of my favorite early stories and also the book that I consider to be one of my best Silhouette Romances.

Bound by a Promise was written in 1979. I had wanted to use a blind hero for a long time, but I couldn't find a reason for his blindness that would contribute to the plot. Then I thought, what if the heroine blinds him accidentally? And what if she's someone he didn't *like* when he could see? What happens if he regains his sight before he finds out that his old enemy has become his best friend?

With those three questions, I built a book. Garet Cambridge was a former pilot, and that profession came out of my father's love for airplanes. Dad had a private pilot's license and owned a Cessna. He and my mother were fanatics on the subject of flying. When they weren't up in an airplane, they were listening to air traffic news on short-wave radio. Both my parents were daredevils, reckless free spirits with very few fears. Neither of them was afraid of dying in a crash—they left those worries to my sister and me. But we knew that if the worst ever happened, it would be the way they wanted to go and we accepted that side of their natures without question. We felt it was their right to live as they pleased.

I remember 1979 well. It was the year my mother got to go aboard the Goodyear Blimp. She was still doing feature articles at the time, and she got a good story out of her ride. About the same time, my Dad totalled a moped and landed in the hospital. My own life was much tamer. I was strapped in a home-built airplane with a jet harness and flew over Toccoa Falls with a pilot I was interviewing. That was before I got involved in the famous Near-Fatal-Chattahoochee-River Inner-Tube Race.

Garet Cambridge's daredevil personality just seemed to come naturally to me; he was a hero I could understand. Kathryn Summers wasn't a reporter, but she did run across a journalist during her stay in St. Martin, where she was working for Mr. Cambridge. I had a field day in Kathryn's mind, trying to picture how it would be for her as she juggled her guilt with her growing love for the boss she'd accidentally blinded. By the time he regained his sight and hurt her unwittingly, I was in tears at my typewriter. It was a very satisfying book to write, although it's very different from the books I write these days.

The lake where Kathryn meets Garet is Georgia's Lake Lanier. I guess I've put this lake in any number of books. I love it, and I keep bringing it back for return engagements. I've spent many a lazy summer day fishing on it, or just sitting on the shore and watching sailboats skipping around its vast expanse. Some of my best and happiest memories revolve around it.

When I was in my early teens, I used to get invited to spend weekends in a cabin on that lake with my best friends Nancy and Brenda Lou and their parents. They were from Kentucky, and we were more like sisters than friends. Pa taught us to track deer and hunt and fish, and Ma taught us how to cook. We got each other through some pretty hard times. We are still friends thirty years later. How time flies!

While I was writing about Kathryn and Garet, I

was thinking back to happy times and my own youth.

The other book in this "Duet" is *Passion Flower*. This book was a real challenge. My first attempt got tossed out. Jenny started out as a rather pathetic figure, and neither my editor nor I liked her that way. So I redid her, and the finished product was a much more self-confident, independent Jenny.

Everett, though, didn't change. He was a hard-headed renegade from the beginning. I liked him. He sort of flowered from a really spiny cactus plant, and he seemed to suit the rugged Texas terrain where he thrived.

In this book, I wanted to show a love of the land, of conservation and responsible management. I also wanted to emphasize traditional values and the changes that inevitably come with progress.

Everett was a die-hard reactionary. He wanted the land left as it was. He looked down his nose at people who sold it for easy money, and he wouldn't accept the fact that there was another viewpoint besides his own. Jenny, on the other hand, was a woman who had a marketable talent and was willing to push it to the limit. Despite her old-fashioned ideals, she was a woman of the future who could see progress working side-by-side with conservation.

Until she came along, Everett had fixed ideas about a woman's place in the world. Events in the storyline forced him to review his own attitude and modify it, to compromise in order to get what he really wanted—and in the end, that was Jenny. The main idea I wanted to communicate is that you have to take people as they are. You can't change them to suit your concept of what they should be. Everett couldn't change Jenny, but he was finally willing to accept her despite his misgivings.

I was very pleased with the way the book turned out, especially since I basically did two entirely different novels with the same characters before I turned out a finished product. The fact that I had that time to review every facet of their personalities in depth made it one of my favorites. It was also very hard to let go when I finished. Characters tend to become part of your life. When you have to turn them loose, it can be very difficult.

That old pickup truck Everett drove was taken from life. When James and I got married, I inherited my grandfather's 1956 red pickup truck. It had a brake line that failed every other week religiously, and it was harder to steer than a stampeding bull. James didn't drive at all back in those days, so the truck was my headache. Until I married, my father looked after all the vehicles in our family. Before he became an educator, he had worked a brief stint as a mechanic, and he could do anything with an engine. But when I left home, all of a sudden I found myself with a husband who was as knowledgable as I was about how vehicles worked.

As a consequence of not realizing that oil has to be replaced periodically, that battery connections corrode, that tires should be rotated and regularly inspected, I had a lot of misfortune with vehicles. I can't tell you how many nice people stopped to help us when we broke down. I have had every single part of a car go bad at one time or another, so as a result, I was determined to learn more about mechanics.

Back in those lean years, I got to the point where I could just listen to an engine and tell if it had a bad speedometer cable, a transmission that was failing or a stuck valve, and I always knew where to find the best mechanics and the lowest prices. I learned how much each part cost and how long it would last. I learned how to check oil and other fluids, and how to pump gas at self-service stations and check air pressure in tires.

About the time I got really good at those things, I started selling books, which meant that I could finally afford a car with less than sixty thousand miles on it. My first really super car was a 1973 white Ford Thunderbird. It had power steering, power brakes and bucket seats. It had a long, elegant nose, an automatic transmission and a V-8 engine, and it was the best car we ever owned. I treated it like a baby. I used to stand back and admire it in parking lots because it was so beautiful.

We've been driving Thunderbirds ever since, and we always have one in the driveway. Right now it's a gorgeous black machine with red racing stripes and a 4-cylinder turbo engine. It can go up sheer cliffs and runs like a scalded dog. It is heaven to drive. But I have never forgotten that beautiful white beast with the black landau roof that was the first Thunderbird and the best car we'd ever owned.

In late 1979 I finally got up enough nerve to send a manuscript over to Silhouette Books, and in early 1980 they accepted the first of my novels to be published by them—*September Morning*.

1990 marks my tenth year as a Silhouette author, and I can't begin to tell you what those years have meant to me. Through all the wonderful editors with whom I have been associated, it has been the best ten years of my life.

Thank you, Silhouette Books, for giving me a chance, for standing behind me, for promoting my work and for putting up with me all these years. I hope that I have deserved such kindness and such loyalty. All that I am, I owe to your faith in my talent.

And to my wonderful readers, thank you for giving me your friendship and your loyalty. If the richness of a life is counted in the love that is given, then mine is wealthy beyond measure.

Love,

Diana Palmer

BOUND BY
A PROMISE

1

*

He was standing alone by the shore, a big, solitary figure against the thin mist that blanketed the silvery water in the early morning. Kathryn had seen him there before a number of times since she and Maude had moved into the lake house for the summer. But keeping up with the famous author's blazing deadlines had only allowed for a few brief outings on the lake for Kate, one of which the man standing there had shattered with his arrogance.

Kathryn Summers was curious about Garet Cambridge, even while she resented everything he stood for. His aircraft corporation was one of the biggest in the country, and his genius for designing new planes had earned him an international reputation. But all it meant to Kathryn was that he could buy people.

She knew too much about prices already, having just been thrown over by the man she loved when he found out that her social pedigree didn't meet his family's exacting standards. The daughter of a small Texas cattle rancher whose parents were divorced was hardly a likely candidate for the social register. In fact, it was only this job, working for the notorious Maude Niccole, that made it possible for her to keep her father's ranch from being put on the auction block. His health was steadily failing, and so were the ranch's profits.

She glared at Cambridge unconsciously from her perch on a log beside the spreading waters of Lake Lanier. She'd come here for the peace and quiet, and she wished he'd decided to spend his summer in Europe or Miami instead of here. Perhaps he thought the reporters who trailed him might not think of looking for him on a North Georgia lake.

And apparently they hadn't, because he was alone; a ghostly figure in brown slacks and a cream open-necked sports shirt, his dark hair lifting in the breeze.

As if he felt the intensity of emotion in the glare of her pale brown eyes, he turned suddenly and saw her sitting there, with her silver blonde hair flowing down like silk around her thin shoulders.

He moved forward with his hands in his pockets until he was standing over her, towering over her, and his leaf green eyes glittered down at her out of a face as dark as an Indian's.

"You're trespassing," he said gruffly, not even bothering with polite conversation.

She cocked her head up at him. "Excuse me, I wasn't aware that you owned the shoreline as well as the lake," she said bitterly, referring to an earlier incident between them, when he'd practically ordered her off the lake.

One dark eyebrow went up at the sarcasm. "I own 50 acres of shoreline," he said quietly. "What you're sitting on is part of it. I came here for privacy, not to be hounded by curiosity seekers."

She'd have given anything at that moment to have had wealth enough, power enough, to tell him where to go. But she had nothing, and he could force her to go easily enough. She got up from the stump without another word, brushing off her blue denim jeans. With a sigh of resignation, she started back toward Maude's luxurious beach house.

"Who are you?" he growled after her.

"Amelia Earhardt," she replied carelessly. "Do keep your eyes peeled for my plane, I seem to have misplaced it," she added, and kept right on walking.

Behind her, she imagined she heard the deep sound of a man's laughter.

Maude was waiting for her in the sprawling living room, her bags packed, her thin face nervous.

"Thank goodness, you're back!" the novelist sighed. "I thought you'd never come home! Kate, I've just gotten a telegram. My father's in the hospital, and I've got to fly to Paris immediately.''

"I'm sorry," Kate said with genuine concern.

"So am I," Maude said sadly. "I'm very fond of the old scalawag, even if he did disown me when I announced that I'd decided to become a romance writer. Honey, will you be okay here until I get back? I don't have any idea how long it's going to take.''

Kate nodded and smiled, hating that drawn, hurt look on her employer's face, the sadness in Maude's pale blue eyes framed by salt and pepper curly hair. "I'll finish typing the manuscript while you're gone.''

Maude nodded, looking around to see if she'd forgotten anything. "Don't overlook that page of changes I wrote last night—I think it's in the top desk drawer. And, for goodness sake, keep your door locked at night!''

"I will. Don't worry about me.''

"I can't help it," Maude said with a quick smile. "You're so reckless lately, Kate. Is it the job? Do you want out?''

"No, it's not that," came the quick reply. "I...oh, I don't know, maybe it's the weather. It's so hot.''

"The weather, or memories?" the older woman probed. "Jesse Drewe was a triple-A heel, my love, you deserve better.''

Kate shifted from one foot to the other restlessly. "I'd have liked to be turned down for myself," she said softly, "not for my lack of money and social standing. It hurt.''

"I know, but we don't always love to order," Maude said, "and more's the pity. You'll get over it. I know you don't think so now, but you will.''

"Of course," Kate said, even though she didn't believe it. "Have a safe trip, and let me know you got there all right.''

"I'll send you a cable, I promise," Maude replied. "Where were you, anyway?" she asked idly as she picked up one suitcase, leaving the other for Kate to bring as she went out the door and headed for the rented car.

"On the beach," she replied. "At least I was until Mr. Cambridge Aircraft Corporation ordered me off his lake.''

"Garet again?" Maude sighed. "Oh, Kate, why can't you be kind to that man? You've already had one run-in with him over the way you were speeding in the boat...."

"He doesn't own the lake," Kate said stubbornly, remembering too well the cold voice telling her if she didn't stop 'driving over the lake like a maniac' he'd have the lake patrol after her. She'd told him where to go, recognizing him immediately from photos she'd seen in news magazines, and zoomed off in Maude's little light cruiser. Since that day, she'd seen him often walking alone on the beach, but he'd never spoken to her again, and she'd never allowed him close enough to make it possible.

"He owns enough of the lake," Maude replied. She took Kate by the shoulders, smiling at her sullen look. "Don't match wits with him. He can hurt you. Don't try to make him pay for Jesse's behavior. Jesse was only a boy. Garet..." she paused, searching for the words, "Garet's a law unto himself. He makes up his own rules as he goes along. Be careful you don't break any of them. He makes an utterly ruthless enemy."

"How do you know?" Kate asked.

"I was a reporter before I got smart and started writing books," Maude explained. "I did a story about Garet and misquoted one of his top advisers. He had me fired, and every time I tried to apply for another position, I seemed to be wrong for the job. Finally, in desperation, I sent Garet a lengthy, tearful apology, and the next thing I knew, editors were calling me in for interviews." She smiled. "It was a rough way to learn the necessity for accuracy. I never forgot the lesson."

Kate felt chills run up and down her spine despite the heat. "He sounds like a bulldozer."

"He is," Maude agreed. "It takes a ruthless man to build an empire, and to hold it."

"I pity his wife."

"He doesn't have one."

"I'm not surprised!"

"He has women instead," Maude grinned. "His own personal harem, and they drip jewels and mink."

"Money can buy everything, it seems," Kate grumbled, feeling the hurt all over again.

"Not everything, baby. Not love." Maude got into the rented car and closed the door. "I don't know when I'll get to come home. When you finish the manuscript, mail it to Benny and start working on the next one I've drafted on tape. Okay?"

"Okay." Kate squeezed the thin hand through the open window. "Thank you," she added.

"For what?"

"For hiring me. For caring about me. For putting up with me," Kate said, her eyes like burnished gold in her oval face.

Maude smiled. "Who puts up with whom?" she corrected. "Little one, I'm quite fond of you. If I'd had the good sense to marry in my youth, I'd have a daughter your age. Lonely people seem to find each other."

"I'm not lonely," Kate told her, with a smile. "Not now."

"Yes, you are," the older woman replied kindly, searching the pale brown eyes. "Lonely and hurting. But we have to weather the storms before we can enjoy the sunshine. Don't dwell on the past, and the sun will come out a lot faster."

"Take care," Kate said softly.

Maude only laughed. "I'm indestructible, didn't you know?" she teased.

"I hope it goes well."

"He's seventy-eight," Maude reminded her. "He's lived a long life, and a full one. I won't pretend that I can give him up without tears. But I'll cross that bridge when I have to. Meanwhile, I've got to get there. Remember what I said, and don't speed in the boat," she added, emphasizing each word.

"Killjoy," Kate grinned. "Okay, I'll hunt bears."

Maude lifted her eyes heavenward. "They say that God looks after fools and children. I do hope it's true. Bye, honey."

She was off in a cloud of dust, and Kate watched until the car was a speck in the distance.

The big log beach house was empty without Maude's sparkling personality. Kate mooned around drinking coffee and staring out at the tree-edged lake as it shimmered in the sunlight like silver, rippling cloth.

Maude was right, she did have to let go of the past. But how could she, when every time she closed her eyes she saw Jesse's long, smiling face, the blue eyes that laughed and loved her.

She'd met Jesse in Austin, where she and her father had gone to a cattle sale, and they were fast friends before the day was over. Jesse had a sophistication she'd never been exposed to in the rural area where she lived, a charm that knocked her legs out from under her. By the time he took her back to her hotel, her heart was in bars. And judging by the way he kissed her goodnight, it seemed as if the feeling might be mutual.

The sale had lasted three days, and Kate the rancher's daughter and Jesse the meatpacker's son were inseparable. In between meals, they acted like tourists, seeing every interesting spot in the city and outside it, learning how much they had in common, clinging to each other with a desperation that was like an omen of things to come.

On the third day, he asked her to marry him, and she said yes. She was that sure, even after such a short space of time. What she hadn't counted on was the new social set it would throw her into.

Jesse wanted to take her home with him, to introduce her to his family. Kate was reluctant, but she saw the inevitability of it. And her father let her go readily enough, even though the trip to Chicago would wipe out her savings. He had wished her happiness with twinkling brown eyes.

They'd no sooner arrived at Jesse's family's estate outside Chicago when Kate began to open her eyes to reality. The house was old, and elegant, and dripping in crystal chandeliers, and Victorian wing chairs which weren't reproductions. As if the trappings weren't enough to bring the situation home to her, Jesse's mother came down the stairs in an original Oleg Cassini gown, perfectly coiffed, and reeking of expensive perfume. To say she wasn't impressed with Kate was an understatement. She took the young girl's hand as if she were picking up a dead mouse, dropping it as quickly as possible and calling her husband downstairs with a voice that positively quavered with horror.

Kate was uncomfortable to the point of tears, even with Jesse's half-hearted reassurances. But at the dinner table when his father pinned her down about the actual size of her father's cattle ranch and she told them 100 acres, Jesse looked as if he might faint. That was when she understood the mistaken impression he'd had of the ranch. He'd thought she was one of "his kind" of people, and had suddenly found to his astonishment that she was almost penniless.

The next day, Jesse's mother called Kate into the study, and, with a frozen smile, explained that Jesse had been called away on urgent business. She hoped Kate hadn't taken Jesse seriously, the boy was so young, and a little flighty, and so easily taken in by a pretty face. Kate would get over it, and, anyway, hadn't she enjoyed seeing how the other half lived and having her breakfast served in bed?

Wounded, hurting, dying inside, Kate managed to say the right thing, pack her bag, and with her savings, afford a bus ticket home to Texas. The money she'd had to spend getting home would have gone to help pay off the heavy mortgage on her father's ranch. Only Maude's advertisement in the Austin paper had saved them from foreclosure. That was several months ago, but the wounds were still open and every thought of the Drewe family, or great wealth, rubbed more salt in them.

Rich people could get away with murder. They owned the world and all the little people in it, and they could do as they liked with their victims. Kate only wished she had that kind of power; enough to make the Drewes squirm as they'd made her squirm, enough to teach them an unforgettable lesson in humiliation.

It ached, the memory ached inside her, and she couldn'
stand the confines of the cabin another instant. Despit
Maude's warning, she went straight to the small cabi
cruiser and cranked it. Gently, she eased it away from th
pier and out of the cove, speeding up as she hit the wid
open waters of the lake. There were a few other boats out
but not many this early in the morning. Kate had most o
the wide blue expanse to herself, and she opened up th
throttle, feeling the boat smash through the waves, feelin
the spray in her face, vibrantly biting, taking away the pain
easing the hurt. She drew in a deep breath of the cool, swee
air with its faint fragrance of honeysuckle. A smile touche
her flushed face, the wildness of speed made her eyes spar
kle darkly behind her closed eyelids. What bliss, to let th
spray and the wind cut away the memories!

She opened her eyes again and felt her heart stop. Sh
grabbed feverishly for the throttle as she saw the dark spo
in her path, growing with incredible speed in size, into
recognizable shape.

"Mr. Cambridge, look out!" she screamed, her eye
widening with horror as they gaped at the dark wet head an
wide bronzed shoulders looming just ahead.

He half turned in the water, his eyes spotting her at th
wheel. Just before the bow of the cabin cruiser struck, sh
saw him dive under the surface.

She fought to get the boat under control, her panic send
ing it around in circles before she finally got it stopped an
let it drift aimlessly while she hung over the side with he
heart machine-gunning in her chest, searching the chopp
waters in quiet desperation. Had she killed him?!

2

*

It was the longest ten seconds of her life until Garet Cambridge's dark head appeared above the surface of the water, with blood pouring from a deep gash at the back of his head. He was near the pier that led to his massive cabin and, as she watched, stricken, he felt for the floating pontoons that held the pier up and heaved himself unsteadily onto the weathered gray boards, breathing heavily.

She breathed a sigh of relief. Thank God he was all right! She started the boat and circled it around going slowly now, not rushing, trembling with guilt and fear and relief. She glanced back to see Cambridge sitting up on the pier, sucking in deep breaths.

Almost a tragedy, but not quite. Almost a tragedy, because of her recklessness, because she wanted to use speed to relieve her pain and, in doing so, had almost cost a man his life. The fact that she didn't like Cambridge was no reason to run him down; but she hadn't done it on purpose, she hadn't! What would he do, she wondered. Would he press charges? Would he have her arrested? Did she only imagine that she saw recognition in those dark green eyes just before she plowed over him?

She floated the cruiser and silently watched Cambridge as he raised his husky frame and staggered down the pier to his cabin. She was crying so hard she could hardly think straight, and the words that she wanted to call out to him stuck fast in her throat. Her first impulse was to dock her boat in Cambridge's pier and follow him up to his cabin. But then as she floated nearer, she saw several people meeting Cambridge at the door. Their sounds of surprise and concern drifted across the lake as they crowded around him and ushered him within. Then the door closed and she could only assume that in the excitement, no one had noticed her boat, just a short distance from the dock.

The thought of facing the injured Cambridge was bad enough, but she simply wasn't able to summon the courage it would take to face both him and his crowd of friends. At least she was sure now that he would be well taken care of. She floated the cruiser beside the pier and into the boat house, locking it up. Then she went into the cabin and threw herself down on the couch. She held her face in her hands and allowed her tears to run freely. If only Maude were here, she thought....

When the tears finally passed, she sat up and dried her eyes and tried to decide what to do. Should she call Cambridge and ask how he was and try to explain, to apologize? Should she report the accident to the lake patrol? Should she call a doctor? What if he'd been hurt worse than she thought? It was a hard knock, and a lot of blood...what if he died? She felt panic like a sick lump lodge deep in her throat. If he died, she'd be guilty of murder!

But if she gave herself in, and he wasn't badly hurt at all? What if he hadn't known it was she who hurt him, wouldn't he prosecute her without hesitation, knowing how reckless she'd already been with the boat? And if she was in jail, there'd be no way to help her father out of debt!

Her mind flashed with activity. No one witnessed the accident. She wasn't known on the lake, only Cambridge had even seen her enough to recognize her. Of course, he'd have recognized the boat, possibly, even if he hadn't identified Kate. But the boat was nothing special, and he didn't know Kate's name, after all.

She licked her lips nervously. Still, what if he was badly hurt?

She lifted the phone and waited for the dial tone. By a stroke of luck she didn't expect, Cambridge's number was listed. She dialed the number. She had to know, even it if meant going to prison. She had to make sure he was going to be all right.

A soft, feminine voice answered the phone. "Hello?"

Kate swallowed, and tried to disguise her voice, to deepen it. "Is Mr. Cambridge in?" she asked in what she hoped was a calm, businesslike tone.

"No, he's been taken to the hospital," came the easy reply. "An accident. We think he must have fallen and hit his head on something. He was bleeding pretty badly, but he was cursing pretty badly, too, so Bob and I think he'll be okay. Is this Pattie?"

With closed eyes and a shuddering sigh, Kate hung up. He was alive. He was all right. She hadn't killed him, thank God. But there in the back of her mind, she remembered what Maude had said about the industrial magnate—that he made a ruthless enemy, and he always got even. Would he, somehow, make her pay for what she'd done? Did he know that it was her fault, would he hunt for her?

She didn't go outside again. There were plenty of groceries in the pantry and she could last indefinitely if she had to. She was terrified that if she went on the beach, he might be there, he might recognize her. Even hidden like this, she dreaded the day when a knock on the door would come, or the phone would ring, and she'd be forced to pay for her carelessness. She felt like a condemned criminal. But her own guilt was punishing her more than any court could.

When the phone finally did ring, several days later, she jumped like a thief. She let it ring four times before she summoned enough nerve to lift the receiver.

"H . . . hello?" she whispered.

"Miss Summers? Miss Kathryn Summers?" a woman's voice queried.

"Yes," she managed, her eyes closing with something akin to relief. It was all over now.

"I have a telegram for you from Miss Maude Niccole in Paris," the woman said cheerfully, and Kate's heart stopped, then started beating again. "Father doing well. Stop. Must stay for few weeks. Stop. Close cabin and go home for present. Stop. Will explain in letter. Stop. Love, Maude."

Kate thanked the operator and hung up, feeling lost and alone and afraid. Did she dare go home and expose her father to the possible consequences of her actions? He had a bad heart, and any shock could cost him his life.

What if Garet Cambridge came looking for her and had her prosecuted, could her father bear the shock when he learned what his daughter had done? He'd raised her to care about other people, to be responsible for herself. Was the way she was acting responsible? She sighed. There was only one thing left to do. The thing she should have had the courage to do in the first place. She was going to have to go to Cambridge and tell him the whole story and throw herself on his mercy—if there was any in him. Which she doubted.

Like a lamb heading for the gate to the slaughterhouse, she braved the outside world and strode reluctantly along the beach in her white shorts and top, her eyes downcast as she counted rocks along the shoreline and dreaded the inevitable.

She was so lost in thought that she was almost on top of the big, dark figure before she stopped with a gasp, almost colliding with him in the process.

He turned and she found herself looking straight into Garet Cambridge's dark green eyes, and her heart froze in her chest.

"Excuse me," she managed in a husky whisper, her voice unnaturally tight as she strained for the right words. "I..."

"My fault," he replied with deadly calm. He raised a smoking cigarette to his chiseled mouth and took a long draw. "I can't see you."

She gaped at him incredulously, at the unseeing green eyes, the unblinking gaze of the blind as he stared straight ahead.

"Your...eyes?" she managed. The world was falling in on her.

"An accident," he replied. "They tell me I fell. I'll be damned if I remember anything about it except a blinding pain. Is it dark yet?"

She shook her head dazedly and then, realizing that he couldn't see the gesture, she said, "No, not yet."

He sighed wearily. His dark face was drawn, heavily lined, as if he'd known a great deal of pain in recent days. Kate choked back a sob, the realization of just exactly how much damage she'd done hitting her all at once. She'd blinded him!

"I like this time of day," he said conversationally. "The peace of it. It's a damned far cry from horns and traffic and gaudy music."

She studied him quietly. "Do you . . . do you come from a place like this?" she asked softly, hoping he wouldn't recognize her voice. Although, she thought, he hadn't really heard it enough to recognize it.

A mocking smile curled his lips. "In a sense, I live in the city. You?"

"I grew up on a ranch," she murmured.

"A cowgirl?" he asked.

She laughed. "More of a milkmaid," she admitted, surprised at this very human side of the man she'd hated by reputation, by previous contact.

"Well, milkmaid, what are you doing on the lake?"

Paying for every sin I ever committed, she thought shakily. "I'm having a holiday with a friend," she said.

"Male or female?" he asked with a half smile.

"Female, of course," she told him indignantly.

The smile widened. "There's no 'of course' about it these days," he replied. "Has your life been that sheltered?"

"In a way," she nodded. "Rural people . . . I suppose we aren't very worldly."

"How rural are you?"

"Texas," she grinned involuntarily.

"What part?"

"Near Austin," she said quickly, without thinking, and could have bitten her tongue for it.

"Your family are in cattle, I take it?" he asked carelessly.

"My father," she corrected, "has five hundred cows, most of which he's already had to sell off because of the drought. I'm not well-to-do," she added flatly. "When I was little, it was all Dad could do to keep me in shoes and sweaters."

"Touchy, aren't you?" he asked pleasantly.

"Yes," she admitted, wrapping her arms around her as if she felt a sudden chill. "What do you do for a living?" she asked with practised carelessness.

His dark face clouded, his unseeing eyes narrowed. He took a long draw from his cigarette. "I . . . was a pilot," he said finally.

She gaped at him. He was lying to her, deliberately it seemed, too. Why?

"What kind of planes did you fly?" she probed gently.

He smiled. "Untested ones."

"You were a test pilot?" she asked, and it suddenly came to her that he tested the very planes he designed; a dangerous undertaking for a man with his wealth, and unnecessary.

"That's it." He drew a deep breath. "Needless to say, I won't be doing it any longer. I'm in the market for a new profession."

"Is there…can you do something besides fly?" she asked, studying the tall, brooding figure beside her as she dropped down onto a fallen tree and watched him.

"I thought I might do a book on airplanes," he replied. He laughed softly. "By God, I've had enough experience with them to tell a few tales."

"From test pilot to writer?" she teased softly. "Can you write?"

He turned toward the sound of her voice and looked down his nose in her general direction. "I can do damned near anything that pleases me, Miss," he replied coolly. "You're an impertinent brat, aren't you?"

"How do you know I'm a brat?" she returned.

"Your voice. You sound as if you're barely out of your teens."

"Well, I am," she retorted, shaking back her pale hair. "I'm twenty-two, almost twenty-three."

He lifted his cigarette to his lips. "Twenty-two," he murmured softly. "What a magic age that was. All the world to pick and choose from, and no barriers at all in the way."

"It isn't exactly like that," she replied.

"Wait until you reach my age, little one, and tell me again."

She studied the dark, leonine head with its sprinkling of gray hairs that turned silver in the fading sunset light. "I didn't realize you were such a relic," she murmured with careful irony. "Goodness, I'd never have guessed you were actually in your fifties."

Both dark eyebrows shot up. "What?!"

"Well, you said . . ."

"I'm forty, damn it!" he growled. "And I can still run circles around men half my age!"

She didn't doubt it, that muscular physique didn't have a spare ounce of flab on it. He was strong, and it showed in every line.

"On foot, or on a motorbike?" she asked conversationally.

"Damn you," he laughed, a deep, pleasant sound in the stillness, that was only broken by the lap of water at the shore's edge.

"No manners, either, I see," she teased.

His eyes narrowed, glittered at the sound of her voice. "Women have been drowned for less."

"By you?"

"I've never been tempted like this before," he told her.

"Maybe I'd better go before you get violent," she suggested.

"That might not be a bad idea. Is it dark?"

She glanced toward the horizon. "Very nearly," she said, watching the sun go down in flames behind the silvery lake, the silhouette of tall pines.

"It isn't wise for a young woman to wander around here in the dark," he cautioned.

"What about you?" she asked as she turned to go.

His eyebrows went up. "I don't really expect that a would-be attacker would mistake me for a woman," he said bluntly.

Looking at the big, husky body, she seriously doubted it, too, and the idea tickled her so that a soft laugh broke from her lips.

"What are you snickering at?" he demanded.

"The thought of anyone mistaking you for a woman."

He chuckled softly. "I see your point. Go home."

"But, can you find your way back . . . ?"

"Why? Are you afraid I'll trip over my feet and fall in the lake?" he asked.

"It gets very deep very fast they say," she replied.

"I've only been like this for a little over a week," he told her quietly, "but I'm not helpless. I may burn a few holes in my chair, and I run into door facings and step on the dog's tail, but I . . . what's so damned funny?"

She forced herself to stop giggling. "It's the way you put things," she told him. "I'm not laughing at you, but . . . oh, the poor dog!"

"Oh, the poor dog, hell! He's a 130-pound gray shepherd, and he's got the disposition of a rattlesnake with a can tied to his tail."

"Anyway," she persisted, watching his face, "you don't have anybody to get you home, and no cane . . ."

"I have a houseboy named Yama who'll be out here on his knees with a flashlight and a net, dredging the lake, if I'm not back by dark," he replied smoothly. "Very handy, is Yama. Not at all like some of my faithful few who turned tail and ran when they were told that I couldn't see."

"They couldn't have been very faithful," she observed. "Do . . . do you know if you might regain your sight?"

He drew a deep breath and she stiffened, tensed, waiting for the answer. "There's a chance," he replied. "A very good one, that my sight will return normally, without surgical intervention. But how soon . . . no one knows. It could be days, or weeks, or months—or never. It was a hard blow, however it happened, and a tremendous shock to the optic nerve."

She swallowed. "Can you see at all?"

He smiled wistfully. "Dark blobs; a few shadows."

She blinked back tears. She couldn't cry, she didn't dare. "Well, I'd better go home."

"How far is it?" he asked suddenly.

"Just down the beach," she said carefully.

"What's your name?" The question was sharp, quick.

"Kate," she replied. "Kate...Jones," she added untruthfully, to throw him off the track. "Well, good-bye...."

"Kate!"

She turned. "Yes?"

"Come tomorrow."

The request shocked her—if it was a request. He'd made it sound like a royal command. Getting too close to him now could be horribly dangerous. But when she saw the quiet anguish in his face that peeked for an instant out of the impassive mask he wore, she couldn't refuse.

"Here?" she asked in a thin voice.

"At the cabin. About nine in the morning. I'll have Yama set breakfast for two. How about it?" he added gruffly, as if he wasn't used to making requests and hated even the idea of asking for anything.

"Can I have bacon?" she asked.

"Sure."

"How about coffee?"

"Done."

"Maybe a bagel with dark honey and hand-crushed mangoes?" she teased.

"Keep it up and all you'll get is the coffee," he returned.

"Coffee's better than nothing, I suppose. Good night."

There was a pause as she started off down the beach. "Good night...Kate," he said softly, and the words echoed along behind her like some ghostly echo.

She slept for the first night in days, relieved that there was even a chance he might recover, even while she was torn by regret and guilt for having done this to him. He was so different from what she'd expected, and plainly reluctant to tell her the truth about himself; that he owned a gigantic corporation, that he was wealthy enough to satisfy almost any material hunger he possessed. It was almost as if he were playing some kind of game... could it be that he knew who she was? She shook her head. No, he wouldn't have been friendly, he wouldn't have invited her to breakfast, if he'd known she was the reckless woman who cost him his sight and so much pain.

She was still worrying over it the next morning when she went to the front door of his spacious beach house and knocked.

A small, slender Oriental opened the door with a smile and welcomed her.

"Come in, come in," he said with only a trace of an accent. "Mr. Cambridge been pacing floor since seven. He waits for you on porch, please go ahead. Breakfast is on its way."

She thanked him with a smile and followed the direction he'd pointed out onto a screened in porch with a magnificent view of the lake.

Cambridge was there, his hands locked behind him, wearing white Bermuda shorts and a white knit top that displayed his dark, muscular arms to a distinct advantage. He seemed to be staring out at the lake, but she knew, full well, that he wasn't seeing it.

"Good morning," she said hesitantly.

He turned quickly, his blind eyes searching, as if by looking hard enough he might be able to find her.

"Good morning. Won't you sit down?"

She helped herself to the chair across from what was obviously his. "I like your porch," she told him.

"So do I. The screens keep the mosquitoes away," he chuckled.

"It's so peaceful here," she murmured, closing her eyes so that she could hear, even better, the whisper of wind through the tall pines, the soft lapping sound the water made against the shore.

"That's why I like it," he replied. "Yama, I'm starving to death out here!" he bellowed toward the kitchen.

"No need to shout, I come as quickly as possible," Yama fussed, bringing in a tray laden with food and a huge pot of coffee. He began to arrange it on the table. "Always, you nag, but if I bring the food when you say, you always complain eggs not done enough, bacon not crisp enough...."

"How would you like a nice, fat raise, Yama?" Cambridge asked through narrowed blank eyes.

Yama's lean face brightened. "That would be very nice, sir."

"Good. Maybe when you learn not to complain so much, I'll get around to giving you one."

Yama made a face at him. "One must be saint to put up with you. Instead of pay hike, I should get medal."

Kate couldn't repress a laugh as Yama disappeared. "He's an absolute jewel," she said.

"Amen, but he won't let me take myself seriously, and I suppose that's an asset." He took a long, deep breath. "He's been with me so long, it would be like losing an arm if he left."

"Does he go everywhere with you?"

A slow, easy smile touched his wide mouth. "Not everywhere," he said in a meaningful tone.

"That's not what I meant."

"Do you blush?" he asked suddenly.

"Of course not!" she lied.

He chuckled softly. "Somehow I don't believe you."

"Do you come to the lake a lot?" she asked quickly, sipping the hot, black coffee that Yama had poured.

"Not any more," he replied. He reached for his coffee cup and upset it, blistering his big hand, and let out a string of blue words.

Kate got to her feet automatically with her napkin and wrapped it around the warm hand, gently removing the liquid from his broad, strong fingers. It was a beautifully masculine hand, she thought involuntarily, noticing the dark, crisp hairs that grew on its back, the square, well-manicured nails. It was warm and a little calloused, and holding it made her tingle with a strange, unfamiliar excitement.

"I'm all right," he said gruffly, but he didn't try to pull his hand away.

"Hurt, didn't it?" she asked with a smile.

"Like hell. I told you I knocked things over."

"I would have taken your word for it, you know," she teased, and let go of his hand to mop up the dark stains growing on the pure white tablecloth.

He chuckled softly. "You're good for me, you little brat. No sympathy in you, is there?"

"Do you want me to coo and fuss over you?"

He scowled in her general direction. "What did you say you do for a living?" he asked, ignoring her attempt at humor.

"I'm a secretary, usually," she replied. "Why?"

"Are you tied up for the rest of the summer?" he persisted.

"Well, not for a few weeks," she admitted, confused by his dogged tone.

"Then why don't you move in with me?" he asked bluntly.

3

She sat gaping at him, her voice gone, her eyes about to pop with the shock.

A slow, knowing smile touched the wide contours of his mouth. "I'm not asking you to share my bed, if that's what produced this deafening silence," he said. "The idea of making love to a woman I can't see doesn't have much appeal right now, Kate."

She blushed, and turned her face away before she remembered that he couldn't see her. What was he asking? And she didn't dare live under the same roof with him. What if she trapped herself, and she might, by giving away that she'd been the maniac in the boat that struck him. What might he do? She remembered Maude's warning, about how ruthless he could be, and she was afraid of what his power could do, not only to her, but to her father. Yet, how could she turn her back on him now, when just about everybody else in his life seemed to have done just that? And Maude had told her to take a few weeks off and close up the cabin. . . .

"I'd pay you your regular salary, plus," Cambridge said quietly. "Although I won't promise you regular hours, Kate. Sometimes I hurt like hell in the middle of the night, and dictating something for the book might ease the pain."

"You...want me to help you put the book together?" she asked.

"I can't do it alone, and Yama can cook, but he can't type." His lips set. "Is it the thought of working for a blind man that puts you off, Kate?" he asked tightly.

"Why should it?" she asked without thinking.

He seemed to relax a little. "You'd have free time," he promised. "You like the lake, don't you? If your friend wouldn't mind...?"

"Oh, she wouldn't mind, that's not it." She searched for an excuse that wouldn't wound him. "It's just...we don't know each other."

"I'm not proposing marriage," he chuckled. "We don't have to be on intimate terms for you to be my secretary."

"I'm glad of that," she said uneasily, "because I wouldn't know how."

There was a long pause. "I wish I could see you," he said finally. "But you don't sound very worldly, Kate, if that's anything to go on."

"I never wanted to be. I don't care much for material things."

"What do you care for?" he probed.

"Gardens," she said with a smile. "Cows gathering in a pasture late in the afternoon. Children in clean pajamas right after a bath. Those kinds of things."

He leaned back in his chair. "I've never known any of those," he said matter-of-factly. "I live my life on a roller coaster that never stops. If I'm not on the phone, I'm in conference. If I'm not sleeping, I'm traveling."

"I guess a pilot's life does get pretty hectic," she remarked, as she remembered the half-truth he'd told her and played along with him.

He reached in his pocket for a cigarette and rolled it absently in his strong fingers. "That wasn't exactly the whole truth. I designed planes, and did my own testing most of the time. I...needed the element of danger, milkmaid," he sighed. Something painful came and went in his eyes. "Have you ever felt that way?"

"Yes, I have," she admitted, hating the memory of what she'd done to this man, whose eyes were everything to him.

"Why?" he asked bluntly.

She shifted restlessly in her chair, cupping her slender hands around her coffee cup. "I was in love with a man who thought I had money. When he found out I didn't, he couldn't get rid of me fast enough.'' Put like that, it sounded so simple, so uncomplicated, and yet it had tormented her for months.

"Not good enough for him, Kate?" he asked. He put the cigarette to his mouth and fumbled with his lighter until he managed to light it. "What did his family own?"

"A meat processing plant."

He chuckled softly. "Only one? My God, they were low on the social ladder."

"I don't understand."

"I'll teach you about stocks and investments one day, and you will." He drew in a breath of smoke. "Baby, one meat processing plant is like owning one tiny business in a town where another man owns a city block. Does that clarify it a little?"

"A little," she said. "I don't know about being rich. I never was. I don't think I'd like it. I'm a lot more comfortable in jeans and T-shirts than I am in evening gowns."

"Money has advantages and disadvantages," he agreed. "Well, Kate, are you going to move in with me or not?"

"I probably ought to have my head examined..."

"Assuredly, both of us should. Yes or no?"

"Yes."

"Good girl. Finish your breakfast and I'll introduce you to the hairy member of my family."

"Hairier than you?" she asked in mock astonishment, her eyes on the thick pelt of black hair that showed in the neck of his open-throated white shirt.

"I hope you can keep that sense of humor, Kate," he remarked, "because I've got one hell of a black temper and I'm not in the least embarrassed about losing it. I'm impatient and bullheaded, and I can wring you out like a wet cloth before you know it. If you tend to be a crier, you won't last here two days."

"Would you like to bet on how long I'll last?" she asked him.

"We'll wait and see about that."

"Whatever you say, boss," she teased.

She thought she'd seen big dogs before, but the gray shadow that rose ominously by the big chair in the den of the big cabin caused her heart to rise in her throat.

There was a soft, dangerous deep growl as she and Cambridge moved into the room.

"Stop showing off, Hunter," he growled at the animal. "Come here and try to pretend you're a pet."

"He's awfully big, isn't he?" Kate asked nervously, but she knelt and held out a hand for the dog to sniff, hoping he wouldn't consider it an invitation to a quick snack.

"Do you like dogs?" Cambridge asked.

"I like cats better, but I'm afraid of them. Dogs, I mean," she added as Hunter came up and sniffed at her hand. His tail started wagging and she let out a deep breath, not realizing that she'd been holding it.

"You'll get used to him. Here, boy," he coaxed, and the big animal came up to sit at his feet, nuzzling contentedly. "He was just a pet until I had the accident," he explained. "Now, he's my eyes most of the time."

"You didn't have him with you yesterday."

"I was trying something new...navigating without aids." He chuckled. "Not very successfully, I have to admit. Yama finally did come after me. Nagging, as usual."

"I guess it beats having a wife nag you. Or, are you married?" she asked, remembering that she wasn't supposed to know anything about him.

A shadow passed over his face and his eyes glittered like green fires for an instant. "No," he growled, "I'm not married."

"I'm sorry," she said, placing an apologetic hand on his sleeve, "I didn't mean to pry."

The light contact seemed to make him stiffen even more, and she quickly removed her hand. He didn't like to be touched, that was apparent, and she mentally filed that fact for future reference.

"How soon do you want me to start?" Kate asked quietly.

"Tomorrow."

"So soon? But I'll need to pack, and get in touch with my father..."

"You can call him from here," he told her.

"But he lives in Austin, Texas...well not exactly in it, but as near as not!" she protested.

"Kate, I'm not a poor man," he said quietly, drawing on the cigarette in his hand. "You're bound to find that out sooner or later. I'm as prone to sudden whims as a politician is to platform changes. You may wake up in the morning and find yourself on a plane to the Bahamas. I'm restless and I like to travel and I've got the wealth to make it feasible. One long distance phone call isn't likely to break me." He turned toward where he thought she should be. "Are you afraid of planes?"

"Why...no," she admitted.

"Are you afraid of traveling?"

"I've never done much of it...."

"Is your passport in order?"

"But I haven't got one, I've never...."

"It doesn't matter, I'll have Pattie take care of it," he said. He frowned at her silence. "Pattie," he emphasized, "is my office secretary. She's young, enthusiastic, and disgustingly efficient."

"And madly in love with the boss, I'll bet," she taunted.

"God, I hope not! She's married to one of my assistant vice presidents."

"Oh," she said.

He smiled. "Sorry to disillusion you, honey, but I don't seduce the office staff."

She blushed furiously. "I'd better go home and start packing," she said, watching the way his big hand was ruffling the dog's soft fur.

"Don't take too much time. I've been idle long enough. I want to get my mind back on something constructive."

She felt a twinge of conscience. "Of course. I won't be long."

She brooded while she packed, praying that she was doing the right thing. There were so many pitfalls. What if his memory came back and somebody described her to him, wouldn't he remember what she looked like? What if . . . ?

She forced herself to stop thinking about it. Tomorrow would take care of tomorrow, and worrying wasn't going to change anything. Besides, it was time she stopped thinking about herself and started thinking about someone else. It was just beginning to occur to her that she'd done very little of that in recent months. She'd been too buried in bitterness and self-pity to turn her thoughts outward at all. Perhaps it would be good therapy, working for someone like Garet Cambridge. He wasn't the kind of man to tolerate self-pity in any form, even his own.

He puzzled her. She'd never known anyone quite like him, and despite his wealth and her lack of it, she felt a strange kinship with him. He made her comfortable with herself and the world around her. He made her feel somehow secure and protected. Perhaps he, too, needed companionship for a little while. Someone to make his path a little easier. If only, she thought, she hadn't made the path so rough for him in the first place!

She sent Maude a telegram before she left the cottage, and that night she called her father from her new bedroom in Cambridge's spacious beach house.

"I thought you might get home for a visit between jobs," her father chuckled. "No hope, I guess."

"I'll make it next month, I promise," she said. "Oh, Dad, I've been such a pill, and I'm so sorry! I'm going to make it all up to you, I promise."

"Kate," he said gently, "you're my best girl and I love you. Don't feel you owe me anything."

"But I do! I do! All those years you put in on me when I was growing up, after Mama left, all the sacrifices you made . . . and for what? So I could run off half cocked with a status-seeking meat packer and leave you with a mortgage you can't pay. . . ."

"Now, hush," he scolded. "I made the payment all right. I sold some of the cattle and got a handsome deal. I'm doing just fine, and you can stop sending me so much of your check. I don't need it now."

"But, Dad...."

"No buts, daughter, I wouldn't lie to you. I'm not about to starve." He paused for an instant, and she could almost see the lines in his thin, leathery face. "Kate, are you happy, are you getting over it?"

"I'm...just fine," she lied, feeling tears prick at her eyes. "Honest I am. Will you write me if I give you the address?"

"You know I'm not much on writing, but you send me a letter first and I just might answer it, all right?"

"All right, Daddy, I love you," she said tightly.

"I love you, too, girl. Be happy, Kate. Life's so short."

"I will. You, too. Dad, are you doing okay?" she asked suddenly.

"Just fine, honey," he said. "You say about another month before you get here? I'll do my best to wait for you. I was going on a cruise to Europe, you know, but if that was a promise...."

"Oh, Dad," she laughed through her tears. "Yes, just a month or so, and please cancel your cruise."

"I'll see what I can do. Good night, child."

"Good night, Daddy."

Working for Garet Cambridge was like nothing she'd ever experienced. He was impatient, demanding, and utterly a perfectionist; but at the same time, he made the work so interesting that she didn't have time to get bored.

Before her stunned eyes, the book began to take shape as he roughed out the first draft and an outline, and her heart came into her throat when she realized that he'd actually done the things he was writing about.

"What's wrong?" he asked at one point, relaxed in his padded armchair with one brow raised curiously. "I can't imagine a woman being as quiet as you are today without some reason."

"Shell shock," she teased, glancing at the pantherish look of his big body in the armchair that seemed to fit perfectly the contours of that body.

"From what?" he asked, and his heavy brows drew together.

"Your life. Here," she added, glancing down at the paragraph that dealt with a plane whose engine caught fire and was forced down. "This part, where the engine burned and you had to bring the plane down in a swamp."

He smiled. "I brought it in between two trees and tore the wings off. That was a close one."

"It really happened, didn't it?" she asked.

"Yes, little one. It really happened." He looked thoughtful. "I'd been going for eighteen hours straight when I got into that plane. It was the dumbest move I ever made. But the board of directors were waiting for a test before they approved construction. They had to know if the plane was skyworthy." He shrugged. "There was a small fault in the engine design that gave it the tendency to short out and burn after the first few minutes of use. We corrected the malfunction and put it into production. It was our best selling executive jet for four years."

"Do you want to put that in?" she asked him.

"Might as well. Kate, how does it read?" he asked, suddenly intent as he leaned forward to stare with unseeing eyes in the direction of her voice. "Is it comprehensible to a lay person?"

"It is to me, and I don't know anything about airplanes."

"I have a feeling," he murmured with a half smile, "that airplanes aren't the only things you're ignorant about."

"How would you know?"

"Never mind." He leaned back again. "Ready for more, milkmaid?"

"Any time, Boss," she said lightly.

He liked the beach. Leaving Yama to tend the house and listen for the phone, she helped Garet down to the pier every evening, where they sat on chaise lounges and listened to the dark quiet sounds of night for hours on end.

"God, I love it here," he said on one of their better evenings. "I'd forgotten how quiet the night could be."

"Didn't you ever sit outside and listen to crickets?" she teased, glancing at him where he lazed back in the floral chaise with his blue shirt unbuttoned, baring his bronzed muscular chest, and his white shorts revealing his powerful, hair-covered thighs.

"Honey, I didn't know there was an outside," he replied as he sipped his whiskey sour idly. "You know what my life was like. I seem to have mentioned it a time or two."

"Cocktail parties, business meetings, phones that never stopped ringing... have I got it?" she asked.

"In a nutshell. Not much of an existence, but it was all I knew. Until now."

She lowered her eyes to her lap, her hands just visible in the yellow light from the cabin. "I'm sorry you had to find out...this way."

He drew a long breath. "So am I, honey. Blindness is hell to try and live with. But I've slowed down enough to get a new perspective on life. I didn't realize how much of it I was missing."

"Can I ask you something?"

"Fire away, Kate."

"You mentioned once that you needed the element of danger...."

"And you want to know why, is that it, Kate?" he asked in a deceptively soft voice, as his knuckles whitened around the glass, his body tensed. "What the hell business is it of yours?" he demanded.

She flinched at the harshness she'd never heard in his deep voice before. "I...only wanted..." she faltered.

"To pry? To pump me for old memories that are better left dead? You're just like every other damned woman, you've got to know everything there is to know about a man!"

She swallowed nervously. "I wasn't trying to pry."

"The hell you weren't!"

"I'm sorry!" she managed in a shaky voice. "Mr. Cambridge, I'm sorry, I don't know why I asked that!"

There was a harsh, throbbing silence between them, and she wished she could get up and run. But she sat stiffly on the edge of the chaise, her fingers gripping each other, her body rigid.

He took out a cigarette from the package in his pocket and felt for a lighter, managing easily to put the fire to it.

"I told you I had a black temper," he said finally. "If you want out, now's the time to say so. But I won't have my personal life picked to pieces. Let's get that clear between us right now."

She pulled her pride together and wrapped it around her. "I won't ask again," she whispered, hating the tears that beaded on her eyelashes as she held back the muffled sound that would have told him she was crying.

"Pouting, milkmaid?" he asked in an unpleasant tone. "That won't work with me, either. It's been tried, by experts."

She drew in an unsteady breath and tried to concentrate on the night sounds, the soft splash of the lake on the shore, anything but the way she felt inside.

"I'm not pouting," she managed finally, in a voice that just barely wobbled.

He looked toward the sound of her voice, and his heavy brows made a line between his eyes. "My God, you're not crying?" he demanded.

She drew in a long, shaky breath. "Of course not," she replied.

"Kate . . . honey, come here," he coaxed, holding out his big hand, all the anger and impatience gone out of him as if it had never existed.

She hesitated, but he called her name again, softly, and she went to stand beside him, gingerly touching that warm, calloused hand. He drew her down to sit on the chaise, so that her hip touched his bare thigh.

His broad, strong fingers reached up until they found her face, and traced her eyebrows, her straight nose, the bow shape of her trembling young mouth. Then his hands swung upward to find the dampness of her long lashes and he frowned.

"Kate," he whispered softly. "I didn't frighten you, did I?"

"No," she admitted. "But you ... you're such an awful bully, you walk all over people's feelings ... !"

"Do you have feelings, little innocent?" he asked in a low, sensuous tone. His fingers went back down to her mouth and traced its soft lines lazily, with a light, tantalizing pressure. "I thought you were always cool and collected."

"Nobody can be collected when you yell at them!" she returned with a wan display of spirit. "Please, don't do that," she murmured, drawing away from that maddening finger.

He chuckled softly. "Haven't you ever let a man make love to you?"

She stiffened. "Of course I have," she told him with an attempt at sophistication.

"I said make love, not make out," he corrected. "You do know there's a difference?"

She blushed to the roots of her hair. "I don't sleep with men, if that's what you mean," she gulped. "Not," she added haughtily, "that it's any of your business."

"Before I'm through with you," he said in a low, menacing tone, "it may be very much my business."

"I'm your secretary...."

"God, yes, don't let's forget it for a second!" he said, mocking her. His arm shot out and pulled her down on top of his broad, unyielding chest. She gasped, stiffened, and tried to pull away, careful to keep her protesting hands on the cotton of his shirt, not to let them rest on the bare, cool muscles of his chest and the mat of hair where the shirt had fallen open.

She heard him laugh, as if he found her unsuccessful efforts toward freedom some private joke.

"This," he murmured, "is unique. I don't think I've ever had a woman fight to get out of my arms. It's always been the other way around."

"I can't imagine why," she panted, still fighting, "unless they were trying to get close enough to pick your pockets."

He laughed even harder. "You don't think I'm attractive, milkmaid?" he asked.

"No, I don't!" she flashed angrily. "Will you let me go?"

He laughed, folding her even closer. "God, you're good for me," he murmured against her ear. "Kate, how have I managed without you all these years?"

"The same way you've managed without a pride of sons, I imagine," she fumed, giving way finally to lie panting breathlessly in his steely grip.

"How do you know I don't have children?"

She considered that. "I'm sorry," she murmured. "I didn't think...."

He ruffled her hair. "I'm teasing, Kate. I'm not a father, to the best of my knowledge," he added wickedly.

"No doubt. Please will you let me up? I'm dreadfully uncomfortable!"

"Are you?" There was, suddenly, a new note in his voice, a difference in the touch of his big hands against her back as he shifted her gently against him until she was lying half-against, half-beside him.

"You...." she faltered as her hand came into contact with the cool flesh of his massive chest.

His big, warm hand covered hers, pressing it against his body. "Just relax, Kate," he said quietly. "We all need physical contact at one point or another in our lives, and it doesn't have to have sexual overtones."

"I didn't mean . . ." she began quickly.

"I know." He let his drawn shoulders relax back against the cushions of the chaise and lay there just holding her. "My darkness can get lonely, little girl," he said finally, and she closed her eyes against the pain of knowing that she'd caused it. "Lonely and cold. I haven't had anyone to hold on to. I didn't think I needed anyone." He laughed shortly. "Kate, have you ever stopped to think just how alone we all are? Separate, self-contained entities walking around in shells of flesh that hardly ever touch."

"Hardly ever?" she teased gently.

"I've had women," he replied, his hand idly stroking her long hair. "But never the right one. Haven't you ever heard of being alone in a crowd, little girl? Or haven't you ever been lonely?"

She closed her eyes, drinking in the night sounds and the fragrance of his spicy cologne. Her hand, where it lay against the hard unyielding muscles with their wiry covering of hair, could feel the steady, hard rhythm of his heart.

"Oh, yes," she said softly. "I know what it is to be lonely. I think everyone does."

He drew her up, shifting her in his arms. "You aren't used to being touched, are you, Kate?" he murmured.

She frowned. "How did you know that?"

He chuckled gently. "You were so damned rigid when I caught you a minute ago. It was like holding a pine limb."

"You don't like being touched, either," she murmured. "That first morning I had breakfast with you, and I grabbed your arm...."

He laughed. "I remember. But that was because of the blindness, Kate. It's disorienting to have people clutch at you when you can't see it coming." He frowned. "It takes some getting used to, this dark world."

"I'm sorry," she whispered.

"Why? It's not your fault," he growled, and she felt the guilt all the way to her toes. His chest lifted in a heavy sigh. He spread her fingers where they rested against him and moved them in a slow, sensuous motion through that mat of curling hair. She could feel his breathing grow faster with the action.

"Mr. Cambridge..." she whispered shakily, liking the feel of his big, muscular body, the closeness that she'd never shared with any man.

"My name is Garet," he said quietly.

"Yes, but you're my boss," she replied.

"Does that make me a leper?" His free hand pressed her soft cheek against his warm shoulder. "I'm part cat, Kate. I like to be touched and stroked...do you?"

She stiffened in his arms at that sensuous deep note in his voice, afraid of what he might learn about her, what she might learn about him, if this went any further.

"Please, it's late," she said quickly, pushing away, "and I have things to do."

He hesitated for just an instant, as if he was weighing the sincerity in her tone against the soft young tremor of the body in his arms. Then he released his tight grip and let her jump to her feet.

"I won't rush you, Kate," he said as he reached for a cigarette and lit it, almost as well as a sighted person could. "You don't have to be afraid that this is part of the job."

"I never thought that," she replied with as much conviction as she could muster, standing at his elbow on shaky legs. "I...I know it must be lonely for you, and without a woman..."

"I had a woman," he replied tightly, "while I had eyes." His big hand raked through the hair that fell across his broad forehead, and he scowled. "Celibacy isn't one of my virtues. You knew that, I imagine?"

"Yes, sir. It's...very hard not to know it," she replied.

"Oh?" One dark eyebrow lifted, and the fierce black mood seemed to leave him. "How?"

She read that amused inflection, and found her temper pricked by it. "I've got some correspondence to catch up on. Good night, sir," she said without answering the bald question.

"Elusive little cat," he murmured. "I'll catch you one day."

And wish you hadn't, she thought miserably. The memory of the boat colliding with that proud head haunted her as she walked back to the beach house. The woman he'd mentioned he had while he still had his sight . . . had the loss of her embittered him so? That would be another black mark against her if he ever found out his secretary's real identity. And, remembering the blazing black temper she'd seen for the first time tonight, she shuddered at what the discovery would mean.

4

It didn't take Kate long to discover that her new boss was a lonely man. It clung to his darkness like a second skin, a fierce kind of loneliness that made deep lines in his face, narrowed his unseeing green eyes. She wondered if the mysterious woman he'd mentioned, the one who'd run out on him, had been responsible, but she wouldn't dared to have asked. One glimpse of his temper had been enough to convince her not to pry into his personal life again.

Even though he couldn't see, she sensed sometimes that he knew she watched him. She couldn't help it. His dark masculinity drew her eyes like a magnet—the bigness of his husky frame, the proud carriage that didn't falter even in blindness.

The only thing that seemed to dent his proud spirit were the headaches. They came in the night, and she'd hear him pacing his room, back and forth, in the early hours of morning. It made her guilt even worse, because more often than not he suffered in silence. Only on rare occasions would he call for her to bring him something for the pain.

"Have you told the doctor about these headaches?" Kate asked him early in the darkness of the morning while she was handing him two pain capsules.

"What the hell could he do?" he growled as he swallowed them down. "Sympathize? Give me more of these damned painkillers? If he's such a magician, Kate, why the hell can't he give me back my sight? Oh, God, if I could just see ...!"

The anguish in his voice brought her a kind of pain she'd never experienced. Without thinking, she sat down on the bed beside him and wrapped her slender arms around him, holding him to her, rocking him in the stillness.

"I'm sorry, I'm sorry," she whispered, crooning like a mother for a lost child. "I'm so sorry."

He drew a deep, shuddering breath and crushed her against his husky body for just an instant before he pushed her away.

"Don't, Kate," he said quietly. "I might just mistake that well-placed sympathy for an invitation, and then where would you be? I don't have to tell you how long I've been without a woman, and Yama's not likely to interrupt us."

"I only meant to offer you sympathy—not myself," she said in a small, tight voice, hating the naivete responsible for the hot blush of her cheeks.

"I know that. But you don't know what goes on inside a man's head when he feels a soft young body against him," he replied. "Light me a cigarette, honey."

She complied with shaking hands and put it to his firm, chiseled lips with their shadow of surrounding beard. Unshaven, he had a roguish look that suited him.

"Were any of your ancestors pirates?" she asked without thinking.

He laughed, putting a hand to his temples as if the sound had aggravated the pain. "What brought that on?"

"I don't know. Without a fresh shave, you kind of reminded me of Henry Morgan."

One dark eyebrow went up. "I didn't realize you were old enough to have known him."

"I've seen pictures."

"They didn't have cameras on pirate ships."

"There was a movie . . . !"

"With an actor playing a part, and it's the actor I remind you of, not the pirate. Now, isn't that so?" he challenged.

She sighed furiously. "It would be easier to argue with a stone wall!" she burst out.

"Damned straight, you might have a chance of winning." He took a long draw from the cigarette and sighed. "God, it hurts."

Her hand laid gently on his big arm, feeling the hard muscle through the silky pajama top that hung loose over his chest. It was burgundy, and emphasized the darkness of his complexion.

He covered that small, cold hand with one of his. "Stay with me for a while, Kate," he said quietly. "Keep my ghosts at bay while these pills have a chance to work."

Her fingers contracted against his arm. "Do you have ghosts?"

"Don't we all? Don't you?" he asked.

She sighed. "Oh, yes. I have one of my own."

"How big?"

She shrugged. "I hurt someone very much," she admitted, "because of my own stupidity. And there's no way I can ever make it up."

His big hand caught hers where it lay on his arm. "Don't try to live in the past. It's hard enough when you take one day at a time."

"Sage words," she smiled.

"And easier said than done, right, Kate?" he asked quietly.

"Yes, sir."

He caught her small hand and drew it to his chest. "Light me another cigarette, honey."

She took the finished butt from his hand and put it in the ashtray, lighting another for him. She had to do it with one hand, because he didn't show any inclination to let go of the one he held captive. She placed the filter tip between his chiseled lips.

"You smoke too much," she accused softly.

"Don't lecture me."

"Is the pain easing off any?"

He drew in a deep breath. "Some."

Her fingers contracted around his, feeling the warm strength in them. "I'm sorry about the headache."

He laughed shortly as he took a draw from the cigarette. "That makes two of us. Your hands are cold, little one."

"I'm chilly," she said quickly.

"In the middle of summer?" he teased lightly. "I don't think so."

"I am!"

"It's like arguing with a wall, Kate," he reminded her, "and you know you won't win. Why are you so nervous near me?"

Now there, she thought miserably, was a dandy question. "Well..." she murmured.

"I'm sorry I tore into you the other night," he told her, with genuine regret in his deep, measured voice. "I..." He took a long, slow breath. "There was a woman, Kate." His hand contracted around hers painfully. "I suppose it was the closest I've ever come to loving anyone. When this happened," he gestured toward his eyes, "she walked out on me. I told her the blindness was probably only temporary, but she wasn't willing to take the chance. The world is too big, she said, to let herself be tied down to a cripple." His jaw tautened with the hated word. His fingers were crushing hers now, and she grimaced and moaned with the pain. "My God, I'm sorry!" he said quickly, releasing his unconsciously cruel grip to caress the fingers his had punished. "I didn't mean to do that, Kate. Did I hurt you badly?"

She swallowed back the tears. "It's...all right."

"Is it?" His blind eyes stared toward the sound of her voice, a dark, emerald green against the darkness of his face with its leonine contours. "God, I wish I could see you! I can't even tell if you're lying to me."

She blanched at the thought that even the blindness was her fault. "I really am all right," she said reassuringly.

He laid back against the pillows with a heavy sigh. "I'm not a gentle man by nature, Kate. It's another of my faults you'll have to adapt to."

"Along with your green warts and your amusing temper?" she asked, tongue-in-cheek.

The black mood seemed to drop from him and he grinned reluctantly. "Think you're cute, don't you?"

"I have a sterling self-image, thanks," she laughed.

He chuckled, a soft, pleasant sound in the soft light of the bedroom. "You're good for me."

"I won't let you feel sorry for yourself. It goes contrary to your nature, anyway. You're not the kind of man to turn to self-pity, no matter what happens to you."

He drew her hand to his mouth and kissed the soft palm slowly, sensuously, in a way that made her knees go weak. "Am I?" he asked.

She tried to pull her hand away, but he held it firmly, letting his lips travel over her slender fingers, against her wrist, her forearm.

"Mr....Cambridge," she whispered unsteadily, drawn in a way she'd never been by any other man as the slow, dangerous caress worked into her blood.

"Kate," he murmured, "put this out." He handed her the cigarette, clasping her free hand tightly, raising it to his cheek.

With trembling fingers, she crushed it out in the ashtray and started to rise. He felt the movement and checked it easily by slipping a hard, determined arm around her waist to bring her falling down onto the bulk of his hard-muscled body.

"No!" she whispered frantically.

His big arms wrapped around her, holding her, cradling her. "Don't fight me, don't be afraid of me, Kate," he whispered at her ear. "This is all I want right now. Let me hold you."

"Oh, please, you shouldn't...!"

"Why not?" His lips brushed the hair at her temple. "God, I'm lonely," he said huskily. "I'm so damned lonely! Would you deny me the feel of a woman in my arms to make the night just a little more bearable?"

She could feel the heavy, hard thunder of his heart against her through all the layers of clothing. "I...that isn't...all you want," she replied.

He drew in a hard breath and his arms tightened. "No, damn it, that's not all I want! I want you," he growled at her ear. "You, Kate! Every soft inch of you, here, now...!"

"No!"

"Why not?" he persisted. "Let me show you how it could be, Kate...."

He brought her face around and found her lips blindly with his, probing gently, teasing them with a pressure so light and unexpected that it took the hard tension out of her limbs and made her go soft against him. She'd been kissed before, but never like this, never in a way that made her feel giddy and boneless and hungry. The feel of his chiseled lips against hers was intoxicating. She parted her own to tempt them into hardness, to provoke that torturous soft brushing into something far more violent and satisfying.

She felt him ease her yielding body across his until she was on her back and he was looming over her, his breath mingling with hers as he held the slow, tender kiss in the burning silence of the night.

His hand spread against her cheek, his thumb brushed across her mouth roughly. "This can't be all take and no give," he said in a deep, gruff tone. "Damn you, kiss me!"

He crushed his mouth down against hers and she went taut instinctively until that hurting, angry pressure lessened and became caressing, tantalizing, seductive....

With a moan, she opened her mouth under his and slid her arms up and around his neck, yielding to him in a fog of dazed pleasure. His hands deftly untied her robe and she felt them on her waist, burning through the thin gown as he caressed the softness of her body and made it tremble.

"God, you're sweet," he whispered against her eager mouth. "I'll give you a night you'll never forget!"

Sanity came back with a rush at the words. She caught his hands and stilled them as they began to move upward on her body.

"I . . . I can't," she whispered.

"Why?"

She swallowed nervously, breathlessly, forcing the words out through swollen lips. "You know why."

He seemed to stiffen against her and for a long moment there was silence, filled only by his rough, harsh breathing.

"It was true, then?" he asked gruffly. "You've never been with a man?"

"No," she replied miserably.

He tightened his grip for just an instant. Then she felt him relax, felt his arms enfold her gently, with all the frightening ardor gone out of them.

"Just relax," he said quietly. "You won't have to fight me off, honey."

She nestled her face against his shoulder, feeling the sting of hot tears in her eyes.

"I'm sorry," she whispered brokenly.

"Sorry about what?" he asked gently. "That you had to stop me? Kate, I'm only a man. The feel of you went a little to my head, that's all. Don't feel guilty about it. I didn't hire you to keep my bed warm."

"I...I know, but if I'd said something at first..." she murmured.

"You're human enough to enjoy being held and kissed, little girl," he said, tracing her cheek with an absent finger. "You've been alone, too, Kate. Don't be too hard on either one of us." He reached over to kiss, lightly, her closed eyelids. "I like the way you taste, little innocent, but I'm not quite cold-hearted enough to make a meal of you."

She smiled in spite of herself. "You're a nice man sometimes."

"Sometimes," he agreed. "Kiss me one more time and go to bed. At the very least," he added teasingly, "you've managed to take my mind off the headache."

She kissed his rough cheek and started to get up.

He held her back. "Not like that," he said quietly, bending. "Like this...."

His mouth opened on hers, pressing her lips apart, exploring the soft contours of her mouth with a practiced expertise that brought a moan from her throat. He drew back with a wisp of a smile. "You've got a hell of a lot to learn about lovemaking," he said gently.

Even without his sight, he read her too well, and it was unnerving. She drew a sharp breath. "I'm very sleepy," she murmured.

"Coward." He released her. "I'd give anything to see you right now," he added with a tightening of his jaw.

She got quickly to her feet. "Can I bring you anything?" she asked, ignoring the rough comment.

"I've already had everything I need . . . for tonight," he mused. "Unless you'd like to crawl back in here with me, in case the headache comes back?"

"No, thanks," she told him.

"Afraid?"

"I most certainly am."

He smiled. "You flatter me, little one. Sleep well."

"You, too."

She closed the door behind her and leaned back against it, breathless, dazed. Something intangible had changed between them tonight, and she wasn't sure how she was going to adjust to it.

He didn't know that she was responsible for his blindness, and now, more than ever, she dreaded having him find out. But, too, he came from another world; a world of power and success and beauty that no ordinary mortal could fit into; certainly not a small-time Texas rancher's daughter. She reminded herself firmly that, with eyes, he'd never have given her a second look except, perhaps, to order her off his property, as he'd done when he came across her sitting on the log by the lake. Cold shudders wracked her body. This kind of thinking would get her nowhere. She was a secretary. She'd have to remember that from now on and not let her emotions get between her and the debt she was repaying.

For an instant she remembered the woman he'd lost because of the blindness, and thought how much he was going to owe her for that accident if he ever found out. Her eyes closed momentarily. Death would be kinder than his retribution—there wouldn't be any mercy in him for Kate if he learned who his secretary really was.

5

---
*

If Kate had been worried about facing him the next morning, she shouldn't have been. He was all business, as usual, and there were no references at all to what had happened between them in the soft darkness. He was a little more brusque than usual as he dictated, but nothing he said betrayed that his interest in his secretary was anything but professional.

As the days passed, she noticed a new restlessness in him. In the middle of dictation, he'd suddenly seem to forget where he was and drift off into a scowling study. Finally, she dredged up enough courage to ask him what was the matter.

"What makes you think anything is?" he growled at her from behind his massive desk, his sightless eyes narrow, threatening even in their darkness, and she shivered, remembering the power of them before he lost his sight.

"I . . . I don't know. You seem restless," she said finally.

He ran a big hand through the silvered hair at his temples with a rough sigh. "I am—restless, bored, sick of routine." He leaned back in his swivel chair, and it creaked in protest under his weight. "Got your birth certificate with you?"

"My . . . Well, yes, I had to send for it because you told me I'd need a passport . . . ."

"You won't need a passport where we're going; just your birth certificate. We're going to St. Martin this afternoon. We'll leave here after lunch."

She caught her breath. "St. Martin?" she asked numbly.

"It's an island in the Lesser Antilles," he explained. "Half of it's French, the other half, Sint Maarten, is Dutch. I own a villa there."

"Where is St. Martin?"

"In the Caribbean," he said with a half smile. "The bluest waters and the whitest beaches you've ever seen. It'll be an experience for you. For anyone," he added bitterly, "with eyes."

He withdrew into himself, letting the bitterness darken his eyes more than blindness had. Kate left him alone to pack, wondering all the while if the memories he had of the Caribbean island had anything to do with the woman who'd left him.

Kate had never liked airplanes, but there was something special about the small Learstar with its jet engines and its luxurious interior. It made an adventure out of air travel, and its compactness was somehow reassuring when it took to the air under the charter pilot's expert handling.

Her eyes darted to Garet. He hadn't said a word since they boarded the plane. He simply sat there, next to the window, his face dark and brooding, his chiseled mouth compressed, his unseeing eyes staring blankly out the window under a black scowl.

Kate hadn't tried to speak to him, remembering the black temper she'd had the misfortune to run into once already. She kept her silence, but her heart went out to the big, dark man. He looked so alone—so terribly alone. Something inside her ached to reach out and comfort him. It was odd, that compulsion. She'd never cared so much about anyone in her life, except her father. Not even, she admitted finally, Jesse Drewe. It was a new experience, to care like that....

She jerked her eyes away from him, as if she was afraid he might turn and sense her staring with that radar-like sense that compensated him for his lack of vision. She couldn't start caring about him. It was too dangerous! In her own way, she was trying to help repay him for the blindness she'd caused, by acting as his helpmate for the duration of the condition. But sympathy was a far cry from the way she was beginning to feel, and she had to dampen down her new vulnerability. He wasn't safe to get attached to, and he could hurt her.

Time went by in a blue haze. Before she realized it, they were over the Caribbean. Yama pointed out St. Martin to her, with its white beaches like tiny white ribbons from the height; its hotels and smoothly rounded green peaks and coral-colored roofs on dainty houses dotting the island.

"Mr. Cambridge owns villa on French side," Yama explained with a grin. "That because he never learn to speak Dutch. Too lazy. French accent is worst I ever hear, but it get him out of jail, maybe."

"Listen to the linguistics expert," Cambridge chuckled from his seat as the small jet received clearance from the airfield and nosed down for a landing.

"I speak good English," Yama protested.

"So did Tarzan," Cambridge muttered.

"You insult me, and wait to see what I put in front of you for dinner tonight," Yama threatened.

"Oh, God, why don't I ever learn to keep my mouth shut?" Cambridge groaned. "Kate, you make sure I get the same thing you have to eat tonight, or you're fired."

"Yes, sir," she said smartly, but with a conspiratorial wink at Yama that made the small man's face light up like a beacon.

The villa was delightful. Perched high on a green hill overlooking the white beach and its luxury hotel, it stood out from the rest with its graceful Spanish design and white, curving walls. The stone floors were cool and smooth and Kate wondered how it would be to walk on them barefoot. In fact, she kicked off her shoes just inside the front door and gave a sigh at the cold delight of the floor under her hot, tired feet.

"What was that all about?" Cambridge asked, turning to scowl in her general direction.

"I love your floors," she said self-consciously. "They feel good."

One corner of his mouth went up. "Barefoot already, country girl? There's an arbor of bougainvillea at the back door and we're fairly well surrounded by banana trees and hibiscus. I imagine you'll like that."

"I'll like the beach, too, although I'm not much of a swimmer. Are we allowed to use the beach at the hotel?" she asked curiously.

"Since I own the hotel," he replied carelessly, "I suppose we are."

She flushed. "You didn't mention...."

"Was there any reason to?" He scowled. "Kate, money doesn't mean a hell of a lot to me. I've always had it, so I tend to take it for granted. It's no big deal."

"I understand. But you'll have to understand that I've been without it all my life," she returned proudly. "I'm not used to luxury, and it's not in me to take such things for granted."

He pondered that for a minute, taking time to light a cigarette with confident fingers. "Sorry you came?" he asked finally.

"Oh, no," she replied quickly. "I'm very grateful...."

"Stop being so damned subservient," he shot at her. "I don't want gratitude from you, not now, not ever!"

She flinched at the whip in his voice, sensing that whatever was eating at him had nothing to do with her.

She started to apologize again, but quickly thought better of it. He wasn't in any mood for apologies. Something was eating at him like acid. It didn't show in that proud, arrogant stance, but it was in every line of his face, in the dark green eyes that glowered toward her.

"I'd like to unpack," she murmured.

"Well, hell, go do it!" he growled, turning on his heel. He turned toward the doorway and slowly, gingerly, felt for the door facing, the back of a chair, until he reached the long blue brocade of the couch and eased himself down. It was too bad, she thought, that he'd had to leave Hunter in the kennel. No way was he going to bend his pride enough to use cane.

"Send Yama in here with an ashtray," he said stiffly.

"Yes." She turned and left him there, feeling vaguely shaky inside from the attack. If he was going to be like this for the duration of the trip, she was already ready to go home.

But by the time she explored the garden and the peaceful stretch of land around the villa, with the blue Caribbean stretching out to the horizon beyond the sparkling white beach, she wasn't so enthusiastic about leaving. Islanders waved as they passed along the road beside the villa, and Kate waved back, feeling a part of the green paradise. It gave her a sense of peace, this slow, easygoing pace, as though she'd been running all her life and now, finally, there was all the time in the world to just live—no time clocks, no deadlines, no pressure—just peace and sand and sea.

Cambridge was already at the table when Yama called Kate in to supper.

"Where have you been?" he demanded irritably. "Hiding from me?"

She shrugged as she sat down across from him at the hand-crafted table. "It did seem like a good idea at the time," she admitted quietly.

He drew in a deep, short breath. "Enjoy what's left of today," he said tightly. "Tomorrow we start work in earnest. I want to get this damned book finished."

"It shouldn't take much longer," she said conversationally as she sipped her coffee, savoring the rich taste of it.

He nodded. He lifted a forkful of Yama's filet of sole to his mouth and tasted it. "Fried octopus?" he asked with raised eyebrows.

Kate smiled in spite of herself. "Filet of sole," she corrected.

He drew in a deep, slow breath. "Have Yama take you down to the beach after dinner. You haven't seen beauty until you've watched the moon rise above the Caribbean. It's a hell of a sight."

"Mr. Cambridge...."

"Why the hell can't you call me Garet?" he growled, throwing down his linen napkin. "Am I too old to merit a first name basis with you, little girl?"

She stared into her plate. "I don't think of you on a first name basis," she murmured. "You're the boss."

He sighed, and she could feel the barely controlled anger in him. "My God, you make me feel my age."

She didn't answer him, picking at her food with as little appetite as she could ever remember having. He was angry, and it looked very much as if he wanted a whipping post.

"Kate?" he growled.

"Yes, sir?" she asked.

He lifted his coffee cup in a big, steady hand. "I asked her to marry me in this villa," he said after a minute. "We were watching the moon over the endless sea, and I slid the ring onto her finger. I'll never forget the look in her eyes, the light in her face . . . I had eyes, and she wanted me," he said gruffly. "I shouldn't have come back here, but I needed to exorcise the ghost, and I couldn't do it on the lake. Bear with me. Can you do that, Kate? Just . . . bear with me until I can come to grips with it?"

"I'm sorry it happened like that for you," she said in a weak voice.

"So am I." He leaned back in his chair, looking darkly satanic in the subdued light. "She was everything I ever wanted in a woman. Beautiful, talented, passionate . . . her hair was like platinum—long and silky and thick, and she had the bluest eyes . . . God, I loved her! A month away from the altar, and this had to happen." He ran his hand over his eyes. "It's not clearing up. If anything, I'm losing what little vision I managed to retain. The darkness is gaining ground, Kate, and how the hell am I going to make it through life without my eyes?" he asked finally, and the pain was in his voice, in the hard lines of his face.

She closed her eyes against the guilt. "You'll manage," she told him quietly. "You'll manage because you have to, and you won't let it break you. You'll go on, one day at a time, and you'll cope."

He stared in the direction her voice had come from. "Stay with me."

She swallowed. "I will. I'll be here...as long as you need me," she said softly.

"It came back to me today, Kate," he said heavily. "I remembered."

A nagging, uneasy suspicion began to form in her mind. "Remembered?" she asked faintly, gripping the smooth, wooden arms of her chair.

"How this happened," he said, touching his forehead. He scowled, and the look on his face was frightening. "That damned girl," he said heatedly. "I never knew her name, or where she came from but she liked to get reckless in boats and speed. I called her down once, but it didn't stop her. I was out swimming," he recalled, his jaw tightening, "and the last thing I remember is turning to see her at the helm of a speedboat coming straight for me. She didn't even stop, the little maniac! She didn't even come back to see if she'd killed me."

Kate sat there like a statue, her face frozen and white, her heart beating her to death. She'd been terrified of this moment, and here it was. He knew. He knew!

6

_____ * _____

That's going to be my number one priority," he said quietly, "when I finish this book and go back to the States. I'm going to find that girl if it takes me the rest of my life. And when I do, I'll crucify her."

He didn't raise his voice, but that made the statement all the more terrifying.

"How will you start?" she asked in what she hoped was a calm voice.

"By hiring a private detective," he replied calmly. "I know she was staying on the lake. It shouldn't be too hard to locate her. I'll have Pattie get on it today. I don't want to lose her trail, not now. That little blonde assassin!" he growled. "If it takes the rest of my life, I'll get even with her for what she did to me!"

Kate's eyes closed momentarily. So that had been part of what was eating him all the way from Georgia. He'd remembered. And from now on it was going to be like walking on eggshells to live with him, wondering what minute she was going to slip up and give something away.

What if he started remembering that his assailant had been blonde, and so was Kate—that she'd been living on the lake when he hired her—mightn't he remember and recognize her husky voice, even if he'd only heard it briefly before?

She trembled at just the thought of discovery. There'd be no explaining away what she'd done. He'd never believe that it had been an accident. Not when he remembered how she'd defied him when he ran her off the lake, off his property. He'd be sure she'd hit him deliberately with the speedboat.

Anyone, she admitted bitterly, would believe that, given the circumstances.

Tears gathered in her eyes. She'd gotten used to him—to his moods, his deep, quiet voice in the night while he dictated, the sound of his heavy footsteps, the smell of his cigarette smoke in the darkness. It would be hard to leave him. She hadn't realized that before, and it came as something of a shock.

"You're very quiet, Kate," he said, scowling. "Can you blame me for being bitter, for wanting revenge? My God, I may go through the rest of my life like this, and all because of a child's deliberate attempt at revenge!"

"You sound as though...you think she meant to hit you."

"Of course she meant to!" he growled savagely. He caught a deep breath, wrapping his big hands around his coffee cup. "I'd run her off the lake once already when I caught her speeding. To make matters worse, I found her sitting by the lake on my property, and I ran her off again." His lips compressed. "Sassy little brat; she didn't like that. I wanted to pick her up and shake her. Instead, I let her go. It wasn't two hours later that she ran the boat over me, and left me there bleeding after I'd managed to drag myself out of the lake," he recalled gruffly.

"Maybe...maybe she was afraid," Kate suggested casually.

"I hope to God she was," he agreed. "Terrified. I hope she still is. If I can believe that, I'll have something to live for!"

"Being bitter, hating won't help," she said gently.

"How do you know it won't?" he demanded.

She drew a deep breath. "Because I've learned it the hard way," she said in a subdued tone.

"The meat packer's son, Kate?" he asked. His heavy brows drew together as he stared blankly in front of him. "He hurt you pretty badly, didn't he?"

She sighed. "I suppose he did. It hardly seems important anymore. I thought I loved him, but I'm not sure now that I even know what love is—or that I want to know."

"I'll tell you what it is, little girl," he said softly. "It's the sweetest madness this side of hell. When it finally happens for you, you won't have to ask what it's all about. You'll know."

Did he, she wondered? Was it the mysterious woman who'd deserted him that he was thinking about? And had it been remembering the accident that really upset him—or remembering the only woman he'd ever loved?

He finished his coffee. "Go with Yama. I've been on your back ever since we landed. You could do with a break from my temper. He's going to pick up some material for us at the hotel. You can enjoy the beach and see something of the tourist trade while you're there."

She swallowed down a little of her apprehension. Maybe his private detective would strike out, anyway. After all, Maude was presumably still in Paris, and the boat was safely locked away. She smiled.

"That's a first," she murmured as she pushed back her chair and stood up. "Admitting you've been like a bear with a sore head."

"I know my own shortcomings," he told her. A wisp of a smile touched his hard mouth. "You're not still afraid of me, are you?"

"I think I am, a little," she admitted softly.

"I'm glad." Something odd flashed in those sightless green eyes, puzzling her.

"Sir?" she murmured.

"Remind me to tell you about it someday," he said. He leaned back in his chair. "Yama! Ready to go?" he called.

Yama appeared at Cambridge's side from the kitchen. "Yes, boss!" he grinned. "I take good care of Miss Kate, not to worry."

"You'd damned well better," Cambridge grinned. "I'd never find anyone else who'd put up with me this long."

"Pattie last good," Yama reminded him.

"Pattie," he replied, "has nerves of steel and a mind like a bear trap. And," he added, "she works by long distance, which she says is the only way she can get along with me."

"I'd like to meet her someday," Kate laughed. "She sounds like a girl after my own heart."

"Insult me," Cambridge warned, "and you may find yourself typing this book after two a.m. every day."

"Sadist!"

He only grinned. "Go away, little girl. I need my rest."

"Naturally," Kate agreed impishly. "What with your advanced age and all, you have to keep up your strength."

His eyes narrowed. "Kate...." he warned softly.

"Would you like an iron tablet before I go?" she persisted, exchanging an amused grin with Yama.

"Damn it...!" Cambridge growled.

"We'll get you a shawl before we go, so you won't catch a chill in this night air," she went on.

"Out!" he exploded, rising from the chair with his face as hard as stone.

"Yes, sir!" Kate agreed, and took to her heels with Yama only a step behind, laughing all the way to the car in the driveway.

The beach by moonlight was everything Cambridge had promised it would be. Kate stood on the silvered sand, watching the moonlight play on the dark water, the glowing whitecaps rolling in against the shore, and wondered if she'd ever seen anything so narcotically lovely.

She stuck her hands deep in the pockets of her blue denim skirt and sighed, leaning back against one of the curving palms that ran the line of the shore. So beautiful, so lonely.... Even the tourists down the beach enjoying the sight from the comfort of lounge chairs didn't compensate for the terrible sense of loneliness that moonlit seascape fostered.

Suddenly, Kate remembered a night on the lake, a big, warm body drawing hers close against it, and a sweet, breathless shudder went through her. Why should she think of Cambridge when she was lonely? That didn't even bear thinking about! Especially now, with his memory back, when any minute he might regain his sight or recognize Kate as his "blonde assassin" by her voice....

"Worried expressions don't go with moonlight on a tropical beach, wood nymph," a pleasantly deep voice murmured behind her.

She whirled, surprised to find a tall young man in a pair of cutoff denims watching her. It was too dark to make out his facial features very well, except for a flash of white teeth.

"I'm Bart Lindsey," he persisted.

"Kate," she replied, taking the thin hand that was offered just briefly.

"Kate what?"

"Just Kate," she said cautiously.

"Mysterious woman! Are you, by any chance, a beautiful Russian spy?" he asked in a loud whisper.

"I don't think so," Kate told him, warming to his personality. "Although, I suppose I could have amnesia or something. What do you do?"

"I sell sea shells by the sea shore," he replied matter of factly.

"Do you have a sister Sue who does the same thing?"

"How did you ever guess?" he grinned.

"And do you have a white jacket with sleeves that tie in the back?" she wanted to know.

"I have one for casual wear, and one for dress occasions," he admitted. "How about having a drink with me? I'll even wear something decent for the occasion, although I'll have to admit that I prefer what I have on."

"Thanks anyway," she said. "But I have a demanding boss who only lets me out for minutes at a time under guard. I'm due back any minute."

"What does this tyrant do for a living?"

"He owns the hotel, among other things."

"Oh." He sighed. "So much for moonlight seduction. Okay, how about a rain check on the drink, in broad daylight next time? Even your boss couldn't make much out of that."

He wouldn't care at all, she started to say, and realized with a feeling of panic that it hurt.

"Maybe," she agreed.

"Tomorrow?"

She grimaced. "I'll be up to my neck in work tomorrow."

"If I give you my phone number, you could call me when you're free," he prodded. "I'm here for three weeks."

"Well...."

"Be a sport. Say, yes, Bart."

"Yes, Bart," she said agreeably.

"Good girl." He drew her along with him back to the hotel. "I'll get the number for you and write it down. Too bad I don't carry my pad around with me on the beach; I guess I ought to in case I meet any pretty girls," he teased.

"You really carry a pad around with you?" she asked, noticing as they moved into the well-lit hotel property that his face had sharp features and his eyes were a playful green—as different a green from Garet Cambridge's deep set eyes as night from day.

"I'm a reporter," he replied, taking in her expression with a grin. "Don't panic, I don't do news. Just feature material, travel stuff. Right now, I'm doing a piece on the island. Fascinating place, part French, part Dutch, part paradise, and you can see the Atlantic on one side of it, and the Caribbean on the other."

"How long have you been here?" she asked.

"Today. You?"

She laughed, tossing her mane of blonde hair. "Same here."

"Something in common already," he teased. "Sure you won't have that drink?"

"I'd love to," she said, "but here comes my boss's butler now," she added as she saw Yama coming out of the entrance to the hotel. "I'll just come down if I can tomorrow instead of calling, how about that?"

"Suits me," he said with a ready smile.

"If you're really sure...."

His eyes traveled over her appreciatively. "Boy, am I sure. I shall sit alone in my room and not move until I hear from you, even though I may starve and thirst to death."

She shook her head. "How do I get involved with people like you?"

"You have rare good luck," he told her. "Good night."

"Goodnight," she called over her shoulder, and ran to meet Yama.

"You must not tell boss you meet strange man," Yama cautioned as they sped toward the villa on the hill. "He funny about things sometimes and I not like to see you get in way of his temper more than you already have."

"You're nice, Yama," she said genuinely. "I seem to set him off by breathing lately. It's his eyes, of course. He just can't adjust to being blind, even if it's only temporary. Maybe..." she chewed her lip, "maybe his sight will come back."

"Maybe whales fly," Yama said sadly. "Who man you meet on beach?"

"A reporter."

"*Hai?* Oh, no!" Yama burst out. "Boss kill us both!"

"Not that kind of reporter," she replied calmly. "He only does features about tourist meccas like this one. He was careful to make sure I understood that," she added absently, and wondered dazedly why he'd been so careful about that point. "Anyway," she went on, "he doesn't know who I am or who I work for."

"He know by morning, you bet," Yama said. "He ask questions until he finds answers. If he find out who Mr. Cambridge is, we both out of job, Miss Kate. Nothing boss hate more than press, and now that eyes no good...."

"He won't do anything about Mr. Cambridge," Kate said doggedly, "I'll see to that. Yama, I...I like him, and I need some company."

Yama smiled. "You nice lady, Miss Kate. Boss not sweet to you, but it hurt him all same if you leave. He think much of you."

She blushed like a schoolgirl. "He hides it well," she said with a little of her old audacity.

"He hides much. He lonely man, Miss Kate. Fiancee hurt him when she leave, and not first time. When they first become engaged, year ago, he catch her out with some other man. He take her back against much good advice. She not worth his little finger, but it hard to tell man in love that his woman no good. Now maybe he begin to understand what she really like."

"Was she very beautiful, Yama?" Kate asked.

"Only on outside. Inside, she ugliest woman I ever see. Hard and calculating. She like boss's money very much," Yama said coldly. "And he give her plenty. Only time I ever see him let woman get so close. Better he stay like he used to be, hard as nails."

She only nodded, remembering the side of him she'd seen that was ice cold, before she came to work for him. She shuddered in spite of the heat.

7

Well, what did you think of it, Kate?'' Cambridge asked when Yama had left the flat envelope from the hotel on the desk and retired to his room.

"The beach, you mean," she muttered. "It was beautiful."

"I'm glad you could see it," he said deliberately, turning away to light a cigarette.

"I wish you wouldn't be so bitter," she said timidly.

"Do you?" There was a low, threatening note in his deep voice. He blew out a cloud of smoke and shifted the cigarette in his hand. "I don't give a damn what you wish, Kate."

She closed her eyes. "No, sir, I never imagined that you would."

"Don't humor me, damn it!" he growled, whirling toward the sound of her voice. "I've had just about enough of that kowtowing manner of yours, Miss Priss!"

She bit her lip. "I'd like to go to bed...."

"No doubt you would!" He blew out another cloud of smoke. "But we 'old men' have to be humored, didn't you know?"

Her eyes widened and she stared at him. Surely that mild teasing before she and Yama left hadn't pricked his hot temper...or had it?

"Mr. Cambridge, I was only teasing," she said gently.

"Well, for future reference, I don't like that kind of 'teasing'!" he said roughly. He turned away and eased himself over to the open French windows, letting the breeze lift his dark hair. "I'm perfectly aware of my age."

"I'm sorry," she murmured, feeling a little like a whipped pup.

"Are you?" he asked harshly. "You sound watery, Kate. Are you going to cry? Scolded children usually do."

She felt the tears, but she wouldn't give him the satisfaction of hearing her shed them.

"If you're quite through," she said with quiet dignity, "I'm going to bed—Sir."

"Yes, I'm through," he said coldly. "I'd tell you to get out of my sight, but that would be a joke, wouldn't it?"

"Oh, please don't . . . !"

"Get out." He said it with such cold contempt that she felt chill bumps rising on her arms, and she'd have given anything to take back those teasing words.

She turned. "Good night, Garet."

But he didn't even answer.

All night, she'd dreaded this morning. It came relentlessly, and far too soon, and she felt every muscle in her body tense with reaction when she sat down at the breakfast table. Cambridge's mood hadn't improved. If anything, she thought, shooting a glance at him, it had deteriorated even more.

His white sports shirt was open down the front over the broad, bronzed chest with its wedge-shaped sprinkling of thick black hair, and she suppressed a sudden, shocking urge to reach out and touch it. Her eyes wandered up to the firm, chiseled mouth, and she remembered without wanting to how it felt against hers that night in his room. . . . What was happening to her?!

"Still sulking?" he asked shortly as he sipped his coffee.

"I don't sulk."

"All women do." He set the cup down.

She picked at her breakfast with all the enthusiasm of eating cardboard. "What time do you want to start work?" she asked quietly.

"I don't. Having to be shut up in the same room with you all day would drive me out of my mind right now," he said icily. "Go sit on the beach, and don't come back until you're through pouting."

"I'm not pouting!" she said shortly. She stood up, throwing her napkin down on the table. "And you go to hell, Mr. Cambridge!"

She ran out of the room, out of the house, and kept going on the paved road that led down to the hotel. Long before she reached the beach, she wished she'd worn a sunhat with her beige shorts and top. It was so hot that she felt like a broken egg on asphalt.

Without thinking, she entered the hotel, drinking in the luxury around her and asked the desk clerk if Mr. Lindsey was still in his room. He was, and she asked if a message could be passed along that Kate was waiting for him in the lobby. She sat down on one of the plush round sofas and waited.

She couldn't begin to understand Garet's strange behavior. For one mad instant she wondered if he might truly have recognized her, but her mind dismissed that thought as impossible. Still, though, what was the matter with him? And why was he taking it out on her, when she couldn't remember anything she'd done to antagonize him except that remark about his age. And why should that upset him?

She sighed miserably, fighting down tears. He'd warned her what seemed ages ago that he had a black temper, and she almost wished she was back home in Texas. That is, until she remembered that Texas wouldn't have Garet Cambridge, and all of a sudden that prospect was as bleak as a desert.

She looked out the front door where the beach was visible from her seat, and she remembered what he'd said about standing at a window overlooking the Caribbean when he proposed to that faceless woman. She couldn't imagine that hard face softened with emotion, love in those sightless green eyes. Most of all, she couldn't imagine a woman stupid enough to throw him over because he couldn't see. He was so very much a man. Lack of sight didn't change that. But what hurt even more was the fact that he hadn't gotten

over that woman. And Kate was afraid to think too hard
about why it should hurt her.

"Well, hello," came a familiar voice.

She turned in her seat to smile at Bart Lindsey, suavely
dressed in a pair of tan slacks and a patterned shirt that
emphasized his blond fairness. "I hoped you'd be able to
make it."

"I had to fight my way out, and I hope you're suitably
impressed," she said.

He lent her a hand to help her up, his eyes lingering on her
long, tanned legs. "I'm impressed, believe me. Have you
had breakfast?"

She shuddered, remembering the scene at the breakfast
table. "Just coffee," she said truthfully.,

"Come on, then, and I'll feed you. The cuisine here is
magnifique."

"Je ne parle pas Francais, Monsieur," she murmured
demurely, flashing a glance at him as they walked toward the
spacious dining room.

"Moi, aussi," he seconded, and launched into a mono-
logue of French that left her breathless and protesting.

"I wasn't kidding," she laughed, "I really *don't* speak
French—only enough to tell people that I don't."

He grinned at her. "I speak just enough to get myself
slapped or arrested. I don't suppose you brought a swimming suit?"

She shook her head. "I wish I had. I . . . I left the villa in
kind of a hurry," she admitted. "I didn't have time to put
mine on."

"Boss in a bad temper?" he probed. "Mr. Cambridge's
reputation is etched in stone here," he continued, smiling at
her puzzled expression. "To hear the hotel manager talk
about him, you'd think he was the resident holy man. Formidable, black-tempered, generous to a fault, rich as all hell
and the very devil with the ladies. Does that about cover it?"

"Just about," she agreed warily.

He seated her at a small table by the window and dropped
down across from her. The dining room was almost de-

serted at this hour of the morning, but it didn't take long for a waitress to come and ask for their order.

"How about a continental breakfast and a side order of fruit?" Bart asked her, giving the order when she nodded and adding two cups of coffee to it.

She smiled at him over the dainty bougainvillea blossoms in their pretty vase. "How did you know to order coffee for me?"

"Because you look like a caffeine fiend. One can always recognize another," he added wickedly. He reached in his pocket for cigarettes and offered her one, which she politely refused.

"Pity," he observed, lighting up. "Caffeine and nicotine go together like ice and tea."

"So do nicotine and lung cancer," she said smartly.

"*Touche*. But I'm going to die of something eventually," he countered.

"I know, don't preach. My father says the same thing." She toyed with her water glass.

"How long have you worked for Mr. Cambridge?" he asked conversationally.

She eyed him with open suspicion. "Are you sure you're a travel writer?"

He laughed self-consciously. "Sorry. Force of habit. Asking questions is my profession."

"And ignoring them," she replied, "is mine. Especially when they concern Mr. Cambridge."

He eyed her closely. "Afraid of him?"

"He does have a temper," she said with a smile.

"What a waste," he sighed. "Burying yourself in an old man's memoirs...."

"Old man?" she blinked. "Memoirs?"

He toyed with the tablecloth. "Well, Jacques—the hotel manager, you know—said that he was a millionaire several times over. I wouldn't expect him to be a spring chicken. And you know yourself there aren't two pictures of him circulating. He breaks cameras, and reporters, if he can get his hands on them."

She laughed. "You wouldn't think he was old if you had to keep up with him. I imagine he used to go twenty-four hours a day...." She broke off, catching herself just in time. There was something naggingly suspicious about the questions he was asking.

"Used to?" He caught the slip and followed through.

"Well," she amended with deadly calm, "he is forty years old, of course."

"And you're what, Kate, twenty?" he teased.

She shook her head. "Almost twenty-three."

"Old enough to be your father, isn't he?" he laughed.

That had never occurred to her. She couldn't begin to think of Garet in that light, he was too utterly masculine, too vividly male to consider in any family sense. She could no more picture him as her father or a doting uncle than she could picture him with a cup in one hand begging on the streets.

"What's wrong?" Bart asked her.

"I was trying to picture Mr. Cambridge as my father," she said on a sigh. "I think I'd run away from home."

"Would you, really?" he probed. "I don't think so. A look comes into your eyes when you talk about him . . . are his memoirs interesting?"

She leaned her forearms on the table and glared across at him, her pale brown eyes darkening. "If you keep this up, I'm leaving. Mr. Cambridge's private life is none of your business."

He had the grace to look uncomfortable, even a little ashamed. He grinned boyishly. "It's just my nature to be curious. But if it bothers you, I'll be the soul of discretion and not ask any more leading questions. Okay?"

The waitress came with their order in time to save her an answer.

Kate watched what she told him for the rest of the day—she couldn't make herself trust him anymore. But she did enjoy herself. Bart had a built in sense of adventure. He could make a mundane walk along the beach something new and exciting. He told her stories he'd picked up about dolphins and sharks and pirates, and pointed out other islands in the Windward group and rattled off history as if he'd been born there.

"How did you ever get to be a reporter?" she asked him late that afternoon when they wound their way back to the hotel.

"Something to do with full moons, I think," he grinned. "Acutally, I had a little talent and I've used it to the limit, that's all. How did you get to be a secretary?"

"I could type."

"Talk about pat answers! But how," he persisted calculatingly, "did you wind up in St. Martin all the way from Texas?"

And that, she thought, would make a good story, especially if she mentioned her famous former employer and her part in Garet Cambridge's blindness. Nobody knew yet that he was blind, and what a scoop it would make for an ambitious young reporter. Kate decided right then that she'd never go out with Bart again. It was too dangerous. She might accidentally give Garet away. And she couldn't stand the thought of causing him any more anguish than she already had.

"It's getting late," she said, pausing in front of the hotel as she glanced toward the hill she had to climb to get back to the villa. "I hate to go, but...."

"I understand. The beast waits on the hill," he said with a grin. "Tomorrow? Same time, same place?"

"Maybe," she said. "Good night."

She turned and started up the road, her mind already on the villa and her moody employer.

Dark clouds were already blotting out the sun when she walked into the villa, nervously pushing back a windblown strand of her blond hair as she looked cautiously into the study.

"Is that you, Kate?" Cambridge asked from his easy chair by the window.

Her pale brown eyes were apprehensive, but her voice didn't show it as she joined him. "Yes, sir."

"I thought you'd decided to spend the night."

She linked her slender hands in front of her and clasped them tight. His dark face was as impassive as ever, but there was a storm brewing in the green eyes that stared in front of him while gray smoke curled up from the cigarette in his big hand.

"You did tell me I could spend the day, doing whatever I wished," she reminded him diplomatically.

"But I didn't know who you'd be spending it with, did I, Kate?" he asked in the harshest voice she'd ever heard from him.

She felt her face go white, and although there was no reason in the world for her to feel guilty, she did.

"How did you know?" she asked.

"People love to tell me things, Kate," he replied gruffly, his sightless eyes narrowing, his jaw tightening. "Especially about my private staff. You might remember that in the future. You can't make a move on this island that I won't know about."

She lifted her chin. "I haven't done a thing that I'm ashamed of."

"I know that, too." He took a draw from his ever-present cigarette. "What does he look like?" he asked in a deceptively casual voice.

"He . . . he's tall and blond."

"And young?" he asked harshly.

"And young," she replied deliberately.

"You're insolent, Miss."

"You drive me to it!" She took a deep breath, trying not to notice how broad his shoulders were, how massive his chest, how beautifully masculine his strong, broad fingers. "You don't own me, Mr. Cambridge."

"Are you sure about that?" he demanded. "Try to get off the island."

She felt her blood freeze. "Why would I want to get off the island?" she asked in what she hoped was a calm voice.

"Your boyfriend might ask you to go home with him," he replied coldly.

She blushed. "He's not my boyfriend," she told him. "For heaven's sake, I only met him...!"

"Time doesn't have a damned thing to do with emotions, Kate," he growled, as she could feel the tension in him. "One minute with some people is like ten years with others. And he's a damned reporter, too, isn't he? What a story he's sitting on right now!"

"If you really think I'd tell anybody anything about your private life, especially a reporter...!" she began hotly.

"Wouldn't you? He could probably persuade you to open up with a few kisses, or some cold cash," he added in a voice laced with contempt. "You did tell me once that you'd never had money, didn't you? What a golden opportunity this is."

Something seemed to die inside of her, like a freezing of buds in an unexpected cold snap. "You really think I could do that to you? That money means more to me than honor or integrity?" She drew a deep, steadying breath. "Is that part of being rich, Mr. Cambridge, thinking that people only do things for profit? Is it a standard that you measure people by? You're no better than that stuffed-shirt I got myself tangled up with! The only difference is that you're richer!"

His jaw locked, his eyes burned as they turned in her direction. "That's enough," he said icily.

"No, it isn't," she replied in a voice shot with tears. "But it'll have to do!"

"Kate, you aren't crying?" he asked suddenly, his heavy brows drawn into a scowl as his sharp ears caught the difference in her voice. "Kate, answer me!"

"Why?" she wept, turning toward the door. "Aren't you through?"

"Where are you going?"

"To sell you out to the press," she lobbed over her shoulder, "isn't that what you think?"

"What I think of you would scare you to death. Come back here."

"Aren't words enough?" she murmured, leaning her forehead against the door as tears rolled down her cheeks. "Or did you want to beat me before I go upstairs?"

"Don't be theatrical." His footsteps echoed behind her as he followed, accurately, the sound of her voice.

She felt the heat radiating from his big body as he stopped just behind her, felt the tentative searching of his hands as they found her shoulders and contracted gently on her bare, cool upper arms.

"You don't know what's wrong with me, do you?" he asked in a strange, low voice.

"I think I do," she corrected miserably, shaken by the feel of his arms, warm and strong and exciting where they touched her. "It's remembering that girl, the one who hit you on the lake, and you want to take it out on somebody because you can't get to her."

"I'll get to her, Kate. It's just a matter of when," he said with chilling certainty. "Is revenge too violent for you, milkmaid, or does it shock you that I feel the need for it? She took my eyes, damn it!"

Her eyes closed against the guilt. "Yes," she whispered. "I know. But whipping me to death won't bring them back!"

"No, it won't," he said gently. "Kate," he murmured, his breath warm against the back of her head, "I hurt like hell. I feel as if my head's about to burst. Don't leave me alone just yet."

A quick surge of sympathy and compassion welled up in her and she turned to look up into those unseeing eyes. "I forget sometimes that you aren't...that you can't see," she admitted softly.

"Do you forget my age at the same time?" he asked, very gently, and his hands moved up to cup her face. "That I'm almost a generation older than you? That I'm too rich for my own good, and that I've got the disposition of a half mad jungle cat half the time?"

"Mr. Cambridge..." she whispered, pushing at his massive chest in token protest. Her hands accidentally touched his bronzed flesh where his unbuttoned shirt had fallen away. Involuntarily, her fingers tangled in the growth of curling dark hair.

His chest rose and fell more rapidly, and under her hands she could feel the heavy beat of his pulse.

"Touch me, Kate," he said in a deep, tight voice.

Lost in the sensation of being close to him like this, drowning in the warmth of him, the tangy male scent of him, the sensuous feel of him, she obeyed him mindlessly. He was all firm muscle, all vibrant male, and there was a delicious intimacy in being allowed to touch him. Following an instinct as old as time, her face dropped to his broad chest and her lips touched him lightly, tentatively, and she felt him shudder.

His big hands tightened around her head like a vice and he jerked her face up to his blazing dark green eyes, eyes that couldn't see her.

"Don't do that," he whispered huskily. "It sets fires in my blood."

Her lips trembled as they tried to form words. "I'm sorry," she managed finally. "I've never done that before...."

"My God, don't apologize," he replied gently. "I'm trying to protect you, you hopeless little innocent! Do I have to remind you how long I've been without a woman?"

She blushed. "I wouldn't let you...."

"Oh, Kate, you'd let me," he whispered softly, pressing his firm, chiseled mouth to her forehead with a tenderness that was new and shattering. "You tremble all over when I hold you. If I started touching you, we'd both go up in flames."

With a start, she realized that he wasn't kidding. She was trembling from head to toe, and it wasn't out of fear. She swallowed nervously, enveloped in the comforting warmth of his body, drinking in the nearness like a thirsting runner. And as she started to analyze her tumbled emotions, it was like a puzzle suddenly fitting together. She loved him.

Loved him! A man she'd blinded, even though accidentally, a man who'd hate her if he ever found out. A man so far removed from her world in power and wealth that he might as well have come from another planet. But she loved him!

He felt the tremor that ran like quicksilver through the slender body pressed so closely to his, and his arms went around her to hold, to comfort.

"Don't ever be afraid of me," he said quietly. "The longest day I live, I'll never hurt you."

Oh, but you will, she thought miserably. You will, because it's inevitable that you'll find out who I am. And I wish I could run from you now, while there's still time.

"Would...would you like me to get you something for your head?" she asked softly.

"I've got all I need," he said at her ear. "You got rid of the last headache I had in a similar manner, remember Kate? Lying in my arms in bed...."

"It wasn't like that!" she protested, going red at the memory.

He chucked softly. "Oh, yes, it was." He tilted her face up and she felt his breath on her lips. "Kate..." he murmured. He bent and his mouth whispered against hers slowly, warmly, making her aware of him in a silence that seemed to catch fire. The lazy, deceptively comforting way he was kissing her made her hungry. Her nails involuntarily bit into his shoulders as he began to build the kiss, tempting, tantalizing her, until a soft, shocked moan broke from her lips. He knew exactly what he was doing, she thought dizzily, and if she didn't stop him right now, she knew what was going to happen.

She pulled against his slowly tightening arms. "Please...don't," she whispered achingly.

His mouth bit at hers with a slow, easy pressure. "Why not?" he murmured, a teasing note in his voice. "There has to be a first time, Kate."

"I'd hate you," she managed, her voice growing weaker as her knees seemed to buckle under her.

"Afterward, maybe," he whispered gruffly. His big arms tightened around her. "Oh, God, Kate, I could love you out of your mind."

Her eyes closed. If only he could love her, in the nonphysical as well as the physical sense—the thought made silver music in her mind. If he could love her as she loved him...involuntarily, she pressed closer to that big, husky body, feeling the strength of it against her with a sense of wonder, of pleasure that bordered on faintness. She loved him so...!

His arms tightened for just an instant and then relaxed. He moved away from her, back to his deep armchair, and she felt a sense of loss, an emptiness, as she watched him sit in the wide leather chair. He looked older suddenly, and there were hard lines in his face.

"Go to bed, Kate," he said wearily. "It was a nice interlude, but you don't have to humor the blind man any more tonight. Tomorrow we'll get back to work."

"But, I wasn't...!" she burst out when she realized the direction his thoughts had taken. He thought her response was...pity!

"Get the hell to bed! You can't give me what I need," he growled harshly. "But if you stay here, I may ask you to try. I need a woman, damn you! Anything in skirts would do, but you happen to be handy, is that clear enough?" he asked when she hesitated.

She flinched as if he'd struck her. And that was all it had meant to him! Those moments when she felt all of paradise in his arms, his possessive mouth, it had only been an interlude to him—something to satisfy a passing need. She turned and went out the door without another word.

Hours seemed to go by before she slept, and the phone ringing in the middle of the night didn't help her shattered nerves. There was something vaguely ominous about that splintering sound echoing through the dark villa. Something final, like a death knell....

When she went down to breakfast the next morning, she knew why she'd thought that. A woman was sitting beside

Garet Cambridge at the breakfast table, her slender hand possessively on his arm, her eyes sparkling as she chattered away. She turned at Kate's entrance, and her identity was immediately obvious. She had curling blond hair and eyes the blue of a spring sky.

"You must be Kate," the woman said with a flash of ice in the glance she turned on the younger woman, and a smile that only touched her wide mouth.

"Yes," Kate said hesitantly, her eyes going to Garet, who was sitting quietly at the head of the table, his dark face giving nothing away.

"I'm Anna Sutton," the blond said. "Garet's fiancee, you know," she added possessively.

Cambridge stiffened almost imperceptibly. "Ex-fiancee," he said calmly, setting down his emptied coffee cup to light a cigarette.

Anna lifted a perfectly manicured hand to her short, curling hair. "Temporarily only, darling," she cooed, "just until you feel I've been punished enough for walking out on you, we both know that."

Kate sat down across from the newcomer and exchanged a sharp glance with Yama when he brought her breakfast in.

"I didn't know you had a live-in secretary, darling," Anna remarked to Garet as she picked at her breakfast. "Where's Pattie?"

"Still at the office, I suppose," he replied quietly. "I'm working on a book, Anna. I can't dictate it long distance."

That voice... Kate stared at the older woman, and she recognize it all at once. The cabin on the lake, when she'd called to ask about Garet after the accident—this was the woman who'd answered the phone! And if she recognized Kate's voice, it would be all over.

"You're quiet this morning, milkmaid," Garet said speculatively, his sightless eyes narrowing thoughtfully. "Nothing to say?"

Kate stared into her coffee. "No, sir."

"Docile, aren't you?" he growled.

"Yes, sir," she murmured.

"Have I missed something?" Anna asked irritably. She glanced from one to the other of them with a frown between her wide-spaced eyes.

"Only a few knock-down, drag-out arguments," Garet said with a hint of a smile. "Young Kate has a streak of impudence in her."

"Only when I'm pushed over the edge," Kate replied darkly, putting down her fork. "I'd like to be excused."

"No doubt you would, but just sit the hell where you are, Kate," Cambridge said harshly, freezing her as she tried to rise. "I plan to get some work done today. That *is* what I pay your salary for, not to play hookey with that damned journalist!"

Kate bit her lip to keep the hot words back, and the smug look Anna gave her didn't help any. She didn't like Garet's girlfriend. One look was enough to tell her that the older woman's only interest in him was his money. She didn't have the light of love in her pale blue eyes when she looked at the big man beside her. There was only a shrewd, cold look there, as if she was measuring the size of his wallet every time she looked at him.

But Garet couldn't see that. His big hand slid along the wooden finish of the table to catch Anna's and squeeze it. He smiled, and there was no mockery in it.

"Tonight," he told her, "we'll go down to the beach and you can describe the moonlight on the sea to me."

Anna leaned forward with a sigh, and it was a pity, Kate thought bitterly, that Cambridge couldn't have the benefit of Anna's low neckline. "Oh, darling," Anna breathed, "I'll describe everything to you. It'll be just like old times."

Kate wanted to be sick. She wanted to scream at him. But all she could do was sit and pretend not to be affected.

"I'll have to get some work done first, however," Garet said with a grin. "Make yourself scarce while Kate and I finish up the paperwork. Put on your bikini and decorate the beach. Tell Jacques to get you a beach umbrella so you don't burn that delicate complexion."

"Oh, Garet, you remembered," Anna said. She took hi big hand in both of hers. "Darling, I'm so sorry about you eyes," she whispered brokenly, although there wasn't a trace of sorrow in her cold eyes. "I'm sorry I walked out on you it was just such a shock . . . but I'm back now, and I'll tak care of you."

"For how long?" he asked conversationally.

"As long as you need me, darling," she purred.

Garet only smiled, feeling for the ashtray to crush out hi cigarette. "Run along," he told her.

"Yes, darling." Anna got up and reached over to plant sweet, long kiss against his hard mouth. Kate turned he head away, because she couldn't bear the sight.

Then Anna was gone, ignoring Kate completely, and the were alone.

"What do you think of her?" he asked quietly.

"She's lovely, and when do you want to start work?" she asked tightly.

One dark eyebrow went up and he smiled. "Jealous milkmaid?"

"Of what? Your wallet?" she asked flatly, "becaus that's the only part of you *she's* interested in!"

Something like amusement flashed in his dark green eyes. "Not quite," he said softly.

Kate blushed all the way to her throat, almost knockin over her coffee cup in her haste to get out of her seat.

"I'll bet your face is redder than a sunset," he remarked

"I never blush," she told him firmly.

"Of course." He got up, feeling his way to the door an along the passageway to his study, right behind Kate "Someday, Kate. . . ."

"Someday, what?" she asked

He stopped in his tracks, sweat breaking out, beading u on his forehead, and he leaned heavily against the wall, on big hand going to his head.

"Oh, my God . . . !" he groaned, and his eyes close against a pain that Kate could only imagine.

8
*

"Garet, what it it?" she cried, running to him. She caught his big arms and stared up at his contorted face with horror in her pale brown eyes. "Oh, please, tell me what's wrong!"

"My...head," he groaned. His eyes closed tightly, and his hand worried them for several seconds before she felt him relax.

"Are you all right?" she asked, in a voice more laced with emotion than she realized.

"I'm all right. It was just a pain, Kate," he said gently.

"No, it wasn't!" she said, a break in her voice. "Garet, you've got to see a doctor."

"What the hell for?" he growled impatiently. "So he can tell me to learn to live with it? I can't even see the blurs and shadows anymore! It's permanent!"

She wanted to sink through the floor. Her slender body seemed to shrink against his.

"Oh, is something wrong?" Anna asked, joining them in the hallway in a shimmering blue bikini with a towel clutched in one manicured hand.

"Mr. Cambridge is having pain," Kate told her in a cool tone.

Anna shrugged. "One of the unpleasant side effects, I imagine, isn't it darling?" she asked Garet with a smile. "I'm sure it passes. Well, I'm going on down to the beach, I'll be back in a few hours. Bye!"

Kate glared after her even when the door closed and cut her off from view. She couldn't remember feeling such a surge of unbearable rage before.

"Aren't you going to say something, milkmaid?" Garet asked, his deep voice amused even though the hard lines hadn't left his face.

Kate's soft mouth pouted. "Whatever I said would be either too much or too little. Anyway," she added tightly, "she's your business."

"Is she, Kate?" He caught her arms and pulled her against his big, husky body, holding her easily when she struggled instinctively to be let go of.

"Mr. Cambridge...!" she grumbled.

"A few minutes ago, it was 'Garet'," he reminded her smoothly. His big hands spread against her shoulder-blades, drawing her relentlessly closer into an embrace that melted her hunger for freedom.

"A...a few minutes ago, I was worried," she said unsteadily.

"I know." His chest rose and fell against her. "I'm indestructible, didn't you know?"

She rested her cheek against the front of his brown silky shirt with a sigh. "I only wish you were," she said quietly. "I wish you'd see a doctor."

"You *are* worried," he murmured, as if he found the thought unbelievable.

Her eyes closed. "No, I'm not!" she burst out. "What should I care if you're too stubborn and hard-headed too...!"

Soft, deep laughter cut into the impassioned speech and his arms tightened. "Hush," he murmured. "Kiss me."

She felt the blush claim her cheeks and resisted, even knowing he couldn't see it, when he reached down and tilted her face up to his.

"Don't," she murmured.

"Kiss me, you little coward," he teased gently.

"Why?" she asked, but her eyes were already on the broad curve of that chiseled mouth, and she remembered the sweet, hard pressure of it with a sense of wonder.

"Do we need reasons, Kate?" he asked, suddenly serious. There was a strange darkness in the green eyes that she couldn't understand.

"No," she admitted, going on tiptoe to touch her soft mouth to his. "No, we don't need reasons, we don't . . . oh, Garet . . ." she breathed.

She felt a rough hand come up behind her head as he forced her lips hard against his.

"Like this," he ground out against her mouth, his breath coming unsteadily. "Pretend you're in love with me, little girl. Show me how it would be. . . ."

Her arms went up around his neck and she threw caution to the winds. Her body swayed against his like a young willow as the kiss went on and on, a mutual hunger in it that was like nothing she'd ever felt. He cherished her young mouth as if he wanted nothing else in life but the touch and taste of it, his big arms cradling her tenderly. She'd never known that an embrace could be so gentle, that a kiss could be a linking of minds and hearts so intense and pleasurable. There was nothing of lust in it.

When he finally drew away, she stared up at him in a daze, speechless, too shaken for words.

His face was like stone, hard and quiet and utterly devoid of expression. But the hands that pressed against her back were trembling, and the heart beneath his massive chest was shaking him with its hard pulsing.

"Have you ever kissed another man like that?" he asked roughly.

"No," she admitted without thinking.

He drew a steadying breath and let her go. "We'd better get some work done," he said tightly, turning away.

She followed him into the study and automatically picked up her notepad and pen, dropping into the chair beside his desk while he fitted his body into the swivel chair behind it.

"Is . . . is your head better?" she asked softly.

A whisper of a smile touched his mouth. "You have a foolproof method of chasing my headaches away, Kate," he said gently, and when she realized what he meant, she felt her hands grow cold as ice.

"No comeback?" he teased.

"I . . . I shouldn't have . . ." she murmured.

"Why not?" he asked, and the smile faded.

"There's Miss Sutton," she said miserably.

"Yes," he said thoughtfully, scowling. "There's Miss Sutton. You wouldn't be jealous?"

She stiffened. "You're my boss, Mr. Cambridge, not my lover."

"I will be," he said quietly, and there was a wealth of meaning in the lazy smile that touched his chiseled mouth.

She blushed. "No, you won't!" she burst out.

But he only laughed. "Got your pad, Kate? Let's get to work."

Anna Sutton was brilliantly talkative at dinner, monopolizing Garet all through the meal as the vivid sunset filtered in through the French windows and gave the villa a coral glow. Kate picked at her food, hardly tasting anything. Her mind was muddled with thoughts that didn't bear sharing.

She wondered idly what kind of a game Garet Cambridge was playing. He seemed to be as infatuated with Anna as ever, but why had he kissed Kate that way? Was he just playing one woman off against the other? Was it some kind of revenge on womankind because Anna had deserted him?

"You don't talk very much anymore, Kate," Garet remarked suddenly, cutting into her thoughts.

She lifted her face in time to catch the venomous look Anna threw at her.

"I . . . I couldn't think of anything to say," she stammered.

"You aren't pining for the young journalist, are you?" he demanded suddenly, harshly, and the black scowl jutted over those sightless eyes.

Young journalist? She hadn't given Bart Lindsey a thought. . . . "No, sir," she replied quietly.

"A reporter?" Anna burst out. "You're letting your secretary associate with a reporter?"

"'Date' is the word," Cambridge said darkly. "And no, I'm not letting her."

Kate glared at him. "I can date whom I please. You don't own me."

"That isn't the impression I got this afternoon," he said with a smug arrogance that caused her to blush furiously.

Anna stared at her suspiciously. "Is there something I missed?"

"You might say that," Garet grinned. "Is she blushing?"

"Like a fire truck," Anna said angrily.

"I ... I wish you wouldn't," Kate murmured in a husky tone.

Anna frowned. "Your voice is so familiar," she muttered, and Kate felt her heart stop. "I'm almost certain I've heard it somewhere before."

"I don't see how," Cambridge said, finishing Yama's well-turned steak. "Unless you've ever been to Austin?"

Anna shrugged uncomfortably. "I don't travel in those circles," she said haughtily, "if you mean cattle country. I believe that's what you told me your secretary's people were into."

Kate wanted to throttle her, but she kept her temper. She had enough trouble wondering what minute the blonde might remember Kate's unsteady voice asking about Garet Cambridge that day on the lake, after the accident. What if she recognized it? What if....

"Is your headache better, darling?" Anna asked him.

"Much," he said with a secretive smile, and Kate kept her face down so that Anna wouldn't see the blush.

It was later that same night when the phone rang in the study, and Garet picked up the receiver before she could get to it. She watched his face change as he listened, asking an occasional question, and before he was through, Kate knew with chilling certainty what he was hearing.

He hung up and leaned back in his chair, frowning thoughtfully. "How interesting," he muttered to himself.

She looked up from her typing. "Sir?" she asked.

He sighed and lit a cigarette. "Remember that private eye I hired, Kate?" he asked conversationally. "He's traced the girl."

Her blood froze—froze in her veins—and she could feel the temperature of her hands drop degree by degree where they rested on the keys of the typewriter.

"Has he?" she asked in a husky voice.

He smiled, satisfied with himself. "She lived down the beach from me; for a while, at least. She's disappeared now. Probably scared to death I'd go looking for her if I lived." His eyes narrowed. "She worked for a writer—Maude Nic-cole, you might have heard of her, Kate, she writes romantic fiction. Unfortunately," he sighed, "we can't locate her. She was in Paris, but she left with her father and didn't leave a forwarding address. I've got her beach house under surveillance, though. If she comes back, I'll know it."

Kate sat there dying. It was all over now. When he found Maude, and he would, he'd know the truth. Her eyes studied him, drinking in the sight of him, so big and dark and arrogant. Leaving him would be the hardest thing she'd ever have to do. Tears misted her soft eyes. She'd have to leave, and as soon as possible. At least that way she could avoid the confrontation that would be inevitable. Anyway, he had his Anna now, she thought, he won't miss me. Tears rolled down her flushed cheeks at just the thought.

"You're very quiet, Kate," he said.

She wiped away the tears, careful not to sniff and give herself away. "I was just thinking," she said, schooling her voice to calmness. "What...what will you do when you find her?" she asked.

"I haven't quite decided," he said thoughtfully. He linked his hands on the desk, flexing them. His eyes narrowed. "But I'll come up with something unique, believe me. I'll make her pay in ways she couldn't have dreamed of."

I already have, she thought miserably. I've paid in a way you couldn't imagine. I fell in love with you, and my punishment will be spending the rest of my life where I'll never see you, or hear you, again. And death might be kinder. Her eyes traced the lines of his face lovingly, achingly. Oh, I do love you so, she thought.

"You think I'm hard," he remarked when she was silent.

"No," she admitted quietly. "I don't really blame you for feeling that way."

"I can't help it, Kate," he said. "I can't help wanting to get my own back on her. I'll have to go through life in this damned darkness, and for what? Because a spoiled brat pitched a temper tantrum on the lake in a boat!"

Kate's eyes closed. He was right, he was absolutely right, and the pain went all the way to the soles of her feet. But she hadn't known what would happen. She hadn't known him. If only she could tell him the truth, make him understand....

She sighed. He'd never listen. She only had one option, and that was to run. But getting off the island wasn't going to be an easy thing now. She had to keep him from getting suspicious. She had enough money, barely, to get back to her father. She'd saved it carefully. But how to get away long enough? That was going to take some planning. She might be able to get Bart Lindsey to help her.

"What are you plotting, Kate?" he asked suddenly.

She jumped as if she'd been slapped unexpectedly. "Plotting? Why...nothing!" she said quickly.

"All right, I believe you," he laughed. "Come on, honey, let's finish up this last chapter while I've still got a clear head."

"Yes, sir."

Kate didn't sleep. She couldn't. And it didn't help that in the middle of the night, there was one whale of an argument in the hall and the voices roared through the cool silence.

It was Anna and Garet. She could tell that without bothering to open the door of her bedroom, and Anna was clearly getting the worst of it. Kate couldn't make out the words to tell what they were arguing about, but it was loud enough to carry all through the villa. Then, suddenly, there was the sound of a door slamming, and for a few minutes it was quiet. Then there was the sound of the door opening, and slamming again, sharp, angry footsteps, and the sound of another door slamming. Then quiet; an ominous, strange quiet that was suddenly shattered by the sound of a yell. Kate jumped out of bed without bothering to grab for her bathrobe, threw open the door, and ran barefoot down the hall to Garet's room. She thought as long as she lived she'd never get over that sound in the darkness, that harsh scream of pain that echoed through the villa.

Yama was already by the bed when she got there, his face heavily lined, his eyes frightened as they lifted to Kate's.

Garet was as white as cotton, his eyes closed, his face strangely relaxed, strangely youthful looking as he lay there against the pillows. His breathing was shallow, erratic. Kate bit her lip, her eyes wincing.

"Oh, Yama, what happened?" she breathed, her eyes never leaving the still figure on the bed, as she stood trying to catch her breath, to cope with the fear.

"Headaches get closer together since we come here," Yama said worriedly. "He not say so, but I know him and can tell. It why his temper so bad lately. Miss Kate, doctor warn him this may happen if he not rest, and he have fall tonight after Miss Sutton leave. I find him in study and get him to bed. Not know if it cause this or not, but we must get him to a doctor, and quick. I call Pattie. She make arrangements. You stay with him?"

She sat down in the chair by the bed and took his limp, cool hand in hers, her eyes eating him. "Oh, yes," she breathed, "I'll stay with him. Miss Sutton . . . left?"

"Very fast," Yama told her. "She upset him and he tell her to go. Finally show good sense, now this happen! I make call."

She sat beside the big man, watching him breathe, willing him to live. If only she knew what was wrong, if she could do something!

Her hand tightened on his. Her doing—it was all her doing. And if he died, what use would living be, and that would be her fault, too. Oh, what a horrible day it was when she got behind the wheel of that boat and gave vent to her temper. She'd have given ten years of her life to undo it. She'd have given her life. He couldn't die. He couldn't!

It seemed an eternity before Yama came back, quiet and solemn.

"Pattie calling doctor now," he said. "I call charter pilot and he standing by at airport. Also call hotel, manager sending men up to help get him into plane. I go with him, Miss Kate."

Tears rolled hot and wet down her cheeks. "Oh, Yama," she whispered brokenly, her hands grasping that big one of Garet's tightly.

"It be all right," Yama said, awkwardly patting her on the shoulder. "Boss tough. It takes more than this to get him down. Miss Kate, I think it best you come with us back to states. Must refuel in Atlanta, can leave you there to go back to lake house and wait, okay?"

She could barely think at all, and was dimly grateful for somebody to tell her what to do. She only nodded through the tears, her eyes never leaving Garet.

"He's so pale," she whispered.

"I know. You pack, Miss Kate. I stay with him."

"Yes, Yama." She got up slowly, her eyes showing the hurt as plainly as if she'd screamed it the width of the room. She let go of his hand, but it was letting go of life.

Kate hardly remembered the rest of that horrible night. Everything seemed to happen all at once. The hotel employees came to lift the big man onto a stretcher, and they transported him in a station wagon to the waiting Learstar. Kate sat beside him on the plane, holding his hand, her eyes burning with tears, her mind numb with fear. He was still breathing, but he hadn't regained consciousness, not for an instant. She'd never been so afraid before. If he didn't make it....

"He be all right, Miss Kate," Yama said from beside her. He handed her a key and a wad of bills. "You rent car, go back to lake house. This key. It be good idea also if you get Hunter out of kennel to stay with you."

"Yama, I thought I might go home...." she began.

"No, Miss Kate," he shook his head emphatically. "Boss do better if he know where you are. Also, Pattie and I can get to you better. Please, Miss Kate, not to argue."

She sighed. "All right," she said wearily, "I'll do it."

Besides, she thought, it would give her the opportunity to check on Maude's cabin. If Maude was no longer in France, there was a good possibility that she'd come back to the lake, anyway. And Kate was too tired, and too heartsick, to argue anymore.

Her eyes went back to the husky figure on the stretcher. Please live, she pleaded silently. Please, live, even if it's only to get even with me for doing this to you!

It seemed so long ago that she'd had the run-in with Cambridge on the beach, so many weeks since the accident. And in that length of time, she'd come to know the man behind the power, and she liked what she found. He wasn't the tyrant she'd thought him. He was simply a man; a very lonely man who was, despite his black temper, the only man she would ever love.

9
*

They landed in Atlanta, and Kate watched them take Garet away to a waiting charter plane with a sense of emptiness.

"I call you soon as I know something," Yama had promised. "He will be all right, Miss Kate."

"Oh, Yama, I hope so," she whispered as she watched the plane take off, shading her eyes with her hand. "What will I do if he..." She swallowed on the thought and turned slowly away toward the terminal.

It had been a while since she'd driven, but she got to the lake house with barely an effort. Now that there was time to think, she wondered about Bart Lindsey and what he'd think when he discovered that she'd gone in the middle of the night. Not that she really cared; he'd pumped her for information pretty hard, and she still wondered if he really was a travel writer. But when her mind went back to Garet, so still and white on that stretcher, Lindsey went right out of her thoughts again.

She'd stopped by the kennels on the way and picked up Hunter. The big shepherd was actually glad to see her, whining and licking her hand and wagging his tail furiously. She opened the cottage door and let him inside first, following him half-heartedly. The cabin held such memories—of that first morning when Cambridge had asked her to move in with him—of that night when she'd gone in to see about him when he had the headache, of the morning he'd announced that they were going to St. Martin....

She turned, her eyes on the telephone. She picked up the receiver to make sure it was still connected, and was reassured when she heard the dial tone. She put it down again and stared at it. Yama said the specialist Garet saw was in

New York. Had they had time to get to New York? Surely they had. Was he already in the hospital? What would the doctor do?

She put her bags in the bedroom and went back to get the groceries she'd picked up out of the car. It was going to be a long wait, even if it only took an hour or two more for Yama to call her. Every second would seem like hours, every hour like a day. She wanted the phone call and dreaded it at one and the same time. Oh, please, let him live, she prayed silently. Please let him live, and if having him hate me is the price I have to pay, then that's all right, too, but please let him be all right!

She fed Hunter and poured herself a bowl of cereal. It had been almost half a day since she'd eaten anything, but she wasn't hungry. It was just a way to keep body and soul together, that was all. Her heart wasn't in it.

The weather was misty outside and there were dark gray clouds on the horizon, hanging ominously over the lake. Kate sat on the porch where she used to eat breakfast with Garet and watched the shadows play on the lake. Something in the rain was vaguely ominous, foreboding. The sudden ringing out of the phone made her jump.

She ran to answer it with trembling hands. "Hello?" she mouthed.

"Kate? This is Pattie," came a pleasant, soft voice on the other end of the line.

"Hello, Pattie. How is he?" Kate asked quickly.

She held her breath until she heard the reply.

"He's still with us," Pattie said gently. "Although it's going to be touch and go for a few days."

"Is he conscious? What happened? What did the doctor say?" Kate fired away.

"No, he's not conscious, and none of us are quite sure what happened," Pattie replied. "The doctor says the fall could have caused additional pressure on the optic nerve, and then he went into a spate of technical jargon about exactly what he planned to do, and lost me completely. All I got out of it is that Mr. Cambridge will live,"

"Oh, thank God," Kate whispered. Her eyes closed and she smiled through a mist of tears. "Oh, thank God. I've been so worried!"

"Yama told me to call you the instant I knew something," the secretary told her gently. "He was pretty upset when he found Anna Sutton in the boss's apartment here. Of course, she made a beeline for the hospital."

It was like the end of the world. Kate felt suddenly empty and alone. "Oh," she murmured.

"I hear she bombed in on you at St. Martin, too," Pattie probed. "And that the boss threw her out. She never gives up."

"So I noticed." Kate stared at the floor. "She only likes the size of his wallet," she muttered.

"I know," came the reply. "And so does he, Kate. Don't think she'll fool him a second time. He isn't stupid—although he does occasionally give that impression."

Kate laughed in spite of herself. "I noticed that," she said. "Is . . . is there anything I can do?"

"Yes. Sit right there and wait for him to come home," Pattie told her with a smile in her tone. "The doctor says if he does okay, he may be out of here in a couple of weeks."

"Two weeks," Kate murmured. She sighed. She wouldn't be here then. She had enough sense of self-preservation left in her to run, before that private detective made the final connection for her sightless boss, before he threw her out into the street. She thanked Pattie again for calling, and put the receiver gently back in its cradle. Then she sat down, buried her face in Hunter's silky fur, and cried like a baby.

The next morning, she took Hunter and walked down the beach toward Maude's cabin. How long ago it had been since she walked this beach and saw the big, solitary man standing on the beach and was ordered off in no uncertain terms. She'd never have dreamed that she'd go to work for him, that she'd fall in love with him. Fate, she thought, was unpredictable.

The cabin still looked empty, but two of the windows were open, and Kate caught Hunter by the collar and started toward the front porch, almost running in her haste to find out if Maude was really home.

She ran up onto the porch. "Maude!" she called excitedly.

The thin little figure who came running out onto the porch was a welcome sight. Without thinking, Kate went straight into her arms and wept as if she were a hurt child.

"Are you really that glad to see me?" Maude asked, rocking the younger woman in her arms.

"I really am," Kate sniffed, stifling the sobs that rose to her throat. "Did you get my telegram? I sent you one...."

"It didn't catch up to me, baby," Maude said apologetically. "Dad and I left Paris and I dropped him off at my aunt's on the way back here. He wasn't able to stay alone, although he's much improved...anyway, when I got here and there was no sign of you, I called your father. He told me where you were." She drew back and looked straight into Kate's misty eyes. "What happened?"

Kate moved away, wiping her eyes. "I hit Garet Cambridge with the boat and hurt him...blinded him," she said painfully, closing her eyes on the memory of that horrible accident.

"I thought you were working for him!" Maude exclaimed. "Why would he hire you when...?"

"You'd better sit down," Kate told her.

"All right, so sit down and I'll bring some coffee. Then you can explain it to me."

Ten minutes later, sipping coffee in the living room, Kate told Maude what had happened in the last few weeks. When she was through, Maude just sat there shaking her head.

"You mean, he hired you, knowing what you'd done to him?" Maude exclaimed.

"No," Kate replied miserably, wrapping her slender fingers around her coffee cup. "He doesn't know I was responsible. Once or twice, I was tempted to tell him, but at the last minute...."

"Oh, Kate, I warned you," Maude groaned. "If only you'd listened to me. Do you have any idea what that man will do to you when he finds out?"

"A pretty good one." Kate looked at her old employer wearily. "He's hired a private detective, and they've traced me to you."

Maude seemed to go white. "A detective? Oh, Kate!"

"That's right. Has anyone talked to you at all about me?"

"No," Maude sighed. "But it's only a question of time. What are you going to do?"

"Well, he won't be back for a couple of weeks. I've got that long to make a decision." She left her coffee sitting and got up to pace the floor. "I guess I'll go home to Austin for a while. I hate to just walk out on you like this...."

"Don't worry about me," Maude said firmly, "I'll manage. It's you I'm concerned about."

"I just hope he doesn't decide to take out his hatred for me on my poor dad. I've been a constant headache to him lately."

"Poor dad, my foot," Maude said. "Poor you, Kate, I'm so sorry."

"Why? I brought it on myself. If I hadn't tried to take out my temper in the boat...."

"That isn't what I meant," Maude said kindly. Her pale blue eyes were compassionate. "You love him very much, don't you?"

Kate met that level look and sighed achingly. "Oh, Maude, I love him more than life," she admitted quietly. "I'd gladly give him my own eyes if I could! At first, he could see blurs and shadows a little, and they thought his sight might come back. But now, even that little glimmer of hope is gone. He's permanently blind, and it's my fault, and when he finds out, he'll hate me. I can't even blame him for it, but I'm so afraid of what he'll do."

Maude went over to put her thin arm around the younger woman. "That fact that you stayed with him all this time, and looked after him might carry some weight. Kate, he isn't totally heartless, you know. He may decide...."

"I don't think so," she murmured. "Even if this hadn't happened, I wouldn't have had a chance with him. A man that powerful, that rich; Maude, if he'd been able to see, he wouldn't have had anything to do with me, anyway. Look at how fast he ran me off his property that day."

"My darling," Maude said softly, "don't you know that those kind of differences don't matter? Men like Garet Cambridge make their own rules as they go along. They don't conform the way we lesser mortals do."

"If only I'd stayed out of the boat," she whispered, and the tears came again. "At least he'll live. At least I won't have that on my conscience."

Maude hugged her affectionately. "My baby," she said soothingly. "My poor baby."

And Kate cried all the harder.

Two days passed with maddening slowness. Kate kept herself busy around the cabin, working on the manuscript until she had it completely typed and ready to go to the publisher. It would give Garet a little satisfaction to be doing something constructive, she thought miserably. If he couldn't test-fly his planes, or design them on paper, at least he could write about them.

On the third day, the phone rang, and she picked it up with a feel of impending doom.

"Kate?"

Her heart leaped at the sound of that deep, slow voice, a little slurred by drugs, but just as commanding as ever.

"Garet!" she cried, clutching the receiver like a lifeline as she sank down into a chair by the table the phone was resting on. "Oh, Garet," she whispered brokenly, "are you all right?"

"Calm down, milkmaid," he said softly. "I'm doing very well. How are you?"

"I'm fine, of course."

"Of course," he scoffed. "You're crying!"

"I've been worried," she muttered defensively as she dabbed at the tears with a corner of her blouse.

"So Yama told me. What are you doing down there?" he asked conversationally.

Her heart pounded wildly and she stroked the receiver as if she were touching his hard, husky body. "I'm holding down the fort. I . . . I got the manuscript typed and ready to go. Do you want me to mail it?"

"Go ahead. Then just relax and enjoy the lake until I get there." There was a pause. "Missing me, little girl?"

"Terribly," she said without thinking. She drew in a deep, slow breath. "I, uh, I hear Miss Sutton's been to see you."

"Anna? Oh, she's been her constantly. Bringing me flowers, boxes of candy." There was a pause. "Why the hell aren't you here?" he demanded.

"Yama said that it would be better if I waited here," she stammered.

"Never mind, maybe he's right. Pattie tells me you've called twice already."

"Yes, sir."

"Don't ever call me sir, again," he said quietly. "Not ever, Kate."

"I'm sorry. I didn't mean. . . ."

"Oh, hell, I wish you were here with me!" he growled. "I'm no good at polite conversation. Kate, you're not alone at the lake house, are you? You've got Hunter, haven't you?"

"Yes," she told him. "I picked him up at the kennels. He's . . . good company."

"Don't go out alone at night. Promise me."

The concern in his voice made her feel warm all over. "I promise," she said.

There was a muffled curse. "The nurse is here with a shot. I've got to go, honey. I'll call you tomorrow."

"All right. Garet . . ." she searched for something to say, anything but what she really wanted to say.,

"Good night, Kate," he said quietly. The receiver went dead before she could find the right words.

Time seemed to fly after that. Kate lived from day to day, for the late night phone calls from New York lulled into a sense of security by the sound of Garet's deep, quiet voice and the new note in his voice that sent chills down her spine. There was nothing personal in the calls, just idle conversation, but it was wonderful just to hear the sound of his voice.

During the day, she spent her time walking Hunter and talking to Maude. In the back of her mind, she knew the time was rapidly approaching when she'd have to leave. Garet would be home in less than a week. She needed to start making plans now, but it was so easy to put it off, to wait just one more day, for one more phone call....

It was late afternoon when she heard Hunter raising the devil outside the cabin. Kate had just finished grilling herself a steak, and she left it on the stove as she moved quickly to the front of the house to see what Hunter had found.

She walked out the door in her jeans and T-shirt and came face to face with a dream.

Garet Cambridge was standing at the bottom of the steps with his big hand on Hunter's silky head. He looked up as Kate froze on the top step, and his dark green eyes looked directly into hers. They dilated. His face went hard as stone. And she knew, without a word being spoken, that everything between them was over.

"You!" he ground out, and the hatred was in his eyes, his voice, the taut lines of his big body. He'd recognized her. He could see!

10

*

"What the hell are you doing in my house?" he demanded.

She only stared at him, drinking in the dark face above the beige sports shirt, the bigness of him, the eyes that, even hating her, could see again.

"I..." she faltered.

"Did you come back to finish the job?" he demanded, moving up the steps to glare at her relentlessly. "Or were you finally curious enough to come find out if you'd killed me?"

She licked her dry lips. "I'm sorry," she whispered in a voice that didn't even sound like her own. She was frightened of him now, frightened of the power he could wield, of his hatred.

"You're sorry," he scoffed. His eyes narrowed, contemptuous, burning. "My God, you left me for dead, and you're sorry?! What the hell do you expect me to say? That's all right, no hard feelings? Well, I'm fresh out of forgiveness, you little assassin! I want your damned throat!"

She flinched at the tone of his deep voice. Her eyes closed on a flood of tears. "I...did call," she whispered.

"Why?" he growled. "Were you afraid you'd missed?"

She started down the steps, but he caught her arm roughly and dragged her around, hurting her in his anger.

"Damn you, I'm not finished!" he said harshly. He drew her up under his blazing eyes and tightened his cruel grip. He studied her as if she were some new kind of insect.

"Skinny little blonde," he said mockingly. "Little spoiled brat. Did it grate so much that I called you down about speeding in that damned boat? Or were you out to get even because I ran you off my beach?"

"It wasn't like that," she whispered, avoiding his piercing gaze.

"Wasn't it? Oh, God, I dreamed about you," he ground out. "I thought about you every day I was without my eyes, and how I was going to pay you back for it." He jerked her closer and she cried out in pain. "You're in for it, now, you bad-tempered little snake. Now that I know who you work for, and where to find you, I can afford to take my time. I'll let you sit and sweat out what I'm going to do. It'll give you something to do with your nights."

Her eyes met his, misty with tears, pleading, wounded. "Please...."

"Please what?" he asked curtly. "Please forgive you? You little tramp, not until I even the score!"

"I didn't ...!"

He let go of her abruptly, thrusting her away from him. She wasn't expecting it, and she stumbled, losing her balance. With a sharp cry, she went down, falling the rest of the way down the steps to land, bruised and crying, on the pine-needle laden ground at the bottom.

Garet stood there and looked down at her, not a trace of sympathy in his cold green eyes.

"And that," he said quietly, "is where you belong—on your belly in the dirt. Are you hurt?"

A sob broke from her lips as she dragged herself to her feet, biting her lip to keep from crying out at the pain in her elbow where she'd hit the hard ground. She rubbed it gingerly, oblivious to the bits of dirt and pine straw that clung to her pale blonde hair. Her soft brown eyes looked into his accusingly, as innocent and wounded as a scolded child's.

That look seemed to bother him. His eyes narrowed. "Oh, get the hell out of my sight!" he growled. "You can't run far enough that I won't find you, anyway."

She turned away, holding her arm, and walked slowly down the beach, blinded by hot tears as she made her way out of his life. It was over. It was all over, now.

Maude held her while she cried. It took a long time for the tears to pass, and the bruises she'd sustained when she fell were already beginning to pop out all over her delicate skin.

"Are you sure he didn't hit you?" Maude demanded, horrified, as she felt the painful elbow for a break.

"He didn't," Kate said quietly. "I . . . I just fell."

"All by yourself?" the older woman asked shrewdly.

Kate felt the heat rise in her cheeks. She looked down at the heavy rug on the living room floor.

"You could have broken your arm," Maude grumbled. "Or gotten a concussion. You could have broken your neck!"

"But I didn't," Kate said calmly. "In a way, it's a relief to have it out in the open. I haven't slept a full night since it happened. Now that he can see again, maybe I can start to live. Maybe I can put away the guilt."

"Did he threaten you?"

"Not in so many words, no," she said quietly. "I think he's just biding his time right now until he can decide how many pieces he'd like me cut into. Maude, I can't blame him," she said when Maude started to interrupt. "You couldn't possibly know the pain he went through, the mental anguish of knowing he might never see again. I had to watch it, and whether he knows it or not, I paid for what I did in those weeks I was with him."

"Whatever you did, it doesn't give him the right to manhandle you!"

"He didn't manhandle me," Kate protested. "I simply fell, Maude. That's all, I fell."

Maude sighed and turned away. "If you say so."

"Maude, can I stay here tonight?" Kate asked gently. "I . . . I don't want to have to go back to Mr. Cambridge and ask for my things tonight."

"Oh, baby, of course you can stay! And tomorrow, I'll go and get your things for you," she promised.

Kate nodded gratefully. At least she'd be spared the hatred in his eyes that last time.

That night was the longest night she'd ever lived through. Sleep was impossible. She laid in the big double bed in the guest room and stared at the darkened ceiling with tears burning her eyes.

As long as she lived, she'd never forget the look in Garet Cambridge's dark eyes when he came upon her at the cabin. She'd never seen hatred in those eyes before. Even when they were sightless, there had been affection in them for Kate. All that was changed now. He knew who she was and what she'd done, and he wasn't going to rest until he made her pay for it.

Ironically, he'd never know just how fully she had paid for her own reckless behavior. How terrible it was going to be, loving a man who hated her, and having to go through life with only his contempt to remember as the years went by.

If only Yama had been at the cabin, she thought miserably. Yama could always calm him down when nothing else worked. But apparently, Cambridge had left everybody behind in New York. Now he was at the cabin all by himself, and she wondered crazily if he'd had any supper. Maybe he found the steak she'd cooked for herself. At least he'd have some nourishment. The thought of him coming out of the hospital with no warm meal waiting set her off even more, and she bawled.

Finally, when the tears passed, she tried to decide what to do next. The only alternative was to stick to her original decision—pack up and go home. Once she was out of his sight, he might put aside his hatred and go on living. At least he still had Anna, she thought bitterly. Dear Anna, who loved his bank account.

That was what she'd do. She'd go home to her father and start over. It wouldn't be so hard, she told herself. She could learn to live without Garet, it wouldn't take that much effort. She'd see him in every man she met from now on, but she'd just have to learn to cope. If he'd died....

She remembered the silent promise she'd made—that if he lived she wouldn't even mind his contempt, his hatred. She swallowed hard. He was alive. He was in the same world with her. Her eyes closed. Perhaps it was worth it after all.

She overslept the next morning, and the fog was already beginning to lift from the lake when Kate dragged into the kitchen and poured herself a cup of coffee. She looked down with distaste at her blue jeans and T-shirt. She'd had to put the stained, dusty clothes on because they were all she had.

Maude was nowhere in sight, and with a feeling of anguish, she realized what that meant. Maude had already gone to see Garet.

She sat down at the table and sipped her coffee. She wished she'd begged Maude to leave well enough alone. She could have cabled her father to send her the plane fare home, and left the clothes behind. She hoped Maude wouldn't catch the same treatment from him that she'd received.

"Oh, you're up!" Maude said cheerfully as she came in the back door lugging Kate's suitcase. "How's the coffee?"

"It's fine." Kate stared at her wanly, her pale face lined with fatigue, dark circles under her soft brown eyes as she paused, the question on the tip of her tongue.

"As you can see, I'm still in one piece," Maude told her, putting the suitcase down. "If you think you look bad, my dear, you should see him. He didn't even give me an argument when I asked for your things."

"Thank you for going," Kate said gently.

Maude poured herself a cup of coffee and sat down across from Kate at the small kitchen table. "He asked me about you," she said casually.

"Oh?" Kate murmured.

"He wanted to know everything about you. Where you were from, your parents, how you came to work for me...I thought he was going to pass out when I told him your father owned a ranch outside Austin. Does he have some hangup about the cattle industry?"

Kate's eyes closed. "I don't know," she said weakly. But she knew what had happened. He'd realized that Kate and his assailant were the same person. When he knew that her father was in cattle, he made the connection he hadn't made when he saw Kate standing on the porch of his cabin.

"He asked about the bruises, too," Maude said, watching Kate like a hawk. "He wanted to be sure you were all right. You didn't tell me you fell down the steps."

"It wasn't important."

"He thought it was."

Kate got up and went back toward her bedroom. "I want to get the few things together that I left here before you went to Paris. I . . . I'm going back to Austin this morning."

"Are you?" Maude asked with a tiny smile.

But Kate was already out of earshot.

She was just putting the last of her small possessions into the open suitcase on the bed when she felt eyes on the back of her head. With a feeling of uneasiness, she turned to find Garet Cambridge standing in the doorway, looking darker and more haggard than she'd seen him since the first days she worked for him. His white shirt was unbuttoned at the throat over his massive chest, his jacket was gone. He looked as if he hadn't slept at all, and his dark green eyes were bloodshot.

He stared at her, wincing when she instinctively took a step backward as he came further into the room.

"I won't hurt you," he said quietly.

She bit her lower lip, feeling the anguish come back fresh as she remembered what he'd said to her yesterday, and how he'd said it. "What do you want, Mr Cambridge?" she asked in a husky whisper.

"To see how badly I hurt you," he said simply, and he had the look of a man who'd pulled the wings off a butterfly. "To make sure you were all right."

"I didn't break my neck," she said gently. "It might have been better . . . if I had." Her voice broke on the words, and he was beside her in a flash. A muffled curse passed his lips as he caught her up in his big arms and held her fiercely against him.

The tears came like a flood, surging down her cheeks, and she couldn't stop them.

"I'm sorry, I'm sorry," she wept against his shirt, "I'm so sorry! I've lived with it every day, every night, and in my sleep...I could see the boat hitting...I saw you climb onto the pier, and I thought you were all right...and I called, and Anna was there. She said they'd taken you to the hospital and you'd be all right, but I didn't know, I didn't know...!" she whimpered.

His arms tightened. Then he drew back to look down into her damp face, searching her eyes in a static, throbbing silence.

His hands came up to cup her face and his eyes closed while he let his broad, strong fingers touch tentatively, gently, every soft line of her face. It was the way he'd touched her when he was blind, reading with his fingers what, at that time, he hadn't been able to see. He brushed the tears away and bent his head. His mouth whispered across her closed eyelids.

His eyes opened then, staring down into hers. "Kate," he whispered achingly.

She bit her lip. "Don't hate me," she pleaded, pride gone to ashes as he held her and she clung to him.

"Could I hate a part of myself, little girl?" he asked. "Why did you come to work for me, knowing that I could find out about you any day? Why take the risk?"

Her eyes lowered to a button on his shirt. "To make restitution in some small way," she murmured.

"You might have told me the truth in the beginning," he pointed out.

"At first you had amnesia and I was afraid of the damage I might cause," she recalled. "Then you did remember, and you hated me so, I was afraid to."

"It wasn't you I hated," he said quietly. "It was the woman I thought you were. If I'd realized you came with me out of guilt, I wouldn't have made you stay."

But it wasn't guilt, she hadn't stayed out of guilt. And she didn't dare tell him that. She couldn't tell him she'd stayed out of love.

"I...I have to finish packing," she murmured, and pressed gently against his chest.

He let her move away from him, but his eyes held her as surely as his arms had.

"Where will you go?" he asked solemnly.

"Home," she said. "Back to my father's ranch. I never should have left it."

He jammed his hands into his pockets and his jaw tightened. "I thought I might write another book," he remarked. "I enjoyed this one, and I'm getting a little old for test flights." He eyed her speculatively. "We made a good team, Kate."

Her eyes misted over. She nodded. Her slender hands closed the suitcase.

"You could come back to work for me," he persisted gently.

"Oh, no, I couldn't!" she said quickly, and her pulse ran wild.

"Why not?" he growled. His eyes flashed fire at her. "Don't you feel guilty enough anymore?"

She winced, and he caught her by the arms, holding her in front of him as he read the wounding in her tormented pale eyes.

"Oh, God, is that how you used to look when I lost my temper with you?" he asked in a haunted tone, his face contorting with the memory. "Kate, gentle little Kate, I'm not going to hurt you anymore. You don't have to be afraid of me."

"I'm not afraid," she said quietly, but her body was trembling, and he must have been able to feel it.

He smiled half-heartedly. "Are you sure? You're trembling...." The smile faded as he caught her eyes and read them. "You trembled like this the last time I held you," he recalled softly, his brows knitting. His hands tightened on her arms. "It wasn't fear then, either. Kate...!"

She pulled away from him. "I ... I've got to get to the airport," she said quickly.

He studied her in a silence tight with emotion. "Come walk with me. One last time, Kate, and I'll let you go."

I'll let you go. Her eyes closed against the finality of those quiet words. But I don't want you to let me go! she thought miserably. If only I were older and more sophisticated and rich ...

"All right," she agreed softly.

The lake was quiet. Not even a motorboat was stirring, and far away there was the silvery cry of seagulls against the horizon.

Inevitably, they came to Cambridge's land as they walked, to the log where Kate was sitting that long-ago day when he ran her off the beach. She dropped down on it and crossed her arms over her knees as she reached down to pluck a blade of grass to worry in her nervous fingers. She couldn't imagine why he wanted to talk to her, why he was behaving so strangely. He didn't seem to want to hurt her, now. But ... why?

He stood at the lake's edge with a cigarette in his big hand, staring out across the choppy waters of the lake to the thick pine trees on the shore across the cove.

"It's been a long time since we found each other here," he remarked quietly.

"I was just thinking that," she remarked. Chill bumps were rising on her arms, because it was fall weather and the air off the lake was chilly.

"I threw you off my property," he recalled with a smile, "And you didn't even bother to argue with me. I took that for arrogance, little one, but it wasn't, was it? You aren't the argumentative type."

"I was afraid to argue with you," she admitted softly.

He turned. "Am I such an ogre, Kate?" he asked her. His eyes swept over her hunched body. "You're cold!"

"It's all right," she murmured. "Just a chill."

He threw down the cigarette and sat next to her on the log, folding her against his big, warm body.

"Better?" he asked at her ear.

Better?! It was heaven, or as close as she ever hoped to get on earth. Her eyes closed and she savored the feel and scent of him. Unconsciously, her cheek nestled lovingly against his broad chest.

"You're very warm," she murmured softly.

"You're soft," he mused. "Like a warm feather pillow. You may look thin, but you don't feel it."

She smiled in spite of herself. "Skinny was how you put it."

His arms tightened. "Don't remind me of what a fool I was," he muttered. "I feel bad enough about it already."

"Why should you? I deserved it."

"No," he corrected. "No, Kate, you didn't. I should have known weeks ago. The signs were all there. But I was blind, in more ways than one."

"You didn't tell me on the phone that you could see again," she whispered.

"It was going to be a surprise," he told her. "I left Yama in New York, and I'd planned . . . well," he sighed, "never mind. It was a surprise, all right, but not the one I had in mind. I couldn't wait to see you—really see you. I dreamed of what it was going to be like when I walked in the door. And then I had to go blow hell out of my own dream with the first words I said to you." He sighed heavily. "Kate, if there was any way I could take it back. . . ."

"It isn't wise to try and go backward," she said.

"I suppose not." He rocked her gently in his arms. "Why are you going away?"

"I . . . well, I don't work for you anymore, and . . ." she faltered.

"I thought you enjoyed living with me," he mused. "Part of the time, at least."

Her eyes closed. "I did," she admitted. "But it's over now. You'd never forget . . ."

His finger came down to cover her soft mouth and he looked down at her quietly. "Kate, I forget everything when I hold you," he said solemnly. "My God, honey, if you go now, I'll need a reason to get up in the mornings. I'll need a reason to breathe!''

She stared at him incredulously, not sure that she wasn't hearing things. "But you're a millionaire," she whispered. "I've got nothing...!"

"Neither have I, without you," he said shortly. His eyes burned over her face. "I have nothing unless I have you, is that clear enough? What the hell does money matter? Wouldn't you like to live in a cave with me, Kate? Wouldn't you live in a cave with me if I'd been a poor man?"

Tears trembled in her wide, soft eyes and started to overflow. She couldn't even manage an answer through the lump in her throat.

"When Maude told me about you this morning, I wanted to cut my throat," he said tightly. "Remembering what I'd said and done to you, and that look I couldn't understand in your eyes before you walked away from me—as if you could forgive me for killing you!—it hurt like hell...God, Kate!" he groaned, his eyes narrow with pain.

"It's all right," she said gently, sitting quietly in his arms, watching him intently, her heart bursting with the joy of loving him.

He searched her eyes for a long time with an unblinking curiosity that made ripples in her bloodstream.

"All that love I see in your eyes," he whispered huskily, "is it all for me, Kate?"

Her face went scarlet and she tried to hide her eyes from him, but he turned her face back.

"I'm years too old for you," he observed. "Bad tempered, spoiled for my own way. And you're just a baby. It might just be infatuation, Kate."

"Why don't you say what you mean?" she asked, lowering her eyes to his brown throat. "You don't want a little nobody like me who...."

"Don't you ever say that again!" he said harshly, catching her chin in a vicelike grip to force her face up to his blazing eyes. "You're not a nobody. You're my woman. You're the only thing in the world I give a damn about."

She gaped at him, feeling her jaw drop at the content of the statement, and the ferocity with which he said it.

"Don't look so dumbfounded," he growled. "My God, I wonder which of us was the more blind? Didn't it ever occur to you that I already had a secretary? You intrigued me from the first minute. I heard your voice and I had to have you. There was no book. I don't even have a publisher, I did it to keep you busy. And when you got tangled up with that damned reporter, I could have broken your neck for you. I took you to St. Martin for reasons that didn't have the first thing to do with work. But then I got to thinking about how young you were, and about the fact that I might be blind for life, and I got cold feet." He sighed, turning his gaze out toward the lake. "The fall was a blessing in disguise because it made an operation possible that restored my vision. I couldn't wait to get back to you. They wanted to keep me another three or four days but I dismissed myself and came anyway." He looked down at her hungrily, and his eyes said it all. "I needed to see you, to be near you, to touch you. It's been hell being away from you, milkmaid. I never meant to let you get that close. God knows, I fought it every step of the way, even to inviting Anna down for a few days. That backfired, too. She only made me appreciate you more. I wondered when I kicked her out why I'd ever been taken in by her."

She stared up at him with her heart shimmering in her eyes. Unbelievably, he seemed to be telling her that he loved her. A shudder of pure delight ran the length of her soft body.

His eyes darkened suddenly as he caught the intensity of feeling he read in hers. "Don't look at me like that," he said huskily.

Her slender hands linked behind his head. "Don't look at you like what?" she asked, trembling with mingled excitement and fear. The hunger she read in his eyes was monstrous, and she wasn't confident about her ability to satisfy it.

His big hands went to her back, lifting her up against him gently. "You're asking for trouble, milkmaid," he whispered at her mouth.

Her fingers dug into the thick hair at the nape of his neck. "I don't know very much," she murmured against his broad, hard mouth. "You'll have to teach me."

A shudder passed through the hard hands at her back. "What a delicious thought," he laughed softly. "The darkness and you in my bed, loving me..."

"Garet!" she gasped.

His lips parted hers expertly, hungrily. "Tell me you love me."

"Oh, don't you know how much?" she whispered fiercely.

"Not yet," he murmured. "Show me."

"Like this?" she asked, rising in his arms to press her mouth long and hard against his.

"More like this, little innocent," he murmured wickedly, and proceeded to teach her how very intimate a kiss could be.

She blushed when he finally stopped long enough to catch his breath, but a new, soft light was in the eyes that worshipped him openly.

"I'm going to marry you, Kate," he said unsteadily. "No half measures for us."

"Garet, what if I don't fit into your world?" she asked seriously.

"We'll make one of our own," he replied simply. He brushed the wild hair away from her cheek with a tender hand. "I want a son with you," he said huskily. "I want a houseful of children."

Her eyes sketched his face. "Dark-haired little boys with green eyes...."

He crushed her mouth under his, roughly, hungrily, possessively. "Don't tempt me," he said tightly. "I want you like hell."

"I wouldn't stop you," she said softly. "Anything you want, Garet. Anything."

He smiled down at her. "I know that. I want you, for keeps. I could walk through fire to get to you." He pressed his lips to her forehead. "Let's go and tell Maude, before things get out of hand. I want you in white when you walk down that aisle to me, as old-fashioned as that may sound."

She smiled back. "Maude will be glad to know you didn't drown me in the lake."

"She knew better than that." He laughed softly. "The first thing she said to me this morning was that I had a nasty way of treating the people who love me most. When she made me understand who you really were, I couldn't get to you fast enough. You'll never know how I felt when I walked into that room and you backed away from me." His eyes searched hers. "I wanted to go through the damned floor. Kate, I didn't hurt you, did I? Nothing was broken . . . ?"

"You didn't push me," she said gently. "I'm just bruised."

"Later, I'll kiss them all better," he promised.

"Oh, you can't," she said without thinking as her hands went to her blouse.

"Oh, can't I?" he murmured with a glint in his eyes. "God, I'm glad I can see, now!"

She blushed to the roots of her hair and ran ahead of him up the beach.

Far away, on the porch of her cabin, Maude Niccole watched the two of them running along the lake's edge. There were tears in her eyes as she went inside to put on the coffee.

*   *   *   *   *

PASSION FLOWER

To Victoria, Texas, with love

1

*

Jennifer King eyed the closed hotel room door nervously. She hadn't wanted this assignment, but she hadn't had much choice, either. Her recent illness had left her savings account bare, and this job was all she had to hold on to. It was a long way from the brilliant career in interior decorating she'd left behind in New York. But it was a living.

She pushed back a loose strand of blond hair and hoped she looked sedate enough for the cattleman behind the door. The kind of clothes she'd favored in New York were too expensive for her budget in Atlanta.

She knocked at the door and waited. It seemed to take forever for the man inside to get there. Finally, without warning, the door swung open.

"Miss King?" he asked, smiling pleasantly.

She smiled back. He was much younger than she'd expected him to be. Tall and fair and pleasant. "Yes," she said. "You rang for a temporary secretary?"

"Just need a few letters done, actually," he said, taking the heavy portable typewriter from her hand. "I'm buying some cattle for my brother."

"Yes, Miss James at the agency told me it had to do with cattle." She sat down quickly. She was pale and wan, still feeling the after-effects of a terrible bout with pneumonia.

"Say, are you all right?" he asked, frowning.

"Fine, thank you, Mr. Culhane," she said, remembering his name from Miss James's description of the job. "I'm just getting over pneumonia, and I'm a little weak."

He sat down across from her on the sofa, lean and rangy, and smiled. "I guess it does take the whip out of you. I've never had it myself, but Everett nearly died on us one year. He smokes too much," he confided.

"Your brother?" she asked with polite interest as she got her steno pad and pen from her large purse.

"My brother. The senior partner. Everett runs the show." He sounded just a little jealous. She glanced up. Jennifer was twenty-three, and he couldn't have been much older. She felt a kinship with him. Until their deaths three years back, her parents had pretty much nudged her into the job they thought she wanted. By the sound of it, Everett Culhane had done the same with this young man.

She dug out her pad and pen and crossed her thin legs. All of her was thin. Back in New York, before the frantic pace threatened her health, she'd been slender and poised and pretty enough to draw any man's eye. But now she was only a pale wraith, a ghost of the woman she'd been. Her blond hair was brittle and lusterless, her pale green eyes were dull, without their old sparkle. She looked bad, and that fact registered in the young man's eyes.

"Are you sure you feel up to this?" he asked gently. "You don't look well."

"I'm a little frail, that's all," she replied proudly. "I'm only just out of the hospital, you see."

"I guess that's why," he muttered. He got up, pacing the room, and found some notes scribbled on lined white paper. "Well, this first letter goes to Everett Culhane, Circle C Ranch, Big Spur, Texas."

"Texas?" Her pale eyes lit up. "Really?"

His eyebrows lifted, and he grinned. "Really. The town is named after a king-sized ranch nearby—the Big Spur. It's owned by Cole Everett and his wife Heather, and their three sons. Our ranch isn't a patch on that one, but big brother has high hopes."

"I've always wanted to see a real cattle ranch," she confided. "My grandfather went cowboying out to Texas as a boy. He used to talk about it all the time, and about the places he'd seen, and the history..." She sat up straight, poising her pen over the pad. "Sorry. I didn't mean to get off the track."

"That's all right. Funny, you don't look like a girl who'd care for the outdoors," he commented as he sat back down with the sheaf of papers in his hand.

"I love it," she said quietly. "I lived in a small town until I was ten and my parents moved to Atlanta. I missed it terribly. I still do."

"Can't you go back?" he asked.

She shook her head sadly. "It's too late. I have no family left. My parents are dead. There are a few scattered relatives, but none close enough to visit."

"That's rough. Kind of like me and Everett," he added. "We got raised by our aunt and uncle. At least, I did. Everett wasn't so lucky. Our dad was still alive while he was a boy." His face clouded, as if with an unpleasant memory. He cleared his throat. "Well, anyway, back to the letter..."

He began to dictate, and she kept up with him easily. He thought out the sentences before he gave them to her, so there were few mistakes or changes. She wondered why he didn't just call his brother, but she didn't ask the question. She took down several pages of description about bulls and pedigrees and bloodlines. There was a second letter, to a bank executive in Big Spur, detailing the method the Culhane brothers had devised to pay back a sizeable loan. The third letter was to a breeder in Carrollton, outlining transport for a bull the man had evidently purchased from the Culhanes.

"Confused?" he murmured dryly when he stopped.

"It's not my business..." she began gently.

"We're selling off one of our best bulls," he said, "to give us enough down payment on another top breeding bull. Everett is trying for a purebred Hereford herd. But we don't have the cash, so I've come down here to do some fancy trading. I sold the bull we had. Now I'm trying to get a potential seller to come down on his price."

"Wouldn't a phone call to your brother be quicker?" she asked.

"Sure. And Everett would skin my head. I came out here on a bus, for God's sake, instead of a plane. We're just about mortgaged to the hilt, you see. Everett says we can't afford not to pinch pennies." His eyes twinkled. "We've got Highland Scots in our ancestry, you see."

She smiled. "Yes, I suppose so. I can see his point. Phone calls are expensive."

"Especially the kind it would take to relay this much information," he agreed, nodding toward what he'd dictated. "If I get it off today, he'll have it in a day or two. Then, if he thinks it's worth giving what the man wants, he can call me and just say a word or two. In the meantime, I've got other business to attend to."

"Shrewd idea," she murmured.

"'Just a couple more," he continued. He leaned back and studied a magazine. "Okay, this one goes to…" He gave her a name and address in north Georgia, and dictated a letter asking if the breeder could give him a call at the hotel on Friday at 1 p.m. Then he dictated a second letter to a breeder in south Georgia, making the same request for 2 p.m. He grinned at her faint smile.

"Saving money," he assured her. "Although why Everett wants to do it the hard way is beyond me. There's a geologist who swears we've got one hell of a lot of oil on our western boundary, but Everett dug in his heels and refused to sell off the drilling rights. Even for a percentage. Can you beat that? We could be millionaires, and here I sit writing letters asking people to call me, just to save money."

"Why won't he sell?" she asked, curious.

"Because he's a purist," he grumbled. "He doesn't want to spoil the land. He'd rather struggle to make the cattle pay. Fat chance. The way things have been going, we're going to wind up eating those damned purebreds, papers and all."

She laughed helplessly at his phrasing and hid her face in her hand. "Sorry," she mumbled. "I didn't mean to laugh."

"It is kind of funny," he confessed. "But not when ou're cutting corners like we are."

She got up and started to lift the typewriter onto the desk y the window, struggling with it.

"Here, let me do that," he said, and put it onto the flat urface for her. "You're pretty weak, little lady."

"I'm getting back on my feet," she assured him. "Just a ttle wobbly, that's all."

"Well, I'll leave you to it. I'm going down to get a sand-vich. Can I bring you something?"

She'd have loved a sandwich, but she wasn't going to put ny further drain on his resources. "No, thank you," she aid, politely and with a smile. "I just had lunch before I ame over here."

"Okay, then. See you in a half hour or so."

He jammed a straw cowboy hat on his head and went out he door, closing it softly behind him.

Jennifer typed the letters quickly and efficiently, even own to the cattle's pedigrees. It was a good thing she'd aken that typing course when she was going through the chool of interior design in New York, she thought. It had ome in handy when the pressure of competition laid her ut. She wasn't ready to handle that competitive rat race gain yet. She needed to rest, and by comparison typing etters for out-of-town businessmen was a piece of cake.

She felt oddly sorry for this businessman, and faintly ympathetic with his brother, who'd rather go spare than sell ut on his principles. She wondered if he looked like his ounger brother.

Her eyes fell on the name she was typing at the bottom of he letter, Robert G. Culhane. That must be the man who'd ictated them. He seemed to know cattle, from his meticu-ous description of them. Her eyes wandered over what ooked like a production record for a herd sire, and she ighed. Texas and cattle. She wondered what the Circle C .anch was like, and while she finished up the letters, lost erself in dreams of riding horseback over flat plains. Pipe

dreams, she thought, smiling as she stacked the neat letter
with their accompanying envelopes. She'd never see Texas

Just as she rose from the typewriter, the door opened and
Robert Culhane was back. He smiled at her.

"Taking a break?" he asked as he swept off his hat and
whirled it onto a table.

"No, I'm finished," she said, astounding him.

"Already?" He grabbed up the letters and bent over the
desk, proofreading them one by one and shaking his head
"Damn, you're fast."

"I do around a hundred words a minute," she replied
"It's one of my few talents."

"You'd be a godsend at the ranch," he sighed. "It take
Everett an hour to type one letter. He cusses a blue streak
when he has to write anything on that infernal old ma
chine. And there are all the production records we have to
keep, and the tax records, and the payroll..." His head lifted
and he frowned. "I don't suppose you'd like a job?"

She caught her breath. "In Texas?"

"You make it sound like a religious experience," he
murmured on a laugh.

"You can't imagine how much I hate the city," she re
plied, brushing back a strand of dull hair. "I still cough al
the time because of the pollution, and the apartment wher
I live has no space at all. I'd almost work for free just to b
out in the country."

He cocked his head at her and pursed his boyish lips. "I
wouldn't be easy, working for Everett," he said. "An
you'd have to manage your own fare to Big Spur. You see
I'll need a little time to convince him. You'd barely ge
minimum wage. And knowing Everett, you'd wind up doin,
a lot of things besides typing. We don't have a house
keeper..."

Her face lit up. "I can make curtains and cook."

"Do you have a telephone?"

She sighed. "No."

"Kind of in the same boat we are in, aren't you?" he said with a sympathetic smile. "I'm Robert Culhane, by the way."

"Jennifer King," she said for the second time that day, and extended her hand.

"Nice to meet you, Jenny. How can I reach you?"

"The agency will take a message for me," she said.

"Fine. I'll be in town for several more days. I'll be in touch with you before I go back to Texas. Okay?"

She beamed. "You're really serious?"

"I'm really serious. And this is great work," he added, gesturing toward the letters. "Jenny, it won't be an easy life on the Circle C. It's nothing like those fancy ranches you see on television."

"I'm not expecting it to be," she said honestly, and was picturing a ramshackle house that needed paint and curtains and overhauling, and two lonely men living in it. She smiled. "I'm just expecting to be needed."

"You'll be that," he sighed, staring at her critically. "But are you up to hard work?"

"I'll manage," she promised. "Being out in the open, in fresh air, will make me strong. Besides, it'll be dry air out there, and it's summer."

"You'll burn up in the heat," he promised.

"I burn up in the heat here," she said. "Atlanta is a southern city. We get hundred-degree temperatures here."

"Just like home," he murmured with a smile.

"I'd like to come," she said as she got her purse and closed up the typewriter. "But I don't want to get you into any trouble with your brother."

"Everett and I hardly ever have anything except trouble," he said easily. "Don't worry about me. You'd be doing us a big favor. I'll talk Everett into it."

"Should I write you another letter?" She hesitated.

He shook his head. "I'll have it out with him when I get home," he said. "No sweat. Thanks for doing my letters. I'll send the agency a check, you tell them."

"I will. And thank you!"

She hardly felt the weight of the typewriter on her way back to the agency. She was floating on a cloud.

Miss James gave her a hard look when she came back in. "You're late," she said. "We had to refuse a call."

"I'm sorry. There were several letters..." she began.

"You've another assignment. Here's the address. A politician. Wants several copies of a speech he's giving, to hand out to the press. You're to type the speech and get it photostatted for him."

She took the outstretched address and sighed. "The typewriter...?"

"He has his own, an electric one. Leave that one here, if you please." Miss James buried her silver head in paperwork. "You may go home when you finish. I'll see you in the morning. Good night."

"Good night," Jennifer said quietly, sighing as she went out onto the street. It would be well after quitting time when she finished, and Miss James knew it. But perhaps the politician would be generous enough to tip her. If only the Texas job worked out! Jennifer was a scrapper when she was at her peak, but she was weary and sick and dragged out. It wasn't a good time to get into an argument with the only employer she'd been able to find. All the other agencies were overstaffed with out-of-work people begging for any kind of job.

The politician was a city councilman, in a good mood and very generous. Jennifer treated herself to three hamburgers and two cups of coffee on the way back to her small apartment. It was in a private home, and dirt cheap. The landlady wasn't overly friendly, but it was a roof over her head and the price was right.

She slept fitfully, dreaming about the life she'd left behind in New York. It all seemed like something out of a fantasy. The competition for the plum jobs, the cocktail parties to make contacts, the deadlines, the endless fighting to land the best accounts, the agonizing perfecting of color schemes and coordinating pieces to fit fussy tastes... Her nerves had given out, and then her body.

It hadn't been her choice to go to New York. She'd have been happy in Atlanta. But the best schools were up north, and her parents had insisted. They wanted her to have the finest training available, so she let herself be gently pushed. Two years after she graduated, they were dead. She'd never truly gotten over their deaths in the plane crash. They'd been on their way to a party on Christmas Eve. The plane went down in the dark, in a lake, and it had been hours before they were missed.

In the two years since her graduation, Jennifer had landed a job at one of the top interior-decoration businesses in the city. She'd pushed herself over the limit to get clients, going to impossible lengths to please them. The outcome had been inevitable. Pneumonia landed her in the hospital for several days in March, and she was too drained to go back to work immediately after. An up-and-coming young designer had stepped neatly into her place, and she had found herself suddenly without work.

Everything had to go, of course. The luxury apartment, the furs, the designer clothes. She'd sold them all and headed south. Only to find that the job market was overloaded and she couldn't find a job that wouldn't finish killing her. Except at a temporary agency, where she could put her typing skills to work. She started working for Miss James, and trying to recover. But so far she'd failed miserably. And now the only bright spot in her future was Texas.

She prayed as she never had before, struggling from one assignment to the next and hoping beyond hope that the phone call would come. Late one Friday afternoon, it did. And she happened to be in the office when it came.

"Miss King?" Robert Culhane asked on a laugh. "Still want to go to Texas?"

"Oh, yes!" she said fervently, holding tightly to the telephone cord.

"Then pack a bag and be at the ranch bright and early a week from Monday morning. Got a pencil? Okay, here's how to get there."

She was so excited she could barely scribble. She got down the directions. "I can't believe it, it's like a dream!" she said enthusiastically. "I'll do a good job, really I will. I won't be any trouble, and the pay doesn't matter!"

"I'll tell Everett," he chuckled. "Don't forget. You needn't call. Just come on out to the ranch. I'll be there to smooth things over with old Everett, okay?"

"Okay. Thank you!"

"Thank *you*, Miss King," he said. "See you a week from Monday."

"Yes, sir!" She hung up, her face bright with hope. She was actually going to Texas!

"Miss King?" Miss James asked suspiciously.

"Oh! I won't be back in after today, Miss James," she said politely. "Thank you for letting me work with you. I've enjoyed it very much."

Miss James looked angry. "You can't just walk out like this," she said.

"But I can," Jennifer said, with some of her old spirit. She picked up her purse. "I didn't sign a contract, Miss James. And if you were to push the point, I'd tell you that I worked a great deal of overtime for which I wasn't paid," she added with a pointed stare. "How would you explain that to the people down at the state labor department?"

Miss James stiffened. "You're ungrateful."

"No, I'm not. I'm very grateful. But I'm leaving, all the same. Good day." She nodded politely just before she went out, and closed the door firmly behind her.

2
*

It was blazing hot for a spring day in Texas. Jennifer
stopped in the middle of the ranch road to rest for a minute
and to set her burdens down on the dusty, graveled ground.
She wished for the tenth time in as many minutes that she'd
let the cab driver take her all the way to the Culhanes' front
door. But she'd wanted to walk. It hadn't seemed a long way
from the main road. And it was so beautiful, with the wildflowers strewn across the endless meadows toward the flat
horizon. Bluebonnets, which she'd only read about until
then, and Mexican hat and Indian paintbrush. Even the
names of the flowers were poetic. But her enthusiasm had
outweighed her common sense. And her strength.

She'd tried to call the ranch from town—apparently
Everett and Robert Culhane did have the luxury of a telephone. But it rang and rang with no answer. Well, it was
Monday, and she'd been promised a job. She hefted her
portable typewriter and her suitcase and started out again.

Her pale eyes lifted to the house in the distance. It was a
two-story white frame building, with badly peeling paint and
a long front porch. Towering live oaks protected it from the
sun, trees bigger than anything Jennifer had seen in Georgia.
And the feathery green trees with the crooked trunks had to
be mesquite. She'd never seen it, but she'd done her share
of reading about it.

On either side of the long, graveled driveway were fences,
gray with weathering and strung with rusting barbed wire.
Red-coated cattle grazed behind the fences, and her eyes
lingered on the wide horizon. She'd always thought Georgia
was big—until now. Texas was just unreal. In a separate
pasture, a mare and her colt frolicked in the hot sun.

Jennifer pushed back a strand of dull blond hair that had escaped from her bun. In a white shirtwaist dress and high heels, she was a strange sight to be walking up the driveway of a cattle ranch. But she'd wanted to make a good impression.

Her eyes glanced down ruefully at the red dust on the hem of her dress, and the scuff marks on her last good pair of white sling pumps. She could have cried. One of her stockings had run, and she was sweating. She could barely have looked worse if she'd planned it.

She couldn't help being a little nervous about the older brother. She had Everett Culhane pictured as a staid old rancher with a mean temper. She'd met businessmen like him before, and dealt with them. She wasn't afraid of him. But she hoped that he'd be glad of her help. It would make things easier all around.

Her footsteps echoed along the porch as she walked up the worn steps. She would have looked around more carefully weeks ago, but now she was tired and run down and just too exhausted to care what her new surroundings looked like.

She paused at the screen door, and her slender fingers brushed the dust from her dress. She put the suitcase and the typewriter down, took a steadying breath, and knocked.

There was no sound from inside the house. The wooden door was standing open, and she thought she heard the whir of a fan. She knocked again. Maybe it would be the nice young man she'd met in Atlanta who would answer the door. She only hoped she was welcome.

The sound of quick, hard footsteps made her heart quicken. Someone was home, at least. Maybe she could sit down. She was feeling a little faint.

"Who the hell are you?" came a harsh masculine voice from behind the screen door, and Jennifer looked up into the hardest face and the coldest dark eyes she'd ever seen.

She couldn't even find her voice. Her immediate reaction was to turn around and run for it. But she'd come too far, and she was too tired.

"I'm Jennifer King," she said as professionally as she could. "Is Robert Culhane home, please?"

She was aware of the sudden tautening of his big body, a harsh intake of breath, before she looked up and saw the fury in his dark eyes.

"What the hell kind of game are you playing, lady?" he demanded.

She stared at him. It had been a long walk, and now it looked as if she might have made a mistake and come to the wrong ranch. Her usual confidence faltered. "Is this the Circle C ranch?" she asked.

"Yes, it is."

He wasn't forthcoming, and she wondered if he might be one of the hired hands. "Is this where Robert Culhane lives?" she persisted, trying to peek past him—there was a lot of him, all hard muscle and blue denim.

"Bobby was killed in a bus wreck a week ago," he said harshly.

Jennifer was aware of a numb feeling in her legs. The long trip of the bus, the heavy suitcase, the effects of her recent illness—all of it added up to exhaustion. And those cold words were the final blow. With a pitiful little sound, she sank down on the porch, her head whirling, nausea running up into her throat like warm water.

The screen door flew open and a pair of hard, impatient arms reached down to lift her. She felt herself effortlessly carried, like a sack of flour, into the cool house. She was unceremoniously dumped down onto a worn brocade sofa and left there while booted feet stomped off into another room. There were muttered words that she was glad she couldn't understand, and clinking sounds. Then, a minute later, a glass of dark amber liquid was held to her numb lips and a hard hand raised her head.

She sipped at the cold, sweet iced tea like a runner on the desert when confronted with wet salvation. She struggled to catch her breath and sat up, gently nudging the dark, lean hand holding the glass to one side. She breathed in deeply, trying to get her whirling mind to slow down. She was still trying to take it all in. She'd been promised a job, she'd come hundreds of miles at her own expense to work for minimum wage, and now the man who'd offered it to her was dead. That was the worst part, imagining such a nice young man dead.

"You look like a bleached handkerchief," the deep, harsh voice observed.

She sighed. "You ought to write for television. You sure do have a gift for prose."

His dark eyes narrowed. "Walking in this heat without a hat. My God, how many stupid city women are there in the world? And what landed you on my doorstep?"

She lifted her eyes then, to look at him properly. He was darkly tanned, and there were deep lines in his face, from the hatchet nose down to the wide, chiseled mouth. His eyes were deep-set, unblinking under heavy dark brows and a wide forehead. His hair was jet-black, straight and thick and a little shaggy. He was wearing what had to be work clothes: faded denim jeans that emphasized long, powerfully muscled legs, and a matching shirt whose open neck revealed a brown chest thick with short, curling hair. He had the look of a man who was all business, all the time. All at once she realized that this man wasn't the hired hand she'd mistaken him for.

"You're Everett Culhane," she said hesitantly.

His face didn't move. Not a muscle in it changed position, but she had the distinct feeling that the sound of his name on her lips had shocked him.

She took another long sip of the tea and sighed at the pleasure of the icy liquid going down her parched throat.

"How far did you walk?" he asked.

"Just from the end of your driveway," she admitted, looking down at her ruined shoes. "Distance is deceptive out here."

"Haven't you ever heard of sunstroke?"

She nodded. "It just didn't occur to me."

She put the glass down on the napkin he'd brought with it. Well, this was Texas. How sad that she wouldn't see anything more of it.

"I'm very sorry about your brother, Mr. Culhane," she said with dignity. "I didn't know him very well, but he seemed like a nice man." She got up with an odd kind of grace despite the unsteadiness of her legs. "I won't take up any more of your time."

"Why did you come, Miss King?"

She shook her head. "It doesn't matter now in the least." She turned and went out the screen door, lifting her suitcase and typewriter from where they'd fallen when she fainted. It was going to be a long walk back to town, but she'd just have to manage it. She had bus fare back home and a little more. A cab was a luxury now, with no job at the end of her long ride.

"Where do you think you're going?" Everett Culhane asked from behind her, his tone like a whiplash.

"Back to town," she said without turning. "Good-bye, Mr. Culhane."

"Walking?" he mused. "In this heat, without a hat?"

"Got here, didn't I?" she drawled as she walked down the steps.

"You'll never make it back. Wait a minute. I'll drive you."

"No, thanks," she said proudly. "I get around all right by myself, Mr. Culhane. I don't need any handouts."

"You'll need a doctor if you try that walk," he said, and turned back into the house.

She thought the matter was settled, until a battered red pickup truck roared up beside her and stopped. The passenger door flew open.

"Get in," he said curtly, in a tone that made it clear he expected instant obedience.

"I said . . ." she began irritatedly.

His dark eyes narrowed. "I don't mind lifting you in and holding you down until we get to town," he said quietly.

With a grimace, she climbed in, putting the typewriter and suitcase on the floorboard.

There was a marked lack of conversation. Everett smoked his cigarette with sharp glances in her direction when she began coughing. Her lungs were still sensitive, and he seemed to be smoking shucks or something equally potent. Eventually he crushed out the cigarette and cracked a window.

"You don't sound well," he said suddenly.

"I'm getting over pneumonia," she said, staring lovingly at the horizon. "Texas sure is big."

"It sure is." He glanced at her. "Which part of it do you call home?"

"I don't."

The truck lurched as he slammed on the brakes. "What did you say?"

"I'm not a Texan," she confessed. "I'm from Atlanta."

"Georgia?"

"Is there another one?"

He let out a heavy breath. "What the hell did you mean coming this distance just to see a man you hardly knew?" he burst out. "Surely to God, it wasn't love at first sight?"

"Love?" She blinked. "Heavens, no. I only did some typing for your brother."

He cut off the engine. "Start over. Start at the beginning. You're giving me one hell of a headache. How did you wind up out here?"

"Your brother offered me a job," she said quietly. "Typing. Of course, he said there'd be other duties as well. Cooking, cleaning, things like that. And a very small salary," she added with a tiny smile.

"He was honest with you, at least," he growled. "But then why did you come? Didn't you believe him?"

"Yes, of course," she said hesitantly. "Why wouldn't I want to come?"

He started to light another cigarette, stared hard at her and put the pack back in his shirt pocket. "Keep talking."

He was an odd man, she thought. "Well, I'd lost my old job, because once I got over the pneumonia I was too weak to keep up the pace. I got a job in Atlanta with one of the temporary talent agencies doing typing. My speed is quite good, and it was something that didn't wring me out, you see. Mr. Culhane wanted some letters typed. We started talking," she smiled, remembering how kind he'd been, "and when I found out he was from Texas, from a real ranch, I guess I just went crazy. I've spent my whole life listening to my grandfather relive his youth in Texas, Mr. Culhane. I've read everything Zane Grey and Louis Lamour ever wrote, and it was the dream of my life to come out here. The end of the rainbow. I figured that a low salary on open land would be worth a lot more than a big salary in the city, where I was choking to death on smog and civilization. He offered me the job and I said yes on the spot." She glanced at him ruefully. "I'm not usually so slow. But I was feeling so bad, and it sounded so wonderful...I didn't even think about checking with you first. Mr. Culhane said he'd have it all worked out, and that I was just to get on a bus and come on out today." Her eyes clouded. "I'm so sorry about him. Losing the job isn't nearly as bad as hearing that he...was killed. I liked him."

Everett's fingers were tapping an angry pattern on the steering wheel. "A job." He laughed mirthlessly, then sighed. "Well, maybe he had a point. I'm so behind on my production records and tax records, it isn't funny. I'm choking to death on my own cooking, the house hasn't been swept in a month..." He glanced at her narrowly. "You aren't pregnant?"

Her pale eyes flashed at him. "That, sir, would make medical history."

One dark eyebrow lifted and he glanced at her studiously before he smiled. "Little Southern lady, are you really that innocent?"

"Call me Scarlett and, unemployment or no unemployment, I'll paste you one, cowboy," she returned with a glimmer of her old spirit. It was too bad that the outburst triggered a coughing spree.

"Damn," he muttered, passing her his handkerchief. "All right, I'll stop baiting you. Do you want the job, or don't you? Robert was right about the wages. You'll get bed and board free, but it's going to be a frugal existence. Interested?"

"If it means getting to stay in Texas, yes, I am."

He smiled. "How old are you, schoolgirl?"

"I haven't been a schoolgirl for years, Mr. Culhane," she told him. "I'm twenty-three, in fact." She glared at him. "How old are you?"

"Make a guess," he invited.

Her eyes went from his thick hair down the hawklike features to his massive chest, which tapered to narrow hips, long powerful legs, and large, booted feet. "Thirty," she said.

He chuckled softly. It was the first time she'd heard the deep, pleasant sound, and it surprised her to find that he was capable of laughter. He didn't seem like the kind of man who laughed very often.

His eyes wandered over her thin body with amused indifference, and she regretted for a minute that she was such a shadow of her former self. "Try again, honey," he said.

She noticed then the deep lines in his darkly tanned face, the sprinkling of gray hair at his temples. In the open neck of his shirt, she could see threads of silver among the curling dark hair. No, he wasn't as young as she'd first thought.

"Thirty-four," she guessed.

"Add a year and you've got it."

She smiled. "Poor old man," she said with gentle humor.

He chuckled again. "That's no way to talk to your new boss," he cautioned.

"I won't forget again, honestly." She stared at him. "Do you have other people working for you?"

"Just Eddie and Bib," he said. "They're married." He nodded as he watched her eyes become wide and apprehensive. "That's right. We'll be alone. I'm a bachelor and there's no staff in the house."

"Well . . ."

"There'll be a lock on your door," he said after a minute. "When you know me better, you'll see that I'm pretty conventional in my outlook. It's a big house. We'll rattle around like two peas in a pod. It's only on rare occasions that I'm in before bedtime." His dark eyes held hers. "And for the record, my taste doesn't run to city girls."

That sounded as if there was a good reason for his taste in women, but she didn't pry. "I'll work hard, Mr. Culhane."

"My name is Everett," he said, watching her. "Or Rett, if you prefer. You can cook meals and do the laundry and housekeeping. And when you have time, you can work in what passes for my office. Wages won't be much. I can pay the bills, and that's about it."

"I don't care about getting rich." Meanwhile she was thinking fast, sorely tempted to accept the offer, but afraid of the big, angry man at her side. There were worse things than being alone and without money, and she didn't really know him at all.

He saw the thoughts in her mind. "Jenny Wren," he said softly, "do I look like a mad rapist?"

Hearing her name that way on his lips sent a surge of warmth through her. No one had called her by a pet name since the death of her parents.

"No," she said quietly. "Of course you don't. I'll work for you, Mr. Culhane."

He didn't answer her. He only scanned her face and nodded. Then he started the truck, turned it around, and headed back to the Circle C Ranch.

3

*

Two hours later, Jennifer was well and truly in residence, to the evident amusement of Everett's two ranchhands. They apparently knew better than to make any snide comments about her presence, but they did seem to find something fascinating about having a young woman around the place.

Jennifer had her own room, with peeling wallpaper, worn blue gingham curtains at the windows, and a faded quilt on the bed. Most of the house was like that. Even the rugs on the floor were faded and worn from use. She'd have given anything to be robust and healthy and have a free hand to redecorate the place. It had such wonderful potential with its long history and simple, uncluttered architecture.

The next morning she slept late, rising to bright sunlight and a strange sense that she belonged there. She hadn't felt that way since her childhood, and couldn't help wondering why. Everett had been polite, but not much more. He wasn't really a welcoming kind of man. But, then, he'd just lost his brother. That must account for his taciturn aloofness.

He was long gone when she went downstairs. She fixed herself a cup of coffee and two pieces of toast and then went to the small room that doubled as his office. As he'd promised the day before, he'd laid out a stack of production records and budget information that needed typing. He'd even put her electric typewriter on a table and plugged it in. There was a stack of white paper beside it, and a note.

"Don't feel obliged to work yourself into a coma the first day," it read. And his bold signature was slashed under the terse sentence. She smiled at the flowing handwriting and the perfect spelling. He was a literate man, at least.

She sat down in her cool blue shirtwaist dress and got to work. Two hours later, she'd made great inroads into the paperwork and was starting a new sheet when Everett's heavy footsteps resounded throughout the house. The door swung open and his dark eyebrows shot straight up.

"Aren't you going to eat lunch?" he asked.

More to the point, wasn't she going to feed him, she thought, and grinned.

"Something funny, Miss King?" he asked.

"Oh, no, boss," she said, leaving the typewriter behind. He was expecting that she'd forgotten his noon meal, but she had a surprise in store for him.

She led him into the kitchen, where two places were set. He stood there staring at the table, scowling, while she put out bread, mayonnaise, some thick ham she'd found in the refrigerator, and a small salad she'd made with a bottled dressing.

"Coffee?" she asked, poised with the pot in her hand.

He nodded, sliding into the place at the head of the table.

She poured it into his thick white mug and then filled her own.

"How did you know I wanted coffee instead of tea?" he asked with a narrow gaze as she seated herself beside him.

"Because the coffee canister was half empty and the tea had hardly been touched," she replied with a smile.

He chuckled softly as he sipped the black liquid. "Not bad," he murmured, glancing at her.

"I'm sorry about breakfast," she said. "I usually wake up around six, but this morning I was kind of tired."

"No problem," he told her, reaching for bread. "I'm used to getting my own breakfast."

"What do you have?"

"Coffee."

She gaped at him. "Coffee?"

He shrugged. "Eggs bounce, bacon's half raw, and the toast hides under some black stuff. Coffee's better."

Her eyes danced as she put some salad on her plate. "I guess so. I'll try to wake up on time tomorrow."

"Don't rush it," he said, glancing at her with a slight frown. "You look puny to me."

"Most people would look puny compared to you," she replied.

"Have you always been that thin?" he persisted.

"No. Not until I got pneumonia," she said. "I just went straight downhill. I suppose I just kept pushing too hard. It caught up with me."

"How's the paperwork coming along?"

"Oh, I'm doing fine," she said. "Your handwriting is very clear. I've had some correspondence to type for doctors that required translation."

"Who did you get to translate?"

She grinned. "The nearest pharmacist. They have experience, you see."

He smiled at her briefly before he bit into his sandwich. He made a second one, but she noticed that he ignored the salad.

"Don't you want some of this?" she asked, indicating the salad bowl.

"I'm not a rabbit," he informed her.

"It's very good for you."

"So is liver, I'm told, but I won't eat that either." He finished his sandwich and got up to pour himself another cup of coffee.

"Then why do you keep lettuce and tomatoes?"

He glanced at her. "I like it on sandwiches."

This was a great time to tell her, after she'd used it all up in the salad. Just like a man . . .

"You could have dug it out of here," she said weakly.

He cocked an eyebrow. "With salad dressing all over it?"

"You could scrape it off . . ."

"I don't like broccoli or cauliflower, and never fix creamed beef," he added. "I'm more or less a meat and potatoes man."

"I'll sure remember that from now on, Mr. Culhane," she promised. "I'll be careful to use potatoes instead of apples in the pie I'm fixing for supper."

He glared at her. "Funny girl. Why don't you go on the stage?"

"Because you'd starve to death and weigh heavily on my conscience," she promised. "Some man named Brickmayer called and asked did you have a farrier's hammer he could borrow." She glanced up. "What's a farrier?"

He burst out laughing. "A farrier is a man who shoes horses."

"I'd like a horse," she sighed. "I'd put him in saddle oxfords."

"Go back to work. But slowly," he added from the doorway. "I don't want you knocking yourself into a sickbed on my account."

"You can count on me, sir," she promised, with a wry glance. "I'm much too afraid of your cooking to ever be at the mercy of it."

He started to say something, turned, and went out the door.

Jennifer spent the rest of the day finishing up the typing. Then she swept and dusted and made supper—a ham-and-egg casserole, biscuits, and cabbage. Supper sat on the table, however, and began to congeal. Eventually, she warmed up a little of it for herself, ate it, put the rest in the refrigerator, and went to bed. She had a feeling it was a omen for the future. He'd mentioned something that first day about rarely being home before bedtime. But couldn't he have warned her at lunch?

She woke up on time her second morning at the ranch. By 6:15 she was moving gracefully around the spacious kitchen in jeans and a green T-shirt. Apparently, Everett didn't mind what she wore, so she might as well be comfortable. She cooked a huge breakfast of fresh sausage, eggs, and biscuits, and made a pot of coffee.

Everything was piping hot and on the table when Everett came into the kitchen in nothing but his undershorts. Barefooted and bare-chested, he was enough to hold any woman's eyes. Jennifer, who'd seen her share of almost-bare men on the beaches, stood against the counter and stared like a star-struck girl. There wasn't an ounce of fat anywhere on that big body, and he was covered with thick black hair—all over his chest, his flat stomach, his broad thighs. He was as sensuously male as any leading man on television, and she couldn't drag her fascinated eyes away.

He cocked an eyebrow at her, his eyes faintly amused at what he recognized as shocked fascination. "I thought I heard something moving around down here. It's just as well I took time to climb into my shorts." And he turned away to leave her standing there, gaping after him.

A minute later he was back, whipping a belt around the faded blue denims he'd stepped into. He was still barefooted and bare-chested as he sat down at the table across from her.

"I thought I told you to stay in bed," he said as he reached for a biscuit.

"I was afraid you'd keel over out on the plains and your horse wouldn't be able to toss you onto his back and bring you home." She grinned at his puzzled expression. "Well, that's what Texas horses do in western movies."

He chuckled. "Not my horse. He's barely smart enough to find the barn when he's hungry." He buttered the biscuit. "My aunt used to cook like this," he remarked. "Biscuits as light as air."

"Sometimes they bounce," she warned him. "I got lucky."

He gave her a wary glance. "If these biscuits are any indication, so did I," he murmured.

"I saw a henhouse out back. Do I gather the eggs every day?"

"Yes, but watch where you put your hand," he cautioned. "Snakes have been known to get in there."

She shuddered delicately, nodding.

They ate in silence for several minutes before he spoke again. "You're a good cook, Jenny."

She grinned. "My mother taught me. She was terrific."

"Are your parents still alive?"

She shook her head, feeling a twinge of nostalgia. "No. They died several months ago, in a plane crash."

"I'm sorry. Were you close?"

"Very." She glanced at him. "Are your parents dead?"

His face closed up. "Yes," he said curtly, and in a tone that didn't encourage further questions.

She looked up again, her eyes involuntarily lingering on his bare chest. She felt his gaze, and abruptly averted her own eyes back to her empty plate.

He got up after a minute and went back to his bedroom. When he came out, he was tucking in a buttoned khaki shirt, and wearing boots as well. "Thanks for breakfast," he said. "Now, how about taking it easy for the rest of the day? I want to be sure you're up to housework before you pitch in with both hands."

"I won't do anything I'm not able to do," she promised.

"I've got some rope in the barn," he said with soft menace, while his eyes measured her for it.

She stared at him thoughtfully. "I'll be sure to carry a pair of scissors on me."

He was trying not to grin. "My God, you're stubborn."

"Look who's talking."

"I've had lots of practice working cattle," he replied. He picked up his coffee cup and drained it. "From now on, I'll come to the table dressed. Even at six o'clock in the morning."

She looked up, smiling. "You're a nice man, Mr. Culhane," she said. "I'm not a prude, honestly I'm not. It's just that I'm not accustomed to sitting down to breakfast with men. Dressed or undressed."

His dark eyes studied her. "Not liberated, Miss King?" he asked.

She sensed a deeper intent behind that question, but she took it at face value. "I was never unliberated. I'm just old-fashioned."

"So am I, honey. You stick to your guns." He reached for his hat and walked off, whistling.

She was never sure quite how to take what he said. As the days went by, he puzzled her more and more. She noticed him watching her occasionally, when he was in the house and not working with his cattle. But it wasn't a leering kind of look. It was faintly curious and a little protective. She had the odd feeling that he didn't think of her as a woman at all. Not that she found the thought surprising. Her mirror gave her inescapable proof that she had little to attract a man's eye these days. She was still frail and washed out.

Eddie was the elder of the ranchhands, and Jenny liked him on sight. He was a lot like the boss. He hardly ever smiled, he worked like two men, and he almost never sat down. But Jenny coaxed him into the kitchen with a cold glass of tea at the end of the week, when he brought her the eggs before she could go looking for them.

"Thank you, ma'am. I can sure use this." He sighed, and drained almost the whole glass in a few swallows. "Boss had me fixing fence. Nothing I hate worse than fixing fence," he added with a hard stare.

She tried not to grin. With his jutting chin and short graying whiskers and half-bald head, he did look fierce.

"I appreciate your bringing the eggs for me," she replied. "I got busy mending curtains and forgot about them."

He shrugged. "It wasn't much," he murmured. He narrowed one eye as he studied her. "You ain't the kind I'd expect the boss to hire."

Her eyebrows arched and she did grin this time. "What would you expect?"

He cleared his throat. "Well, the boss being the way he is . . . an older lady with a mean temper." He moved restlessly in the chair he was straddling. "Well, it takes a mean temper to deal with him. I know, I been doin' it for nigh on twenty years."

"Has he owned the Circle C for that long?" she asked.

"He ain't old enough," he reminded her. "I mean, I knowed him that long. He used to hang around here with his Uncle Ben when he was just a tadpole. His parents never had much use for him. His mama ran off with some man when he was ten and his daddy drank hisself to death."

It was like having the pins knocked out from under her. She could imagine Everett at ten, with no mother and an alcoholic father. Her eyes mirrored the horror she felt. "His brother must have been just a baby," she burst out.

"He was. Old Ben and Miss Emma took him in. But Everett weren't so lucky. He had to stay with his daddy."

She studied him quietly, and filled the tea glass again. "Why doesn't he like city women?"

"He got mixed up with some social-climbing lady from Houston," he said curtly. "Anybody could have seen she wouldn't fit in here, except Everett. He'd just inherited the place and had these big dreams of making a fortune in cattle. The fool woman listened to the dreams and came harking out here with him one summer." He laughed bitterly. "Took her all of five minutes to give Everett back his ring and tell him what she thought of his plans. Everett got drunk that night, first time I ever knew him to take a drink of anything stronger than beer. And that was the last time he brought a woman here. Until you come along, at least."

She sat back down, all too aware of the faded yellow shirt and casual jeans she was wearing. The shirt was Everett's. She'd borrowed it while she washed her own in the ancient chugging washing machine. "Don't look at me like a contender," she laughed, tossing back her long blond hair. "I'm just a hanger-on myself, not a chic city woman."

"For a hanger-on," he observed, indicating the scrubbed floors and clean, pressed curtains at the windows and the food cooking on the stove, "you do get through a power of work."

"I like housework," she told him. She sipped her own tea. "I used to fix up houses for a living, until it got too much for me. I got frail during the winter and I haven't quite picked back up yet."

"That accent of yours throws me," he muttered. "Sounds like a lot of Southern mixed up with Yankee."

She laughed again. "I'm from Georgia. Smart man, aren't you?"

"Not so smart, lady, or I'd be rich, too," he said with a rare grin. He got up. "Well, I better get back to work. The boss don't hold with us lollygagging on his time, and Bib's waiting for me to help him move cattle."

"Thanks again for bringing my eggs," she said.

He nodded. "No trouble."

She watched him go, sipping her own tea. There were a lot of things about Everett Culhane that were beginning to make sense. She felt that she understood him a lot better now, right down to the black moods that made him walk around brooding sometimes in the evening.

It was just after dark when Everett came in, and Jenny put the cornbread in the oven to warm the minute she heard the old pickup coming up the driveway. She'd learned that Everett Culhane didn't work banker's hours. He went out at dawn and might not come home until bedtime. But he had yet to find himself without a meal. Jenny prided herself in keeping not only his office, but his home, in order.

He tugged off his hat as he came in the back door. He looked even more weary than usual, covered in dust, his eyes dark-shadowed, his face needing a shave.

She glanced up from the pot of chili she was just taking off the stove and smiled, "Hi, Boss. How about some chili and Mexican cornbread?"

"I'm hungry enough to even eat one of those damned salads," he said, glancing toward the stove. He was still wearing his chaps and the leather had a fine layer of dust over it. So did his arms and his dark face.

"If you'll sit down, I'll feed you."

"I need a bath first, honey," he remarked.

"You could rinse off your face and hands in the sink," she suggested, gesturing toward it. "There's a hand towel there, and some soap. You look like you might go to sleep in the shower."

He lifted an eyebrow. "I can just see you pulling me out."

She turned away. "I'd call Eddie or Bib."

"And if you couldn't find them?" he persisted, shedding the chaps on the floor.

"In that case," she said dryly, "I reckon you'd drown, tall man."

"Sassy lady," he accused. He moved behind her and suddenly caught her by the waist with his lean, dark hands. He held her in front of him while he bent over her shoulder to smell the chili. She tried to breathe normally and failed. He was warm and strong at her back, and he smelled of the whole outdoors. She wanted to reach up and kiss that hard, masculine face, and her heart leaped at the uncharacteristic longing.

"What did you put in there?" he asked.

"One armadillo, two rattlers, a quart of beans, some tomatoes, and a hatful of jalapeno peppers."

His hands contracted, making her jump. "A hatful of jalapeno peppers would take the rust off my truck."

"Probably the tires, too," she commented, trying to keep her voice steady. "But Bib told me you Texans like your chili hot."

He turned her around to face him. He searched her eyes for a long, taut moment, and she felt her feet melting into the floor as she looked back. Something seemed to link them for that tiny space of time, joining them soul to soul for one explosive second. She heard him catch his breath and then she was free, all too soon.

"Would...would you like a glass of milk with this?" she asked after she'd served the chili into bowls and put it on the table, along with the sliced cornbread and some canned fruit.

"Didn't you make coffee?" he asked, glancing up.

"Sure. I just thought..."

"I don't need anything to put out the fire," he told her with a wicked smile. "I'm not a tenderfoot from *Jawja*."

She moved to the coffeepot and poured two cups. She set his in front of him and sat down. "For your information, suh," she drawled, "we Georgians have been known to eat rattlesnakes while they were still wiggling. And an aunt of mine makes a barbecued sparerib dish that makes Texas chili taste like oatmeal by comparison."

"Is that so? Let's see." He dipped into his chili, savored it, put the spoon down, and glared at her. "You call this hot?" he asked.

She tasted hers and went into coughing spasms. While she was fanning her mouth wildly, he got up with a weary sigh, went to the cupboard, got a glass, and filled it with cold milk.

He handed it to her and sat back down, with a bottle of Tabasco sauce in his free hand. While she gulped milk, he poured half the contents of the bottle into his chili and then tasted it again.

"Just right." He grinned. "But next time, honey, it wouldn't hurt to add another handful of those peppers."

She made a sound between a moan and a gasp and drained the milk glass.

"Now, what were you saying about barbecued spareribs making chili taste like oatmeal?" he asked politely. "I especially liked the part about the rattlers..."

"Would you pass the cornbread, please?" she asked proudly.

"Don't you want the rest of your chili?" he returned.

"I'll eat it later," she said. "I made an apple pie for dessert."

He stifled a smile as he dug into his own chili. It got bigger when she shifted her chair so that she didn't have to watch him eat it.

4
_____ * _____

It had been a long time since Jennifer had been on a horse, but once Everett decided that she was going riding with him one morning, it was useless to argue.

"I'll fall off," she grumbled as she stared up at the palomino gelding he'd chosen for her. "Besides, I've got work to do."

"You've ironed every curtain in the house, washed everything that isn't tied down, scrubbed all the floors, and finished my paperwork. What's left?" he asked, hands low on his hips, his eyes mocking.

"I haven't started supper," she said victoriously.

"So we'll eat late," he replied. "Now, get on."

With a hard glare, she let him put her into the saddle. She was still weak, but her hair had begun to regain its earlier luster and her spirit was returning with a vengeance.

"Were you always so domineering, or did you take lessons?" she asked.

"It sort of comes naturally out here, honey," he told her with a hard laugh. "You either get tough or you go broke."

His eyes ran over her, from her short-sleeved button-up blue print blouse down the legs of her worn jeans, and he frowned. "You could use some more clothes," he observed.

"I used to have a closetful," she sighed. "But in recent months my clothing budget has been pretty small. Anyway, I don't need to dress up around here, do I?"

"You could use a pair of new jeans, at least," he said. His lean hand slid along her thigh gently, where the material was almost see-through, and the touch quickened her pulse.

"Yours aren't much better," she protested, glancing down from his denim shirt to the jeans that outlined his powerful legs.

"I wear mine out fast," he reminded her. "Ranching is tough on clothes."

She knew that, having had to get four layers of mud off his several times. "Well, I don't put mine to the same use. I don't fix fence and pull calves and vet cattle."

He lifted an eyebrow. His hand was still resting absently on her thin leg. "You work hard enough. If I didn't already know it, I'd be told twice a day by Eddie or Bib."

"I like your men," she said.

"They like you. So do I," he added on a smile. "You brighten up the place."

But not as a woman, she thought, watching him. He was completely unaware of her sexually. Even when his eyes did wander over her, it was in an indifferent way. It disturbed her, oddly enough, that he didn't see her as a woman. Because she sure did see him as a man. That sensuous physique was playing on her nerves even now as she glanced down at it with helpless appreciation.

"All we need is a violin," she murmured, grinning.

He stared up at her, but he didn't smile. "Your hair seems lighter," he remarked.

The oddest kind of pleasure swept through her. He'd noticed. She'd just washed it, and the dullness was leaving it. It shimmered with silvery lights where it peeked out from under her hat.

"I just washed it," she remarked.

He shook his head. "It never looked that way before."

"I wasn't healthy before," she returned. "I feel so much better out here," she remarked, sighing as she looked around, with happiness shining out of her like a beacon. "Oh, what a marvelous view! Poor city people."

He turned away and mounted his buckskin gelding. "Come on. I'll show you the bottoms. That's where I've got my new stock."

"Does it flood when it rains?" she asked. It was hard getting into the rhythm of the horse, but somehow she managed it.

"Yes, ma'am, it does," he assured her in a grim tone. "Uncle Ben lost thirty head in a flood when I was a boy. I watched them wash away. Incredible, the force of water when it's unleashed."

"It used to flood back home sometimes," she observed.

"Yes, but not like it does out here," he commented. "Wait until you've seen a Texas rainstorm, and you'll know what I mean."

"I grew up reading Zane Grey," she informed him. "I know all about dry washes and flash floods and stampeding."

"Zane Grey?" he asked, staring at her. "Well, I'll be."

"I told you I loved Texas," she said with a quick smile. She closed her eyes, letting the horse pick its own way beside his. "Just breathe that air," she said lazily. "Rett, I'll bet if you bottled it, you could get rich overnight!"

"I could get rich overnight by selling off oil leases if I wanted to," he said curtly. He lit a cigarette, without looking at her.

She felt as if she'd offended him. "Sorry," she murmured. "Did I hit a nerve?"

"A raw one," he agreed, glancing at her. "Bobby was forever after me about those leases."

"He never won," she said, grinning. "Did he?"

His broad shoulders shifted. "I thought about it once or twice, when times got hard. But it's like a cop-out. I want to make this place pay with cattle, not oil. I don't want my land tied up in oil rigs and pumps cluttering up my landscape." He gestured toward the horizon. "Not too far out there, Apaches used to camp. Santa Ana's troops cut through part of this property on their way to the Alamo. After that, the local cattlemen pooled their cattle here to start them up the Chisolm Trail. During the Civil War, Confederates passed through on their way to Mexico.

There's one hell of a lot of history here, and I don't want to spoil it.''

She was watching him while he spoke, and her eyes involuntarily lingered on his strong jaw, his sensuous mouth. ''Yes,'' she said softly, ''I can understand that.''

He glanced at her over his cigarette and smiled. ''Where did you grow up?'' he asked curiously.

''In a small town in south Georgia,'' she recalled. ''Edison, by name. It wasn't a big place, but it had a big heart. Open fields and lots of pines and a flat horizon like this out beyond it. It's mostly agricultural land there, with huge farms. My grandfather's was very small. Back in his day, it was cotton. Now it's peanuts and soybeans.''

''How long did you live there?''

''Until I was around ten,'' she recalled. ''Dad got a job in Atlanta, and we moved there. We lived better, but I never liked it as much as home.''

''What did your father do?''

''He was an architect,'' she said, smiling. ''A very good one, too. He added a lot to the city's skyline in his day.'' She glanced at him. ''Your father...''

''I don't discuss him,'' he said matter-of-factly, with a level stare.

''Why?''

He drew in an impatient breath and reined in his horse to light another cigarette. He was chain smoking, something he rarely did. ''I said, I don't discuss him.''

''Sorry, boss,'' she replied, pulling her hat down over her eyes in an excellent imitation of tall, lean Bib as she mimicked his drawl. ''I shore didn't mean to rile you.''

His lips tugged up. He blew out a cloud of smoke and flexed his broad shoulders, rippling the fabric that covered them. ''My father was an alcoholic, Jenny.''

She knew that already, but she wasn't about to give Eddie away. Everett wouldn't like being gossiped about by his employees. ''It must have been a rough childhood for you and Robert,'' she said innocently.

"Bobby was raised by Uncle Ben and Aunt Emma," he said. "Bobby and I inherited this place from them. They were fine people. Ben spent his life fighting to hold this property. It was a struggle for him to pay taxes. I helped him get into breeding Herefords when I moved in with them. I was just a green kid," he recalled, "all big ears and feet and gigantic ideas. Fifteen, and I had all the answers." He sighed, blowing out another cloud of smoke. "Now I'm almost thirty-five, and every day I come up short of new answers."

"Don't we all?" Jennifer said with a smile. "I was lucky, I suppose. My parents loved each other, and me, and we were well-off. I didn't appreciate it at the time. When I lost them, it was a staggering blow." She leaned forward in the saddle to gaze at the horizon. "How about your mother?"

"A desperate woman, completely undomesticated," he said quietly. "She ran off with the first man who offered her an alternative to starvation. An insurance salesman," he scoffed. "Bobby was just a baby. She walked out the door and never looked back."

"I can't imagine a woman that callous," she said, glancing at him. "Do you ever hear from her now? Is she still alive?"

"I don't know. I don't care." He lifted the cigarette to his chiseled lips. His eyes cut around to meet hers, and they were cold with memory and pain. "I don't much like women."

She felt the impact of the statement to her toes. She knew why he didn't like women, that was the problem, but was too intelligent to think that she could pry that far, to mention the city woman who'd dumped him because he was poor.

"It would have left scars, I imagine," she agreed.

"Let's ride." He stuck the cigarette between his lips and urged his mount into a gallop.

Riding beside him without difficulty now, Jennifer felt alive and vital. He was such a devastating man, she thought, glancing at him, so sensuous even in faded jeans and shirt.

He was powerfully built, like an athlete, and she didn't imagine many men could compete with him.

"Have you ever ridden in rodeo competition?" she asked suddenly without meaning to.

He glanced at her and slowed his mount. "Have I what?"

"Ridden in rodeos?"

He chuckled. "What brought that on?"

"You're so big . . ."

He stopped his horse and stared at her, his wrists crossed over the pommel of his saddle. "Too big," he returned. "The best riders are lean and wiry."

"Oh."

"But in my younger days, I did some steer wrestling and bulldogging. It was fun until I broke my arm in two places."

"I'll bet that slowed you down," she murmured dryly.

"It's about the only thing that ever did." He glanced at her rapt face. Live oaks and feathery mesquite trees and prickly pear cactus and wildflowers filled the long space to the horizon and Jennifer was staring at the landscape as if she'd landed in heaven. There were fences everywhere, enclosing pastures where Everett's white-faced Herefords grazed. The fences were old, graying and knotty and more like posts than neatly cut wood, with barbed wire stretched between them.

"Like what you see?" Everett mused.

"Oh, yes," she sighed. "I can almost see it the way it would have been a hundred and more years ago,, when settlers and drovers and cattlemen and gunfighters came through here." She glanced at him. "Did you know that Dr. John Henry Holliday, better known as Doc, hailed from Valdosta, Georgia?" she added. "Or that he went west because the doctors said he'd die of tuberculosis if he didn't find a drier climate quick? Or that he and his cousin were supposed to be married, and when they found out about the TB, he went west and she joined a nunnery in Atlanta? And that he once backed down a gang of cowboys in Dodge City and saved Wyatt Earp's life?"

He burst out laughing. "My God, you do know your history, don't you?"

"There was this fantastic biography of Holliday by John Myers Myers," she told him. "It was the most exciting book I ever read. I wish I had a copy. I tried to get one once, but it was out of print."

"Isn't Holliday buried out West somewhere?" he asked.

"In Glenwood Springs, Colorado," she volunteered. "He had a standing bet that a bullet would get him before the TB did, but he lost. He died in a sanitarium out there. He always said he had the edge in gunfights, because he didn't care if he died—and most men did." She smiled. "He was a frail little man, not at all the way he's portrayed in films most of the time. He was blond and blue-eyed and most likely had a slow Southern drawl. Gunfighter, gambler, and heavy drinker he might have been, but he had some fine qualities, too, like loyalty and courage."

"We have a few brave men in Texas, too," he said, smoking his cigarette with a grin. "Some of them fought a little battle with a few thousand Mexicans in a Spanish mission in San Antonio."

"Yes, in the Alamo," she said, grinning. "In 1836, and some of those men were from Georgia."

He burst out laughing. "I can't catch you out on anything, can I?"

"I'm proud of my state," she told him. "Even though Texas does feel like home, too. If my grandfather hadn't come back, I might have been born here."

"Why did he go back?" he asked, curious.

"I never knew," she said. "But I expect he got into trouble. He was something of a hell-raiser even when I knew him." She recalled the little old man sitting astride a chair in her mother's kitchen, relating hair-raising escapes from the Germans during World War I while he smoked his pipe. He'd died when she was fourteen, and she still remembered going to Edison for the funeral, to a cemetery near Fort Gaines where Spanish moss fell from the trees. It had been a quiet place, a fitting place for the old gentleman to be laid to rest. In his home country. Under spreading oak trees.

"You miss him," Everett said quietly.

"Yes."

"My Uncle Ben was something like that," he murmured, lifting his eyes to the horizon. "He had a big heart and a black temper. Sometimes it was hard to see the one for the other," he added with a short laugh. "I idolized him. He had nothing, but bowed to no man. He'd have approved of what I'm doing with this place. He'd have fought the quick money, too. He liked a challenge."

And so, she would have bet, did his nephew. She couldn't picture Everett Culhane liking anything that came too easily. He would have loved living in the nineteenth century, when a man could build an empire.

"You'd have been right at home here in the middle eighteen hundreds," she remarked, putting the thought into words. "Like John Chisum, you'd have built an empire of your own."

"Think so?" he mused. He glanced at her. "What do you think I'm trying to do now?"

"The same thing," she murmured. "And I'd bet you'll succeed."

He looked her over. "Would you?" His eyes caught hers and held them for a long moment before he tossed his cigarette onto the ground and stepped down out of the saddle to grind it under his boot.

A sudden sizzling sound nearby shocked Jennifer, but it did something far worse to the horse she was riding. The gelding suddenly reared up, and when it came back down again it was running wild.

She pulled back feverishly on the reins, but the horse wouldn't break its speed at all. "Whoa!" she yelled into its ear. "Whoa, you stupid animal!"

Finally, she leaned forward and hung on to the reins and the horse's mane at the same time, holding on with her knees as well. It was a wild ride, and she didn't have time to worry about whether or not she was going to survive it. In the back of her mind she recalled Everett's sudden shout, but nothing registered after that.

The wind bit into her face, her hair came loose from its neat bun. She closed her eyes and began to pray. The jolting pressure was hurting, actually jarring her bones. If only she could keep from falling off!

She heard a second horse gaining on them, then, and she knew that everything would be all right. All she had to do was hold on until Everett could get to her.

But at that moment, the runaway gelding came to a fence and suddenly began to slow down. He balked at the fence, but Jennifer didn't. She sailed right over the animal's head to land roughly on her back in the pasture on the other side of the barbed wire.

The breath was completely knocked out of her. She lay there staring up at leaves and blue sky, feeling as if she'd never get a lungful of air again.

Nearby, Everett was cursing steadily, using words she'd never heard before, even from angry clients back in New York City. She saw his face come slowly into focus above her and was fascinated by its paleness. His eyes were colorful enough, though, like brown flames glittering at her.

"Not...my...fault," she managed to protest in a thin voice.

"I know that," he growled. "It was mine. Damned rattler, and me without a gun..."

"It didn't...bite you?" she asked apprehensively, her eyes widening with fear.

He blew out a short breath and chuckled. "No, it didn't. Sweet Jenny. Half dead in a fall, and you're worried about me. You're one in a million, honey."

He bent down beside her. "Hurt anywhere?" he asked gently.

"All over," she said. "Can't get...my breath."

"I'm not surprised. Damned horse. We'll put him in your next batch of chili, I promise," he said on a faint smile. "Let's see how much damage you did."

His lean, hard hands ran up and down her legs and arms, feeling for breaks. "How about your back?" he asked, busy with his task.

"Can't . . . feel it yet."

"You will," he promised ruefully.

She was still just trying to breathe. She'd heard of people having the breath knocked out of them, but never knew what it was until now. Her eyes searched Everett's quietly.

"Am I dead?" she asked politely.

"Not quite." He brushed the hair away from her cheeks. "Feel like sitting up?"

"If you'll give me a hand, I'll try," she said huskily.

He raised her up and that was when she noticed that her blouse had lost several buttons, leaving her chest quite exposed. And today of all days she hadn't worn a bra.

Her hands went protectively to the white curves of her breasts, which were barely covered.

"None of that," he chided. "We don't have that kind of relationship. I'm not going to embarrass you by staring. Now get up."

That was almost the final blow. Even half dressed, he still couldn't accept her as a woman. She wanted to sit down on the grass and bawl. It wouldn't have done any good, but it might have eased the sudden ache in her heart.

She let him help her to her feet and staggered unsteadily on them. Her pale eyes glanced toward the gelding, now happily grazing in the pasture across the fence.

"First," she sputtered, "I'm going to dig a deep pit. Then I'm going to fill it with six-foot rattlesnakes. Then I'm going to get a backhoe and shove that stupid horse in there!"

"Wouldn't you rather eat him?" he offered.

"On second thought, I'll gain weight," she muttered. "Lots of it. And I'll ride him two hours every morning."

"You could use a few pounds," he observed, studying her thinness. "You're almost frail."

"I'm not," she argued. "I'm just puny, remember? I'll get better."

"I guess you already have," he murmured dryly. "You sure do get through the housework."

"Slowly but surely," she agreed. She tugged her blouse together and tied the bottom edges together.

When she looked back up, his eyes were watching her hands with a strange, intent stare. He looked up and met her puzzled gaze.

"Are you okay now?" he asked.

"Just a little shaky," she murmured with a slight grin.

"Come here." He bent and lifted her easily into his arms, shifting her weight as he turned, and walked toward the nearby gate in the fence.

She was shocked by her reaction to being carried by him. She felt ripples of pleasure washing over her body like fire, burning where his chest touched her soft breasts. Even through two layers of fabric, the contact was wildly arousing, exciting. She clamped her teeth together hard to keep from giving in to the urge to grind her body against his. He was a man, after all, and not invulnerable. She could start something that she couldn't stop.

"I'm too heavy," she protested once.

"No," he said gently, glancing down into her eyes unsmilingly. "You're like feathers. Much too light."

"Most women would seem light to you," she murmured, lowering her eyes to his shirt. Where the top buttons were undone, she saw the white of his T-shirt and the curl of dark, thick hair. He smelled of leather and wind and tobacco and she wanted so desperately to curl up next to him and kiss that hard, chiseled mouth...

"Open the gate," he said, nodding toward the latch.

She reached out and unfastened it, and pushed until it came free of the post. He went through and let her fasten it again. When she finished, she noticed that his gaze had fallen to her body. She followed it, embarrassed to find that the edges of her blouse gaped so much, that one creamy pink breast was completely bare to his eyes.

Her hand went slowly to the fabric, tugging it into place. "Sorry," she whispered self-consciously.

"So am I. I didn't mean to stare," he said quietly, shif'
ing her closer to his chest. "Don't be embarrassed, Jenny.

She drew in a slow breath, burying her red face in h
throat. He stiffened before he drew her even closer, his arm
tautening until she was crushed to his broad, warm chest.

He didn't say a word as he walked, and neither did she
But she could feel the hard beat of his heart, the ragged sigl
of his breath, the stiffening of his body against her tar
breasts. In ways she'd never expected, her body sang to her
exquisite songs of unknown pleasure, of soft touches an
wild contact. Her hands clung to Everett's neck, her eye
closed. She wanted this to last forever.

All too soon, they reached the horses. Everett let her slid
down his body in a much too arousing way, so that she coul
feel the impact of every single inch of him on the way to th
ground. And then, his arms contracted, holding her, brin
ing her into the length of him, while his cheek rested on he
hair and the wind blew softly around them.

She clung, feeling the muscles of his back tense under he
hands, loving the strength and warmth and scent of hin
She'd never wanted anything so much as she wanted th
closeness. It was sweet and heady and satisfying in a wil
new way.

Seconds later, he let her go, just as she imagined she fe
a fine tremor in his arms.

"Are you all right?" he asked softly.

"Yes," she said, trying to smile, but she couldn't look u
at him. It had been intimate, that embrace. As intimate a
a kiss in some ways, and it had caused an unexpected shif
in their relationship.

"We'd better get back," he said. "I've got work to do."

"So have I," she said quickly, mounting the gelding wit
more apprehension than courage. "All right, you ugl
horse," she told it. "You do that to me again, and I'll bac
the pickup truck over you!"

The horse's ears perked up and it moved its head slightl
to one side. She burst into laughter. "See, Rett, he hear
me!"

But Everett wasn't looking her way. He'd already turned his mount and was smoking another cigarette. And all the way back to the house, he didn't say a word.

As they reached the yard she felt uncomfortably tense. To break the silence, she broached a subject she'd had on her mind all day.

"Rett, could I have a bucket of paint?"

He stared at her. "What?"

"Can I have a bucket of paint?" she asked. "Just one. I want to paint the kitchen."

"Now, look, lady," he said, "I hired you to cook and do housework and type." His eyes narrowed and she fought not to let her fallen spirits show. "I like my house the way it is, with no changes."

"Just one little bucket of paint," she murmured.

"No."

She glared at him, but he glared back just as hard. "If you want to spend money," he said curtly, "I'll buy you a new pair of jeans. But we aren't throwing money away on decorating." He made the word sound insulting.

"Decorating is an art," she returned, defending her professional integrity. She was about to tell him what she'd done for a living, but as she opened her mouth, he was speaking again.

"It's a high-class con game," he returned hotly. "And even if I had the money, I wouldn't turn one of those fools loose on my house. Imagine paying out good money to let some tasteless idiot wreck your home and charge you a fortune to do it!" He leaned forward in the saddle with a belligerent stare. "No paint. Do we understand each other, Miss King?"

Do we ever, she thought furiously. Her head lifted. "You'd be lucky to get a real decorator in here, anyway," she flung back. "One who wouldn't faint at the way you combine beautiful old oriental rugs with ashtrays made of old dead rattlesnakes!"

His dark eyes glittered dangerously. "It's my house," he said coldly.

"Thank God!" she threw back.

"If you don't like it, close your eyes!" he said. "Or pack your damned bag and go back to Atlanta and turn your nose up..."

"I'm not turning my nose up!" she shouted. "I just wanted a bucket of paint!"

"You know when you'll get it too, don't you?" he taunted. He tipped his hat and rode off, leaving her fuming on the steps.

Yes, she knew. His eyes had told her, graphically. When hell froze over. She remembered in the back of her mind that there was a place called Hell, and once it did freeze over and made national headlines. She only wished she'd saved the newspaper clipping. She'd shove it under his arrogant nose, and maybe then she'd get her paint!

She turned to go into the house, stunned to find Eddie coming out the front door.

He looked red-faced, but he doffed his hat. "Mornin', ma'am," he murmured. "I was just putting the mail on the table."

"Thanks, Eddie," she said with a wan smile.

He stared at her. "Boss lost his temper, I see."

"Yep," she agreed.

"Been a number of days before when he's done that."

"Yep."

"You going to keep it all to yourself, too, ain't you?"

"Yep."

He chuckled, tipped his hat, and went on down the steps. She walked into the house and burst out laughing. She was getting the hang of speaking Texan at last.

5

Jennifer spent the rest of the day feverishly washing down the kitchen walls. So decorators were con artists, were they? And he wouldn't turn one loose in his home, huh? She was so enraged that the mammoth job took hardly any time at all. Fortunately, the walls had been done with oil-based paint, so the dirt and grease came off without taking the paint along with them. When she was through, she stood back, worn out and damp with sweat, to survey her handiwork. She had the fan going full blast, but it was still hot and sticky, and she felt the same way herself. The pale yellow walls looked new, making the effort worthwhile.

Now, she thought wistfully, if she only had a few dollars' worth of fabric and some thread, and the use of the aging sewing machine upstairs, she could make curtains for the windows. She could even buy that out of her own pocket, and the interior-decorator-hating Mr. Everett Donald Culhane could just keep his nasty opinions to himself. She laughed, wondering what he'd have said if she'd used his full name while they were riding. Bib had told her his middle name. She wondered if anyone ever called him Donald.

She fixed a light supper of creamed beef and broccoli, remembering that he'd told her he hated both of those dishes. She deliberately made weak coffee. Then she sat down in the kitchen and pared apples while she waited for him to come home. Con artist, huh?

It was getting dark when he walked in the door. He was muddy and tired-looking, and in his lean, dark hand was a small bouquet of slightly wilted wildflowers.

"Here," he said gruffly, tossing them onto the kitchen table beside her coffee cup. The mad profusion of bluebonnets and Indian paintbrush and Mexican hat made blue and orange and red swirls of color on the white tablecloth. "And you can have your damned bucket of paint."

He strode toward the staircase, his face hard and unyielding, without looking back. She burst into tears, her fingers trembling as they touched the unexpected gift.

Never in her life had she moved so fast. She dried her tears and ran to pour out the pot of weak coffee. She put on a pot of strong, black coffee and dragged out bacon and eggs and flour, then put the broccoli and chipped beef, covered, into the refrigerator.

By the time Everett came back down, showered and in clean denims, she had bacon and eggs and biscuits on the table.

"I thought you might like something fresh and hot for supper," she said quickly.

He glanced at her as he sat down. "I'm surprised. I was expecting liver and onions or broccoli tonight."

She flushed and turned her back. "Were you? How strange." She got the coffeepot and calmly filled his cup and her own. "Thank you for my flowers," she said without looking at him.

"Don't start getting ideas, Miss King," he said curtly, reaching for a biscuit. "Just because I backed down on the paint, don't expect it to become a habit around here."

She lowered her eyes demurely to the platter of eggs she was dishing up. "Oh, no, sir," she said.

He glanced around the room and his eyes darkened, glittered. They came back to her. He laid down his knife. "Did you go ahead and buy paint?" he asked in a softly menacing tone.

"No, I did not," she replied curtly. "I washed down the walls."

He blinked. "Washed down the walls?" He looked around again, scowling. "In this heat?"

"Look good, don't they?" she asked fiercely, smiling. "I don't need the paint, but thank you anyway."

He picked up his fork, lifting a mouthful of eggs slowly to his mouth. He finished his supper before he spoke again. "Why did it matter so much about the walls?" he asked. "The house is old. It needs thousands of dollars' worth of things I can't afford to have done. Painting one room is only going to make the others look worse."

She shrugged. "Old habits," she murmured with a faint smile. "I've been fixing up houses for a long time."

That went right past him. He look preoccupied. Dark and brooding.

"Is something wrong?" she asked suddenly.

He sighed and pulled an envelope from his pocket and tossed it onto the table. "I found that on the hall table on my way upstairs."

She frowned. "What is it?"

"A notice that the first payment is due on the note I signed at the bank for my new bull." He laughed shortly. "I can't meet it. My tractor broke down and I had to use the money for the payment to fix it. Can't plant without the tractor. Can't feed livestock without growing feed. Ironically, I may have to sell the bull to pay back the money."

Her heart went out to him. Here she sat giving him the devil over a bucket of paint, and he was in serious trouble. She felt terrible.

"I ought to be shot," she murmured quietly. "I'm sorry I made such a fuss about the paint, Rett."

He laughed without humor. "You didn't know. I told you times were hard."

"Yes. But I didn't realize how hard until now." She sipped her coffee. "How much do you need . . . can I ask?" she said softly.

He sighed. "Six hundred dollars." He shook his head. "I thought I could swing it, I really did. I wanted to pay it off fast."

"I've got last week's salary," she said. "I haven't spent any of it. That would help a little. And you could hold back this week's . . ."

He stared into her wide, soft eyes and smiled. "You're quite a girl, Jenny."

"I want to help."

"I know. I appreciate it. But spend your money on yourself. At any rate, honey, it would hardly be a drop in the bucket. I've got a few days to work it out. I'll turn up something."

He got up and left the table and Jennifer stared after him, frowning. Well, she could help. There had to be an interior-design firm in Houston, which was closer than San Antonio or Austin. She'd go into town and offer her services. With any luck at all, they'd be glad of her expert help. She could make enough on one job to buy Everett's blessed bull outright. She was strong enough now to take on the challenge of a single job. And she would!

As luck would have it, the next morning Eddie mentioned that his wife Libby was going to drive into the city to buy a party dress for his daughter. Jennifer hitched a ride with her after Everett went to work.

Libby was a talker, a blond bearcat of a woman with a fine sense of humor. She was good company, and Jennifer took to her immediately.

"I'm so glad Everett's got you to help around the house," she said as they drove up the long highway to Houston. "I offered, but he wouldn't hear of it. Said I had enough to do, what with raising four kids. He even looks better since you've been around. And he doesn't cuss as much." She grinned.

"I was so delighted to have the job," Jennifer sighed, smiling. She brushed back a stray wisp of blond hair. She was wearing her best blue camisole with a simple navy-blue skirt and her polished white sling pumps with a white purse. She looked elegant, and Libby remarked on it.

"Where are you going, all dressed up?" she asked.

"To get a second job," Jennifer confessed. "But you mustn't tell Everett. I want to surprise him."

Libby looked worried. "You're not leaving?"

"Oh, no! Not until he makes me! This is only a temporary thing," she promised.

"Doing what?"

"Decorating."

"That takes a lot of schooling, doesn't it?" Libby asked, frowning.

"Quite a lot. I graduated from interior-design school in New York," Jennifer explained. "And I worked in the field for two years. My health gave out and I had to give it up for a while." She sighed. "There was so much pressure, you see. So much competition. My nerves got raw and my resistance got low, and I wound up flat on my back in a hospital with pneumonia. I went home to Atlanta to recuperate, got a job with a temporary talent agency, and met Robert Culhane on an assignment. He offered me a job, and I grabbed it. Getting to work in Texas was pretty close to heaven, for me."

Libby shook her head. "Imagine that."

"I was sorry about Robert," Jennifer said quietly. "I only knew him slightly, but I did like him. Everett still broods about it. He doesn't say much, but I know he misses his brother."

"He was forever looking out for Bobby," Libby confirmed. "Protecting him and such. A lot of the time, Bobby didn't appreciate that. And Bobby didn't like living low. He wanted Everett to sell off those oil rights and get rich. Everett wouldn't."

"I don't blame him," Jennifer said. "If it was my land, I'd feel the same way."

Libby looked surprised. "My goodness, another one."

"I don't like strip-mining, either," Jennifer offered. "Or killing baby seals for their fur or polluting the rivers."

Libby burst out laughing. "You and Everett were made for each other. He's just that way himself." She glanced at Jennifer as the Houston skyline came into view. "Did Bobby tell you what Everett did the day the oil man came out here to make him that offer, after the geologists found what they believe was oil-bearing land?"

"No."

"The little oil man wanted to argue about it, and Everett had just been thrown by a horse he was trying to saddle-break and was in a mean temper. He told the man to cut it off, and he wouldn't. So Everett picked him up," she said, grinning, "carried him out to his car, put him in, and walked away. We haven't seen any oil men at the ranch since."

Jennifer laughed. It sounded like Everett, all right. She sat back, sighing, and wondered how she was going to make him take the money she hoped to earn. Well, that worry could wait in line. First, she had to find a job.

While Libby went into the store, Jennifer found a telephone directory and looked up the addresses of two design shops. The first one was nearby, so she stopped to arrange a time and place to rendezvous with Libby that afternoon, and walked the two blocks.

She waited for fifteen minutes to see the man who owned the shop. He listened politely, but impatiently, while she gave her background. She mentioned the name of the firm she'd worked with in New York, and saw his assistant's eyebrows jump up. But the manager was obviously not impressed. He told her he was sorry but he was overstaffed already.

Crestfallen, she walked out and called a taxi to take her to the next company. This time, she had better luck. The owner was a woman, a veritable Amazon, thin and dark and personable. She gave Jennifer a cup of coffee, listened to her credentials, and grinned.

"Lucky me," she laughed. "To find you just when I was desperate for one more designer!"

"You mean, you can give me work?" Jennifer burst out, delighted.

"Just this one job, right now, but it could work into a full-time position," she promised.

"Part-time would be great. You see, I already have a job I'd rather not leave," Jennifer replied.

"Perfect. You can do this one in days. It's only one room. I'll give you the address, and you can go and see the lady yourself. Where are you staying?"

"Just north of Victoria," Jennifer said. "In Big Spur."

"How lovely!" the lady said. "The job's in Victoria! No transportation problem?"

She thought of asking Libby, and smiled. "I have a conspirator," she murmured. "I think I can manage." She glanced up. "Can you estimate my commission?"

Her new employer did, and Jennifer grinned. It would be more than enough for Everett to pay off his note. "Okay!"

"The client, Mrs. Whitehall, doesn't mind paying for quality work," came the lilting reply. "And she'll be tickled when she hears the background of her designer. I'll give her a ring now, if you like."

"Would I! Miss . . . Mrs . . . Ms . . . ?"

"Ms. Sally Ward," the owner volunteered. "I'm glad to meet you, Jennifer King. Now, let's get busy."

Libby was overjoyed when she heard what Jennifer was plotting, and volunteered to drive her back and forth to the home she'd be working on. She even agreed to pinch-hit in the house, so that Everett wouldn't know what was going on. It would be risky, but Jennifer felt it would be very much worth the risk.

As it turned out, Mrs. Whitehall was an elderly lady with an unlimited budget and a garage full of cars. She was more than happy to lend one to Jennifer so that she could drive back and forth to Victoria to get fabric and wallcoverings and to make appointments with painters and carpetlayers.

Jennifer made preliminary drawings after an interview with Mrs. Whitehall, who lived on an enormous estate called Casa Verde.

"My son Jason and his wife Amanda used to live with me," Mrs. Whitehall volunteered. "But since their marriage, they've built a house of their own further down the road. They're expecting their first child. Jason wants a boy and Amanda a girl." She grinned. "From the size of her, I'm expecting twins!"

"When is she due?" Jennifer asked.

"Any day," came the answer. "Jason spends part of the time pacing the floor and the other part daring Amanda to lift, move, walk, or breathe hard." She laughed delightedly. "You'd have to know my son, Miss King, to realize how out of character that is for him. Jason was always such a calm person until Amanda got pregnant. I think it's been harder on him than it has on her."

"Have they been married long?"

"Six years," Mrs. Whitehall said. "So happily. They wanted a child very much, but it took a long time for Amanda to become pregnant. It's been all the world to them, this baby." She stared around the room at the fading wallpaper and the worn carpet. "I've just put this room off for so long. Now I don't feel I can wait any longer to have it done. Once the baby comes, I'll have so many things to think of. What do you suggest, my dear?"

"I have some sketches," Jennifer said, drawing out her portfolio.

Mrs. Whitehall looked over them, sighing. "Just what I wanted. Just exactly what I wanted." She nodded. "Begin whenever you like, Jennifer. I'll find somewhere else to sit while the workmen are busy."

And so it began. Jennifer spent her mornings at Casa Verde, supervising the work. Afternoons she worked at Everett's ranch. And amazingly, she never got caught.

It only took a few days to complete the work. Luckily, she found workmen who were between jobs and could take on a small project. By the end of the week, it was finished.

"I can't tell you how impressed I am," Mrs. Whitehall sighed as she studied the delightful new decor, done in soft green and white and dark green.

"It will be even lovelier when the furniture is delivered tomorrow." Jennifer grinned. "I'm so proud of it. I hope you like it half as much as I do."

"I do, indeed," Mrs. Whitehall said. "I..."

The ringing of the phone halted her. She picked up the extension at her side. "Hello?" She sat up straight. "Yes,

Jason! When?" She laughed, covering the receiver. "It's a
boy!" She moved her hand. "What are you going to name
him? Oh, yes, I like that very much. Joshua Brand Whitehall. Yes, I do. How is Amanda? Yes, she's tough, all right.
Dear, I'll be there in thirty minutes. Now you calm down,
dear. Yes, I know it isn't every day a man has a son. I'll see
you soon. Yes, dear."

She hung up. "Jason's beside himself," she said, smiling. "He wanted a boy so much. And they can have others.
Amanda will get her girl yet. I must rush."

Jennifer stood up. "Congratulations on that new grand-
baby," she said. "And I've enjoyed working with you very
much."

"I'll drop you off at the ranch on my way," Mrs. Whitehall offered.

"It's a good little way," Jennifer began, wondering how
she'd explain it to Everett. Mrs. Whitehall drove a Mer-
cedes-Benz.

"Nonsense." Mrs. Whitehall laughed. "It's no trouble at
all. Anyway, I want to talk to you about doing some more
rooms. This is delightful. Very creative. I never enjoyed re-
decorating before, but you make it exciting."

After that, how could Jennifer refuse? She got in the car.

Luckily enough, Everett wasn't in sight when she reached
the ranch. Mrs. Whitehall let her out at the steps and Jennifer rushed inside, nervous and wild-eyed. But the house
was empty. She almost collapsed with relief. And best of all,
on the hall table was an envelope addressed to her from
Houston, from the interior-design agency. She tore it open
and found a check and a nice letter offering more work. The
check was for the amount Everett needed, plus a little. Jennifer endorsed it, grinning, and went in to fix supper.

6

* * *

Everett came home just before dark, but he didn't come into the house. Jennifer had a light supper ready, just cold cuts and bread so there wouldn't be anything to reheat. When he didn't appear after she heard the truck stop, she went out to look for him.

He was standing by the fence, staring at the big Hereford bull he'd wanted so badly. Jennifer stood on the porch and watched him, her heart aching for him. She'd decided already to cash her check first thing in the morning and give it to him at breakfast. But she wondered if she should mention it now. He looked so alone . . .

She moved out into the yard, the skirt of her blue shirtwaist dress blowing in the soft, warm breeze.

"Rett?" she called.

He glanced at her briefly. "Waiting supper on me again?" he asked quietly.

"No. I've only made cold cuts." She moved to the fence beside him and stared at the big, burly bull. "He sure is big."

"Yep." He took out a cigarette and lit it, blowing out a cloud of smoke. He looked very western in his worn jeans, batwing chaps, and close-fitting denim shirt, which was open halfway down his chest. He was a sensuous man, and she loved looking at him. Her eyes went up to his hard mouth and she wondered for what seemed the twentieth time how it would feel on her own. That made her burn with embarrassment, and she turned away.

"Suppose I offered you what I've saved?" she asked.

"We've been through all that. No. Thank you," he added. "I can't go deeper in debt, not even to save my bull.

I'll just pay off the note and start over. The price of beef is expected to start going up in a few months. I'll stand pat until it does."

"Did anyone ever tell you that you have a double dose of pride?" she asked, exasperated.

He looked down at her, his eyes shadowed in the dusk by the brim of his hat. "Look who's talking about pride, for God's sake," he returned. "Don't I remember that you tried to walk back to town carrying a suitcase and a typewriter in the blazing sun with no hat? I had to threaten to tie you in the truck to get you inside it."

"I knew you didn't want me here," she said simply. "I didn't want to become a nuisance."

"I don't think I can imagine that. You being a nuisance, I mean." He took another draw from the cigarette and crushed it out. "I've had a good offer for the bull from one of my neighbors. He's coming over tomorrow to talk to me about it."

Well, that gave her time to cash the check and make one last effort to convince him, she thought.

"Why are you wearing a dress?" he asked, staring down at her. "Trying to catch my eye, by any chance?"

"Who, me?" she laughed. "As you told me the other day, we don't have that kind of relationship."

"You were holding me pretty hard that day the rattlesnake spooked your horse," he said unexpectedly, and he didn't smile. "And you didn't seem to mind too much that I saw you without your shirt."

She felt the color work its way into her hairline. "I'd better put supper on the...oh!"

He caught her before she could move away and brought her gently against the length of his body. His hand snaked around her waist, holding her there, and the other one spread against her throat, arching it.

"Just stand still," he said gently. "And don't start anything. I know damned good and well you're a virgin. I'm not going to try to seduce you."

Her breath was trapped somewhere below her windpipe. She felt her knees go wobbly as she saw the narrowness of his eyes, the hard lines of his face. She'd wanted it so much, but now that it was happening, she was afraid.

She stilled and let her fingers rest over his shirt, but breathing had become difficult. He felt strong and warm and she wanted to touch his hair-roughened skin. It looked so tantalizing to her innocent eyes.

He was breathing slowly, steadily. His thumb nudged her chin up so that he could look into her eyes. "You let me look at you," he said under his breath. "I've gone half mad remembering that, wondering how many other men have seen you that way."

"No one has," she replied quietly. She couldn't drag her eyes from his. She could feel his breath, taste the smokiness of it, smell the leather and tobacco smells of his big, hard body so close to hers. "Only you."

His chest rose heavily. "Only me?"

"I was career-minded," she said hesitantly. "I didn't want commitment, so I didn't get involved. Everett . . ."

"No. I don't want to fight." He took her hands and slid them up and down over the hard muscles of his chest. His breathing changed suddenly.

He bent and drew her lower lip down with the soft pressure of his thumb. He fit his own mouth to it with exquisite patience, opening it slowly, tempting it, until she stood very still and closed her eyes.

His free hand brought her body close against his. The other one slowly undid the top two buttons of her dress and moved inside to her throat, her shoulder, her collarbone. His mouth increased its ardent pressure as his fingers spread, and his breathing became suddenly ragged as he arched her body and found the soft rise of her breast with his whole hand.

She gasped and instinctively caught his wrist. But he lifted his mouth and looked into her eyes and slowly shook his head. "You're old enough to be taught this," he said quietly. "I know how delicate you are here," he breathed, brushing his fingers over the thin lace. "I'm going to be very gentle, and you're going to enjoy what I do to you. I promise. Close your eyes, honey."

His mouth found hers again, even as he stopped speaking. It moved tenderly on her trembling lips, nibbling, demanding, in a silence bursting with new sensations and promise.

She clung to his shirtfront, shocked to find that her legs were trembling against his, that her breath was coming quick enough to be audible. She tried to pull away, but his fingers slid quietly under the bra and found bare, vulnerable skin, and she moaned aloud.

Her nails bit into his chest. "Rett!" she gasped, on fire with hunger and frightened and embarrassed that he could see and feel her reaction to him.

"Shhhh," he whispered at her mouth, gentling her. "It's all right. It's all right to let me see. You're so sweet, Jenny Wren. Like a bright new penny without a single fingerprint except mine." His mouth touched her closed eyelids, her forehead. His fingers contracted gently, his palm feeling the exquisite tautening of her body as she clung to him and shuddered. "Yes, you like that, don't you?" he breathed. His mouth brushed her eyelids again, her nose, her mouth. "Jenny, put your hand inside my shirt."

His voice was deep and low and tender. She obeyed him blindly, on fire with reckless hunger, needing to touch and taste and feel him. Her hands slid under his shirt and flattened on hair and warm muscle, and he tautened.

"Does that...make you feel the way...I feel?" she whispered shakily, looking up at him.

"Exactly," he whispered back. He moved his hand from her breast to her neck and pressed her face slowly against his bare chest.

She seemed to sense what he wanted. Her mouth touched him there tentatively, shyly, and he moaned. He smelled of faint cologne and tobacco, and she liked the way his hard muscles contracted where she touched them with her hands and her lips. He was all man. All man. And her world was suddenly narrowed to her senses, and Everett.

He took her face in his hands and tilted it, bending to kiss her with a hungry ferocity that would have frightened her minutes before. But she went on tiptoe and linked her arms around his neck and gave him back the kiss, opening her mouth under his to incite him to further intimacy, shivering wildly when he accepted the invitation and his tongue went into the sweet darkness in a slow, hungry tasting.

When he finally released her, he was shaking too. His eyes burned with frustrated desire, his hands framed her face, hot and hard.

"We have to stop. Now."

She took a slow, steadying breath. "Yes."

He took his hands away and moved toward the house, lighting a cigarette eventually after two fumbles.

She followed him, drunk on sensual pleasure, awed by what she'd felt with him, by what she'd let him do. She felt shy when they got into the house, into the light, and she couldn't quite meet his eyes.

"I'll get supper on the table," she said.

He didn't even reply. He followed her into the kitchen, and with brooding dark eyes watched her move around.

She poured coffee and he sat down, still watching her.

Her hand trembled as she put the cream pitcher beside his cup. He caught her fingers, looking up at her with a dark, unsmiling stare.

"Don't start getting self-conscious with me," he said quietly. "I know you've never let another man touch you like that. I'm proud that you let me."

She stared at him, eyes widening. Of all the things she'd expected he might say, that wasn't one of them.

His nostrils flared and his hand contracted. "After supper," he said slowly, holding her eyes, "I'm going to carry you into the living room and lay you down on the sofa. And I'm going to make love to you, in every way I know. And when I get through, you'll shudder at the thought of another man's hands on you."

His eyes were blazing, and her own kindled. Her lips parted. "Rett, I can't . . . you know."

He nodded. "We won't go that far." His fingers caressed her wrist and his face hardened. "How hungry are you?" he asked under his breath.

Her heart was beating wildly. She looked at him and it was suicide. She felt shaky to her toes.

"Make love to me," she whispered blindly as she reached for him.

He twisted her down across his lap and found her mouth in a single motion. He groaned as he kissed her, his breath sighing out raggedly.

"Oh, God, I need you," he ground out, standing with her in his arms. "I need you so much!"

He turned, still kissing her, and carried her through into the living room, putting her gently down on the worn couch. After giving her a hot stare, he turned and methodically drew all the curtains and closed and locked the door. Then he came back, sitting down so that he was facing her.

"Now," he whispered, bending with trembling hands to the bodice of her dress. "Now, let's see how much damage we can do to each other's self-control, Jenny Wren. I want to look at you until I ache to my toes!"

He unbuttoned it and she sank back against the pillows, watching unprotestingly. He half lifted her and slipped the dress down her arms. Her bra followed it. And then he leaned over her, just looking at the soft mounds he'd uncovered.

His fingers stroked one perfect breast, lingering on the tip until she cried out.

"Does that hurt?" he whispered, looking into her eyes.

She was trembling, and it was hard to talk. "No," she breathed.

He smiled slowly, in a tender, purely masculine way, and repeated the brushing caress. She arched up, and his eyes blazed like dark fires.

"Jenny!" he growled. He lifted her body up to his hard mouth. He took her by surprise, and she moaned wildly as she felt the warm moistness envelop her. Her hands dug into his hair and she dragged his head closer, whimpering as if she were being tortured.

"Not so hard, baby," he whispered raggedly, lifting his head. "You're too delicate for that, Jenny."

"Rett," she moaned, her eyes wild.

"Like this, then," he whispered, bending to grind his mouth into hers. His hand swallowed her, stroking, molding, and she trembled all over as if with a fever, clinging to him, needing something more than this, something closer, something far, far more intimate . . .

Her hands moved against his chest, trembling as they explored the hard muscles.

"Be still now," he whispered, easing her back into the cushions. "Don't move under me. Just lie still, Jenny Wren, and let me show you . . . how bodies kiss."

She held her breath as his body moved completely onto hers. She felt the blatant maleness of it, the warmth, the tickle of hair against her soft breasts, the exquisite weight, and her hungry eyes looked straight into his as they joined.

"Oh," she whispered jerkily.

"Sweet, sweet Jenny," he breathed, cupping her face in his hands. "It's like moving on velvet. Do you feel me . . . all of me?"

"Yes." Her own hands went to his back, found their way under his shirt. "Rett, you're very heavy," she said with a shaky smile.

"Too heavy?" he whispered.

"Oh, no," she said softly. "I . . . like the way it feels."

"So do I." He bent and kissed her tenderly, in a new and delicious way. "Not afraid?"

"No."

"You will be," he whispered softly. His hands moved down, sliding under her hips. He lifted his head and looked down at her just as his fingers contracted and ground her hips up into his in an intimacy that made her gasp and cry out.

He shuddered, and she buried her face in his hot throat, dizzy and drowning in deep water, burning with exquisite sensation and blinding pleasure.

"Jenny," he groaned. His hands hurt. "Jenny, Jenny, if you weren't a virgin, I'd take you. I'd take you, here, now, in every way there is...!"

She barely heard him, she was shaking so badly. All at once, he eased himself down beside her and folded her into his arms in a strangely protective way. His hands smoothed her back, his lips brushed over her face in tiny, warm kisses. All the passion was suddenly gone, and he was comforting her.

"I never believed... what my mother used to say about... passion," Jenny whispered at his ear, still trembling. "Rett, it's exquisite... isn't it? So explosive and sweet and dangerous!"

"You've never wanted a man before?" he breathed.

"No."

"I'll tell you something, Jenny. I've never wanted a woman like this. Not ever." He kissed her ear softly. "I want you to know something. If it ever happened, even accidentally, you'd never want to forget it. I'd take you so tenderly, so slowly, that you'd never know anything about pain."

"Yes, I know that," she murmured, smiling. Her arms tightened. "You could have had me, then, lofty principles and all," she added ruefully. "I didn't realize how easy it was to throw reason to the wind."

"You're a very passionate woman." He lifted his head and searched her eyes. "I didn't expect that."

"You didn't seem much like a passionate man either," she confessed, letting her eyes wander slowly over his hard, dark face. "Oh, Rett, I did want you in the most frightening way!"

His chest expanded roughly. "Jenny, I think we'd better get up from here. My good intentions only seem to last until I get half your clothes off."

She watched him draw away, watched how his eyes clung to her bare breasts, and she smiled and arched gently.

"Oh, God, don't do that!" he whispered, shaken, as he turned away.

She laughed delightedly and sat up, getting back into her clothes as she stared at his broad back. He was smoking a cigarette, running a restless hand through his hair. And he was the handsomest man she'd ever seen in her life. And the most . . . loved.

I love you, she thought dreamily. I love every line and curve and impatient gesture you make. I'd rather live here in poverty, with you than to have the world in the bank.

"I'm decent now," she murmured, smiling when he turned hesitantly around. "My gosh, you make me feel good. I was always self-conscious about being so small."

His eyes narrowed. "You're not small, baby," he said in a gruff tone. "You're just delicate."

Her face glowed with pride. "Thank you, Rett."

"Let's see if the coffee's still warm," he said softly, holding out his hand.

She took it, and he pulled her up, pausing to bend and kiss her slowly, lingering over the soft, swollen contours of her warm mouth.

"I've bruised your lips," he whispered. "Are they sore?"

"They're delightfully sensitive," she whispered back, going on tiptoe. "You know a lot about kissing for a cattle man."

"You know a lot for a virgin," he murmured, chuckling.

"Pat yourself on the back, I'm a fast study." She slid her hand pertly inside his shirt and stroked him. "See?"

He took her hand away and buttoned his shirt to the throat. "I'm going to have to watch you, lady," he murmured, "or you'll wrestle me down on the couch and seduce me one dark night."

"It's all right," she whispered. "I won't get you pregnant. You can trust me, honey," she added with a wicked smile.

He burst out laughing and led her into the kitchen. "Feed me," he said, "before we get in over our heads."

"Spoilsport. Just when things were getting interesting."

"Another minute, and they'd have gone past interesting to educational," he murmured dryly, with a pointed glance. "Men get hot pretty fast that way, Jenny. Don't rely on my protective instincts too far. I damned near lost my head."

"Did you, really?" she asked, all eyes. "But I don't know anything."

"That's why," he sighed. "I . . . haven't touched a virgin since I was one myself. Funny, isn't it, that these days it's become a stigma. Back when I was a kid, decent boys wouldn't be seen with a girl who had a reputation for being easy. Now it's the virgins who take all the taunting." He stopped, turning her, and his face was solemn. "I'm glad you're still innocent. I'm glad that I can look at you and make you blush, and watch all those first reactions that you've never shown anybody else. To hell with modern morality, Jenny. I love the fact that you're as old-fashioned as I am."

"So do I. Now," she added, studying him warmly. "Rett. . ." Her fingers went up and touched his hard mouth. "Rett, I think I . . ." She was about to say "love you" when a piece of paper on the floor caught his eye.

"Hey, what's this?" he asked, bending to pick it up.

Her heart stopped. It was the check she'd gotten in the mail. She'd stuck it in her pocket, but it must have fallen out. She watched him open it and read the logo at the top with a feeling of impending disaster. She hadn't meant to tell him where it came from just yet. . . .

His lean hand closed around the check, crumpling it. "Where did you get this kind of money, and what for?" he demanded.

"I . . . I worked part-time for a design house in Houston, decorating a lady's living room," she blurted out. "It's for you. To pay off your bull," she said, her face bright, her eyes shining. "I went to Houston and got a part-time job decorating a living room. That's my commission. Surprise! Now you won't have to sell that mangy old Hereford bull!''

He looked odd. As if he'd tried to swallow a watermelon and couldn't get it down. He stood up, still staring at the crumpled check, and turned away. He walked to the sink, staring out the darkened window.

"How did you get a job decorating anything?"

"I studied for several years at an excellent school of interior design in New York," she said. "I got a job with one of the leading agencies and spent two years developing my craft. That's why I got so angry when you made the remark about interior decorators being con artists," she added. "You see, I am one."

"New York?"

"Yes. It's the best place to learn, and to work."

"And you got pneumonia..."

"And had to give it up temporarily," she agreed. She frowned. He sounded strange. "Thanks to you, I'm back on my feet now and in fine form. The lady I did the design for was really pleased with my work, too. But the reason I did it was to get you enough money to pay off your note..."

"I can't take this," he said in a strained tone. He put it gently on the table and started out the door.

"But, Everett, your supper...!" she called.

"I'm not hungry." He kept walking. A moment later, the front door slammed behind him.

She sat there at the table, alone, staring at the check for a long time, until the numbers started to blur. Her eyes burned with unshed tears. She loved him. She loved Everett Culhane. And in the space of one night, her good intentions had lost her the pleasure of being near him. She knew almost certainly that he was going to fire her now. Too late, she remembered his opinion of city women. She hadn't had time to explain that it was her parents' idea for her to study and work in New York, not her own. Nor that the pressure had been too much. He thought it was only pneumonia. Could she convince him in time that she wasn't what he was sure she was? That she wanted to stay here forever, not just as a temporary thing? She glanced toward the door with a quiet sigh. Well, she'd just sit here and wait until the shock wore off and he came back.

She did wait. But when three o'clock in the morning came, with no sign of Everett, she went reluctantly upstairs and lay down. It didn't help that she still smelled leather and faint cologne, and that her mind replayed the fierce ardor she'd learned from him until, exhausted, she slept.

When her eyes slowly opened the next morning, she felt as if she hadn't slept at all. And the first thing she remembered was Everett's shocked face when she'd told him what she used to do for a living. She couldn't understand why he'd reacted that way. After the way it had been between them, she hadn't expected him to walk off without at least discussing it. She wondered if it was going to be that way until he fired her. Because she was sure he was going to. And she knew for a certainty that she didn't want to go. She loved him with all her heart.

7

If she'd hoped for a new start that morning, she was disappointed. She fixed breakfast, but Everett went out the front door without even sticking his head in the kitchen. Apparently, he'd rather have starved than eat what she'd cooked for him.

That morning set the pattern for the next two days. Jennifer cooked and wound up eating her efforts by herself. Everett came home in the early hours of the morning, arranging his schedule so that she never saw him at all.

He'd sold the bull. She found it out from Eddie, who was in a nasty temper of his own.

"I practically begged him to wait and see what happened," Eddie spat as he delivered the eggs to Jennifer the second morning. "When that neighbor didn't want the bull, Everett just loaded it up and took it to the sale without a word. He looks bad. He won't talk. Do you know what's eating him?"

She avoided that sharp look. "He's worried about money, I think," she said. "I offered him what I had. He got mad and stomped off and he hasn't spoken to me since."

"That don't sound like Everett."

"Yes, I know." She sighed, smiling at him. "I think he wants me to go away, Eddie. He's done everything but leave the ranch forever to get his point across."

"Money troubles are doing it, not you." Eddie grinned. "Don't back off now. He needs us all more than ever."

"Maybe he does," Jennifer said. "I just wish he'd taken the money I offered to lend him."

"That would be something, all right, to watch Everett take money from a lady. No offense, Miss Jenny, but he's too much man. If you know what I mean."

She did, unfortunately. She'd experienced the male in him, in ways that would haunt her forever. And worst of all was the fact that she was still hungry for him. If anything, that wild little interlude on the sofa had whetted her appetite, not satisfied it.

For lunch, she put a platter of cold cuts in the refrigerator and left a loaf of bread on the table along with a plate and cup; there was coffee warming on the stove. She pulled on a sweater and went down to visit Libby. It was like baiting a trap, she thought. Perhaps he'd enjoy eating if he didn't have to look at a city woman.

Libby didn't ask any obvious questions. She simply enjoyed the visit, since the children were in school and she could talk about clothes and television programs with the younger woman.

At one o'clock, Jennifer left the house and walked slowly back up to see if Everett had eaten. It was something of a shock to find him wandering wildly around the kitchen, smoking like a furnace.

"So there you are!" he burst out, glaring at her with menacing brown eyes. "Where in hell have you been? No note, no nothing! I didn't know if you'd left or been kidnapped, or stepped into a hole . . ."

"What would you care if I had?" she demanded. "You've made it obvious that you don't care for my company!"

"What did you expect?" he burst out, his eyes dangerous. "You lied to me."

"I didn't," she said in defense.

"I thought you were a poor little secretary in danger of starving if I didn't take you in," he said through his teeth. He let his eyes wander with slow insolence over the white blouse and green skirt she was wearing. "And what do I find out? That you lived and worked in New York at a job that would pay you more in one week than I can make here in two months!''

So that was it. His pride was crushed. He was poor and she wasn't, and that cut him up.

But knowing it wasn't much help. He was as unapproachable as a coiled rattler. In his dusty jeans and denim shirt, he looked as wild as an outlaw.

"I had pneumonia," she began. "I had to come south..."

"Bobby didn't know?" he asked.

"No," she said. "I didn't see any reason to tell him. Everett...!''

"Why didn't you say something at the beginning?" he demanded, ramming his hand into his pocket to fish for another cigarette.

"What was there to say?" she asked impotently. She took the sweater from around her shoulders, and her green eyes pleaded with him. "Everett, I'm just the same as I always was.''

"Not hardly," he said. His jaw clenched as he lit the cigarette. "You came here looking like a straggly little hen. And now..." He blew out a cloud of smoke, letting his eyes savor the difference. They lingered for a long time on her blouse, narrowing, burning. "I brought a city girl here once," he said absently. His eyes caught hers. "When she found out that I had more ideas than I had money, she turned around and ran. We were engaged," he said on a short laugh. "I do have the damndest blind spot about women.''

She wrapped her arms around her chest. "Why does it make so much difference?" she asked. "I only took the designing job to help, Rett," she added. She moved closer. "I just wanted to pay you back, for giving me a job when I needed it. I knew you couldn't afford me, but I was in trouble, and you sacrificed for me." Her eyes searched his dark, hard face. "I wanted to do something for you. I wanted you to have your bull.''

His face hardened and he turned away, as if he couldn't bear the sight of her. He raised the cigarette to his lips and his back was ramrod straight.

"I want you to leave," he said.

"Yes, I know," she said on a soft little sigh. "When?"

"At the end of the week."

So soon, she thought miserably? Her eyes clouded as she stared at his back, seeing the determination in every hard line of it. "Do you hate me?" she asked in a hurting tone.

He turned around slowly, the cigarette held tautly in one hand, and his eyes slashed at her. He moved closer, with a look in his dark eyes that was disturbing.

With a smooth motion, he tossed the unfinished cigarette into an ashtray on the table and reached for her.

"I could hate you," he said harshly. "If I didn't want you so damned much." He bent his head and caught her mouth with his.

She stiffened for an instant, because there was no tenderness in this exchange. He was rough and hurting, deliberately. Even so, she loved him. If this was all he could give, then it would be enough. She inched her trapped hands up to his neck and slid them around it. Her soft mouth opened, giving him all he wanted of it. She couldn't respond, he left her no room. He was taking without any thought of giving back the pleasure.

His hard hands slid roughly over her breasts and down to her hips and ground her against him in a deep, insolent rhythm, letting her feel what she already knew—that he wanted her desperately.

"Was it a lie?" he ground out against her mouth. "Are you really a virgin?"

Her lips felt bruised when she tried to speak. "Yes," she said shakily. He was still holding her intimately, and when she tried to pull back, he only crushed her hips closer.

"No, don't do that," he said with a cruel smile. "I like to feel you. Doesn't it give you a sense of triumph, city girl, knowing how you affect me?"

Her hands pushed futilely at his hard chest. "Everett, don't make me feel cheap," she pleaded.

"Could I?" He laughed coldly. "With your prospects?" His hands tightened, making her cry out. His mouth lowered. This time it was teasing, tantalizing. He brushed it against her own mouth in whispery motions that worked like a narcotic, hypnotizing her, weakening her. She began to follow those hard lips with her own, trying to capture them in an exchange that would satisfy the ache he was creating.

"Do you want to stay with me, Jenny?" he whispered.

"Yes," she whispered back, her whole heart in her response. She clutched at his shirtfront with trembling fingers. Her mouth begged for his. "Yes, Everett, I want to stay...!"

His breath came hard and fast at her lips. "Then come upstairs with me, now, and I'll let you," he breathed.

It took a minute for his words to register, and then she realized that his hands had moved to the very base of her spine, to touch her in ways that shocked and frightened her.

She pulled against his hands, her face red, her eyes wild. "What do you mean?" she whispered.

He laughed, his eyes as cold as winter snow. "Don't you know? Sleep with me. Or would you like to hear it in a less formal way?" he added, and put it in words that made her hand come up like a whip.

He caught it, looking down at her with contempt and desire and anger all mixed up in his hard face. "Not interested?" he asked mockingly. "You were a minute ago. You were the other night, when you let me strip you."

Her teeth clenched as she tried to hang on to her dignity and her pride. "Let me go," she whispered shakily.

"I could please you, city girl," he said with a bold, slow gaze down her taut body. "You're going to give in to a man someday. Why not me? Or do I need to get rich first to appeal to you?"

Tears welled up in her eyes. His one hand was about to crack the delicate bone in her wrist, and the other was hurting her back. She closed her eyelids to shut off the sight of his cold face. She loved him so. How could he treat her this way? How could he be so cruel after that tenderness they'd shared!

"No comment?" he asked. He dropped his hands and retrieved his still-smoking cigarette from the ashtray. "Well, you can't blame a man for trying. You seemed willing enough the other night. I thought you might like some memories to carry away with you."

She'd had some beautiful ones, she thought miserably, until now. Her hands reached, trembling, for her sweater. She held it over her chest and wouldn't look up.

"I've got some correspondence on the desk you can type when you run out of things to do in the kitchen," he said, turning toward the door. He looked back with a grim smile on his lips. "That way you can make up some of the time you spent decorating that woman's house for her."

She still didn't speak, didn't move. The world had caved in on her. She loved him. And he could treat her like this, like some tramp he'd picked up on the street!

He drew in a sharp breath. "Don't talk, then," he said coldly. "I don't give a damn. I never did. I wanted you, that's all. But if I had the money, I could have you and a dozen like you, couldn't I?"

She managed to raise her ravaged face. He seemed almost to flinch at the sight of it, but he was only a blur through the tears in her eyes, and she might have been mistaken.

"Say something!" he ground out.

She lifted her chin. Her pale, swollen eyes just stared at him accusingly, and not one single word left her lips. Even if he threw her against the wall, she wouldn't give him the satisfaction of even one syllable!

He drew in a furious breath and whirled on his heel, slamming out the door.

She went upstairs like a zombie, hardly aware of her surroundings at all. She went into her room and took the uncashed checks that he'd signed for her salary and put them neatly on her dresser. She packed very quickly and searched

in her purse. She had just enough pocket money left to pay
a cab. She could cash the design firm's check in town when
she got there. She called the cab company and then lifted her
case and went downstairs to wait for it.

Everett was nowhere in sight, neither were Eddie and Bib,
when the taxi came winding up the driveway. She walked
down the steps, her eyes dry now, her face resolved, and got
inside.

"Take me into town, please," she said quietly.

The cab pulled away from the steps, and she scanned the
ranchhouse and the corrals one last time. Then she turned
away and closed her eyes. She didn't look back, not once.

Fortunately, Jennifer had no trouble landing a job. Sally
Wade had been so impressed with the work that she'd done
for Mrs. Whitehall that she practically created a position for
Jennifer in her small, and still struggling, design firm. Jennifer loved the work, but several weeks had passed before
she was able to think about Everett without crying.

The cup of coffee at Jennifer's elbow was getting cold. She
frowned at it as her hand stilled on the sketch she was doing
for a new client.

"Want some fresh?" Sally Wade asked from the doorway, holding her own cup aloft. "I'm just going to the pot."

"Bless you," Jennifer laughed.

"That's the first time you've really looked happy in the
three months since you've been here," Sally remarked,
cocking her head. "Getting over him?"

"Over whom?" came the shocked reply.

"That man, whoever he was, who had you in tears your
first week here. I didn't pry, but I wondered," the older
woman confessed. "I kept waiting for the phone to ring, or
a letter to come. But nothing did. I kind of thought that he
had to care, because you cared so much."

"He wanted a mistress," Jennifer said, putting it into
words. "And I wanted a husband. We just got our signals
crossed. Besides," she added with a wan smile, "I'm feel-

ing worlds better. I've got a great job, a lovely boss, and even a part-time boyfriend. If you can call Drew a boy.''

"He's delightful." Sally sighed. "Just what you need. A live wire.''

"And not a bad architect, either. You must be pleased he's working with us.'' She grinned. "He did a great job on that office project last month.''

"So did you," Sally said, smiling. She leaned against the doorjamb. "I thought it a marvelous idea, locating a group of offices in a renovated mansion. It only needed the right team, and you and Drew work wonderfully well together.''

"In business, yes.'' Jennifer twirled her pencil around in her slender fingers. "I just don't want him getting serious about me. If it's possible for him to get serious about anyone.'' She laughed.

"Don't try to bury yourself.''

"Oh, I'm not. It's just…'' She shrugged. "I'm only now getting over… I don't want any more risks. Not for a long time. Maybe not ever.''

"Some men are kind-hearted," Sally ventured.

"So why are you single?'' came the sharp reply.

"I'm picky,'' Sally informed her with a sly smile. "Very, very picky. I want Rhett Butler or nobody.''

"Wrong century, wrong state.''

"You're from Georgia. Help me out!''

"Sorry,'' Jennifer murmured. "If I could find one, do you think I'd tell anybody?''

"Point taken. Give me that cup and I'll fill it for you.''

"Thanks, boss.''

"Oh, boy, coffee!'' a tall, redheaded man called from the doorway as he closed the door behind him. "I'll have mine black, with two doughnuts, a fried egg…''

"The breakfast bar is closed, Mr. Peterson,'' Jennifer told him.

"Sorry, Drew,'' Sally added. "You'll just have to catch your own chicken and do it the hard way.''

"I could starve,'' he grumbled, ramming his hands in his pockets. He had blue eyes, and right now they were glaring

at both women. "I don't have a wife or a mother. I liv
alone. My cook hates me..."

"You're breaking my heart," Sally offered.

"You can have the other half of my doughnut," Jennife
said, holding up a chunk of doughnut with chocolate cling
ing to it.

"Never mind." Drew sighed. "Thanks all the same, bu
I'll just wither away."

"That wouldn't be difficult," Jennifer told him. "You're
nothing but skin and bones."

"I gained two pounds this week," he said, affronted.

"Where is it," Sally asked with a sweeping glance, "in
your big toe?"

"Ha, ha," he laughed as she turned to go to the coffee
pot.

"You *are* thin," Jennifer remarked.

He glared at her. "I'm still a growing boy." He stretched
lazily. "Want to ride out to the new office building with m
this morning?"

"No, thanks. I've got to finish these drawings. What d
you think?"

She held one up, and he studied it with an architect'
trained eye. "Nice. Just remember that this," he said
pointing to the vestibule, "is going to be a heavy-traffi
area, and plan accordingly."

"There goes my white carpet," she teased.

"I'll white carpet you," he muttered. He pursed his lip
as he studied her. "Wow, lady, what a change."

She blinked up at him. "What?"

"You. When you walked in here three months ago, yo
looked like a drowned kitten. And now..." He only sighed.

She was wearing a beige suit with a pink candy-stripe
blouse and a pink silk scarf. Her blond hair was almos
platinum with its new body and sheen, and she'd had i
trimmed so that it hung in wispy waves all around he
shoulders. Her face was creamy and soft and she was wear
ing makeup again. She looked nice, and his eyes told her so.

"Thanks."

He pursed his lips. "What for?"

"The flattery," she told him. "My ego's been even with my ankles for quite awhile."

"Stick with me, kid, I'll get it all the way up to your ears," he promised with an evil leer.

"Sally, he's trying to seduce me!" she called toward the front of the office.

She expected some kind of bantering reply, but none was forthcoming. She looked up at Drew contemplatively. "Reckon she's left?"

"No. She's answered the phone. You still aren't used to the musical tone, are you?"

No, she wasn't. There were quite a lot of things she wasn't used to, and the worst of them was being without Everett. She had a good job, a nice apartment, and some new clothes. But without him, none of that mattered. She was going through the motions, and little more. His contempt still stung her pride when she recalled that last horrible scene. But she couldn't get him out of her mind, no matter how she tried.

"Well!" Sally said, catching her breath as she rejoined them. "If the rest of him looks like his voice, I may get back into the active part of the business. That was a potential client, and I think he may be the Rhett Butler I've always dreamed of. What a silky, sexy voice!"

"Dream on," Jennifer teased.

"He's coming by in the morning to talk to us. Wants his whole house done!" the older woman exclaimed.

"He must have a sizeable wallet, then," Drew remarked.

Sally nodded. "He didn't say where the house was, but I assume it's nearby. It didn't sound like a long-distance call." She glanced at Jennifer with a smile. "Apparently your reputation has gotten around, too," she laughed. "He asked if you'd be doing the project. I had the idea he wouldn't have agreed otherwise." She danced around with her coffee cup in her hand. "What a godsend. With the office building and this job, we'll be out of the red, kids! What a break!"

"And you were groaning about the bills just yesterday,"
Jennifer laughed. "I told you something would turn up,
didn't I?"

"You're my lucky charm," Sally told her. "If I hadn't
hired you, I shudder to think what would have happened."

"You know how much I appreciated getting this job,"
Jennifer murmured. "I was in pretty desperate circumstances."

"So I noticed. Well, we did each other a lot of good. We
still are," Sally said warmly. "Hey, let's celebrate. Come on.
I'll treat you two to lunch."

"Lovely!" Jennifer got up and grabbed her purse.
"Come on, Drew, let's hurry before she changes her mind!"

She rushed out the door, with Drew in full pursuit, just
ahead of Sally. And not one of them noticed the man sitting quietly in the luxury car across the street, his fingers idly
caressing a car phone in the back seat as he stared intently
after them.

8

*

Drew had asked Jennifer to go out with him that night, but she begged off with a smile. She didn't care for the nightlife anymore. She went to company functions with Sally when it was necessary to attract clients or discuss new projects, but that was about the extent of her social consciousness. She spent most of her time alone, in her modest apartment, going over drawings and planning rooms.

She enjoyed working for Sally. Houston was a big city, but much smaller than New York. And while there was competition, it wasn't as fierce. The pressure was less. And best of all, Jennifer was allowed a lot of latitude in her projects. She had a free hand to incorporate her own ideas as long as they complemented the client's requirements. She loved what she did, and in loving it, she blossomed into the woman she'd once been. But this time she didn't allow herself to fall into the trap of overspending. She budgeted, right down to the pretty clothes she loved—she bought them on sale, a few at a time, and concentrated on mix-and-match outfits.

It was a good life. But part of her was still mourning Everett. Not a day went by when she couldn't see him, tall and unnerving, somewhere in her memory. They'd been so good for each other. She'd never experienced such tenderness in a man.

She got up from the sofa and looked out at the skyline of Houston. The city was bright and beautiful, but she remembered the ranch on starry nights. Dogs would howl far in the distance, crickets would sing at the steps. And all around would be open land and stars and the silhouettes of Everett's cattle.

She wrapped her arms around her body and sighed. Perhaps someday the pain would stop and she could really forget him. Perhaps someday she could remember his harsh accusations and not be wounded all over again. But right now, it hurt terribly. He'd been willing to let her stay as his mistress, as a possession to be used when he wanted her. But he wouldn't let her be part of his life. He couldn't have told her more graphically how little he thought of her. That had hurt the most. That even after all the caring, all the tenderness, she hadn't reached him at all. He hadn't seen past the shape of her body and his need of it. He hadn't loved her. And he'd made sure she knew it.

There were a lot of nights, like this one, when she paced and paced and wondered if he thought of her at all, if he regretted what had happened. Somehow, she doubted it. Everett had a wall like steel around him. He wouldn't let anyone inside it. Especially not a city woman with an income that could top his.

She laughed bitterly. It was unfortunate that she had fallen in love for the first time with such a cynical man. It had warped the way she looked at the world. She felt as if she, too, were impregnable now. Her emotions were carefully wrapped up, where they couldn't be touched. Nobody could reach her now. She felt safe in her warm cocoon. Of course, she was as incapable of caring now as he'd been. And in a way, that was a blessing. Because she couldn't be hurt anymore. She could laugh and carry on with Drew, and it didn't mean a thing. There was no risk in dating these days. Her heart was safely tucked away.

With a last uncaring look at the skyline, she turned off the lights and went to bed. Just as she drifted off, she wondered who the new client was going to be, and grinned at the memory of Sally's remark about his sexy voice.

She overslept the next morning for the first time in months. With a shriek as she saw the time, she dressed hastily in a silky beige dress and high heels. She moaned over her unruly hair that would curl and feather all around her shoulders instead of going into a neat bun. She touched up her face, stepped into her shoes, and rushed out into the chill autumn morning without a jacket or a sweater. Oh, well, maybe she wouldn't freeze, she told herself as she jumped into the cab she'd called and headed for the office.

"So there you are," Drew said with mock anger as she rushed breathlessly in the door, her cheeks flushed, her eyes sparkling, her hair disheveled and sexy around her face. "I ought to fire you."

"Go ahead. I dare you." She laughed up at him. "And I'll tell Sally all about that last expense voucher you faked."

"Blackmailer!" he growled. He reached out and lifted her up in the air, laughing at her.

"Put me down, you male chauvinist." She laughed gaily. Her face was a study in beauty, her body lusciously displayed in the pose, her hands on his shoulders, her hair swirling gracefully as she looked down at him. "Come on, put me down," she coaxed. "Put me down, Drew, and I'll take you to lunch."

"In that case," he murmured dryly.

"Jennifer! Drew!" Sally exclaimed, entering the room with a nervous laugh. "Stop clowning. We've got business to discuss, and you're making a horrible first impression."

"Oops," Drew murmured. He turned his head just as Jennifer turned hers, and all the laughter and brightness drained out of her like air out of a balloon. She stared down at the newcomer with strained features and eyes that went from shock to extreme anger.

Drew set her down on her feet and turned, hand extended, grinning. "Sorry about that. Just chastising the staff for tardiness." He chuckled. "I'm Andrew Paterson, resident architect. This is my associate, Jennifer King."

"I know her name," Everett Culhane said quietly. His dark eyes held no offer of peace, no hint of truce. They were angry and cold, and he smiled mockingly as his eyes went from Jennifer to Drew. "We've met."

Sally looked poleaxed. It had just dawned on her who Everett was, when she got a look at Jennifer's white face.

"Uh, Mr. Culhane is our new client," Sally said hesitantly. Jennifer looked as if she might faint. "You remember, Jenny, I mentioned yesterday that he'd called."

"You didn't mention his name," Jennifer said in a cool voice that shook with rage. "Excuse me, I have a phone call to make."

"Not so fast," Everett said quietly. "First we talk."

Her eyes glittered at him, her body trembled with suppressed tension. "I have nothing to say to you, Mr. Culhane," she managed. "And you have nothing to say to me that I care to hear."

"Jennifer..." Sally began nervously.

"If my job depends on working for Mr. Culhane, you can have my resignation on the spot," Jennifer said unsteadily. "I will not speak to him, much less work with him. I'm sorry."

She turned and went on wobbly legs to her office, closing the door behind her. She couldn't even sit down. She was shaking like a leaf all over and tears were burning her eyes. She heard voices outside, but ignored them. She stared at an abstract painting on the wall until she thought she'd go blind.

The sound of the door opening barely registered. Then it closed with a firm snap, and she glanced over her shoulder to find Everett inside.

It was only then that she noticed he was wearing a suit. A very expensive gray one that made his darkness even more formidable; his powerful body was streamlined and elegant in its new garments. He was holding a silverbelly Stetson in one lean hand and staring at her quietly, calculatingly.

"Please go away," she said with as much conviction as she could muster.

"Why?" he asked carelessly, tossing his hat onto her desk. He dropped into an armchair and crossed one long leg over the other. He lit a cigarette and pulled the ashtray on her desk closer, but his eyes never left her ravaged face.

"If you want your house redone, there are other firms," she told him, turning bravely, although her legs were still trembling.

He saw that, and his eyes narrowed, his jaw tautened. "Are you afraid of me?" he asked quietly.

"I'm outraged," she replied in a voice that was little more than a whisper. Her hand brushed back a long, unruly strand of hair. "You might as well have taken a bullwhip to me, just before I left the ranch. What do you want now? To show me how prosperous you are? I've noticed the cut of your suit. And the fact that you can afford to hire this firm to redo the house does indicate a lot of money." She smiled unsteadily. "Congratulations. I hope your sudden wealth makes you happy."

He didn't speak for a long minute. His eyes wandered over her slowly, without any insult, as if he'd forgotten what she looked like and needed to stare at her, to fill his eyes. "Aren't you going to ask me how I came by it?" he demanded finally.

"No. Because I don't care," she said.

One corner of his mouth twitched a little. He took a draw from the cigarette and flicked an ash into the ashtray. "I sold off the oil rights."

So much for sticking to your principles, she wanted to say. But she didn't have the strength. She went behind her desk and sat down carefully.

"No comment?" he asked.

She blanched, remembering with staggering clarity the last time he'd said that. He seemed to remember it, too, because his jaw tautened and he drew in a harsh breath.

"I want my house done," he said curtly. "I want you to do it. Nobody else. And I want you to stay with me while you work on the place."

"Hell will freeze over first," she said quietly.

"I was under the impression that the firm wasn't operating in the black," he said with an insolent appraisal of her office. "The commission on this project will be pretty large."

"I told you once that you couldn't buy me," she said on a shuddering breath. "I'd jump off a cliff before I'd stay under the same roof with you!"

His eyes closed. When they opened again, he was staring down at his boot. "Is it that redheaded clown outside?" he asked suddenly, jerking his gaze up to catch hers.

Her lips trembled. "That's none of your business."

His eyes wandered slowly over her face. "You looked different with him," he said deeply. "Alive, vibrant, happy. And then, the minute you spotted me, every bit of life went out of you. It was like watching water drain from a glass."

"What did you expect, for God's sake!" she burst out, her eyes wild. "You cut me up!"

He drew in a slow breath. "Yes. I know."

"Then why are you here?" she asked wearily. "What do you want from me?"

He stared at the cigarette with eyes that barely saw it. "I told you. I want my house done." He looked up. "I can afford the best, and that's what I want. You."

There was an odd inflection in his voice, but she was too upset to hear it. She blinked her eyes, trying to get herself under control. "I won't do it. Sally will just have to fire me."

He got to his feet and loomed over the desk, crushing out the cigarette before he rammed his hands into his pockets and glared at her. "There are less pleasant ways to do this," he said. "I could make things very difficult for your new employer." His eyes challenged her. "Call my bluff. See if you can skip town with that on your conscience."

She couldn't, and he knew it. Her pride felt lacerated. "What do you think you'll accomplish by forcing me to come back?" she asked. "I'd put a knife in you if I could. I won't sleep with you, no matter what you do. So what will you get out of it?"

"My house decorated, of course," he said lazily. His eyes wandered over her. "I've got over the other. Out of sight, out of mind, don't they say?" He shrugged and turned away with a calculating look on his face. "And one body's pretty

much like another in the dark,'' he added, reaching for his
Stetson. His eyes caught the flutter of her lashes and he
smiled to himself as he reached for the doorknob. ''Well,
Miss King, which is it? Do you come back to Big Spur with
me or do I give Ms. Wade the sad news that you're leaving
her in the lurch?''

Her eyes flashed green sparks at him. What choice was
there? But he'd pay for this. Somehow, she'd make him.
''I'll go,'' she bit off.

He didn't say another word. He left her office as though
he were doing her a favor by letting her redecorate his house!

Sally came in the door minutes later, looking troubled and
apologetic.

''I had no idea,'' she told Jennifer. ''Honest to God, I had
no idea who he was.''

''Now you know,'' Jennifer said on a shaky laugh.

''You don't have to do it,'' the older woman said curtly.

''Yes, I'm afraid I do. Everett doesn't make idle threats,''
she said, rising. ''You've been too good to me, Sally. I can't
let him cause trouble for you on my account. I'll go with
him. After all, it's just another job.''

''You look like death warmed over. I'll send Drew with
you. We'll do something to justify him ...''

''Everett would eat him alive,'' she told Sally with a level
stare. ''And don't pretend you don't know it. Drew's a nice
man but he isn't up to Everett's weight or his temper. This
is a private war.''

''Unarmed combat?'' Sally asked sadly.

''Exactly. He has this thing about city women, and I
wasn't completely honest with him. He wants to get even.''

''I thought revenge went out with the Borgias,'' Sally
muttered.

''Not quite. Wish me luck. I'm going to need it.''

''If it gets too rough, call for reinforcements,'' Sally said.
''I'll pack a bag and move in with you, Everett or no Everett.''

''You're a pal,'' Jennifer said warmly.

"I'm a rat," came the dry reply. "I wish I hadn't done this to you. If I'd known who he was, I'd never have told him you worked here."

Jennifer had hoped to go down to Big Spur alone, but Everett went back to her apartment with her, his eyes daring her to refuse his company.

He waited in the living room while she packed, and not one corner escaped his scrutiny.

"Looking for dust?" she asked politely, case in hand.

He turned, cigarette in hand, studying her. "This place must cost you an arm," he remarked.

"It does," she said with deliberate sarcasm. "But I can afford it. I make a lot of money, as you reminded me."

"I said a lot of cruel things, didn't I, Jenny Wren?" he asked quietly, searching her shocked eyes. "Did I leave deep scars?"

She lifted her chin. "Can we go? The sooner we get there, the sooner I can get the job done and come home."

"Didn't you ever think of the ranch as home?" he asked, watching her. "You seemed to love it at first."

"Things were different then," she said noncommittally, and started for the door.

He took her case, his fingers brushing hers in the process, and producing electric results.

"Eddie and Bib gave me hell when they found out you'd gone," he said as he opened the door for her.

"I imagine you were too busy celebrating to notice."

He laughed shortly. "Celebrating? You damned little fool, I...!" He closed his mouth with a rough sigh. "Never mind. You might have left a nasty note or something."

"Why, so you'd know where I went?" she demanded. "That was the last thing I wanted."

"So I noticed," he agreed. He locked the door, handed her the key, and started down the hall toward the elevator. "Libby told me the name of the firm you'd worked for. It wasn't hard to guess you'd get a job with them."

She tossed her hair. "So that was how you found me."

"We've got some unfinished business," he replied as they waited for the elevator. His dark eyes held hers and she had to clench her fists to keep from kicking him. He had a power over her that all her anger couldn't stop. Deep beneath the layer of ice was a blazing inferno of hunger and love, but she'd die before she'd show it to him.

"I hate you," she breathed.

"Yes, I know you do," he said with an odd satisfaction.

"Mr. Culhane..."

"You used to call me Rett," he recalled, studying her. "Especially," he added quietly, "when we made love."

Her face began to color and she aimed a kick at his shins. He jumped back just as the elevator door opened.

"Pig!" she ground out.

"Now, honey, think of the kids," he drawled, aiming a glance at the elevator full of fascinated spectators. "If you knock me down, how can I support the ten of you?"

Red-faced, she got in ahead of him and wished with all her heart that the elevator doors would close right dead center on him. They didn't.

He sighed loudly, glancing down at her. "I begged you not to run off with that salesman," he said in a sad drawl. "I told you he'd lead you into a life of sin!"

There were murmured exclamations all around and a buzz of conversation. She glared up at him. Two could play that game.

"Well, what did you expect me to do, sit at home and knit while you ran around with that black-eyed hussy?" she drawled back. "And me in my delicate condition..."

"Delicate condition...?" he murmured, shocked at her unexpected remark.

"And it's your baby, too, you animal," she said with a mock sob, glaring up at him.

"Darling!" he burst out. "You didn't tell me!"

And he grabbed her and kissed her hungrily right there in front of the whole crowd while she gasped and counted to ten and tried not to let him see that she was melting into the floor from the delicious contact with his mouth.

The elevator doors opened and he lifted his head as the other occupants filed out. He was breathing unsteadily and his eyes held hers. "No," he whispered when she tried to move away. His arm caught her and his head bent. "I need you," he whispered shakily. "Need you so . . . !"

That brought it all back. Need. He needed her. He just needed a body, that was all, and she knew it! She jerked herself out of his arms and stomped off the elevator.

"You try that again and I'll vanish!" she threatened, glaring up at him when they were outside the building. Her face was flushed, her breath shuddering. "I mean it! I'll disappear and you won't find me this time!"

He shrugged. "Suit yourself." He walked alongside her, all the brief humor gone out of his face. She wondered minutes later if it had been there at all.

9

He had a Lincoln now. Not only the car, but a driver to go with it. He handed her bag to the uniformed driver and put Jennifer in the back seat beside him.

"Aren't we coming up in the world, though?" she asked with cool sarcasm.

"Don't you like it?" he replied mockingly. He leaned back against the seat facing her and lit a cigarette. "I didn't think a woman alive could resist flashy money."

She remembered reluctantly how he'd already been thrown over once for the lack of wealth. Part of her tender heart felt sorry for him. But not any part that was going to show, she told herself.

"You could buy your share now, I imagine," she said, glancing out the window at the traffic.

He blew out a thin cloud of smoke. The driver climbed in under the wheel and, starting the powerful car, pulled out into the street.

"I imagine so."

She stared at the purse in her lap. "They really did find oil out there?" she asked.

"Sure did. Barrels and barrels." He glanced at her over his cigarette. "The whole damned skyline's cluttered with rigs these days. Metal grasshoppers." He sighed. "The cattle don't even seem to mind them. They just graze right on."

Wouldn't it be something if a geyser blew out under one of his prize Herefords one day, she mused. She almost told him, and then remembered the animosity between them. It had been a good kind of relationship that they'd had. If only Everett hadn't ruined it.

"It's a little late to go into it now," he said quietly. "But I didn't mean to hurt you that much. Once I cooled down, I would have apologized."

"The apology wouldn't have meant much after what you said to me!" she said through her teeth, flushing at the memory of the crude phrase.

He looked away. For a long minute he just sat and smoked. "You're almost twenty-four years old, Jenny," he said finally. "If you haven't heard words like that before, you're overdue."

"I didn't expect to hear them from you," she shot back, glaring at him. "Much less have you treat me with less respect than a woman you might have picked up on the streets with a twenty-dollar bill!"

"One way or another, I'd have touched you like that eventually!" he growled, glaring at her. "And don't sit there like lily white purity and pretend you don't know what I'm talking about. We were on the verge of becoming lovers that night on the sofa."

"You wouldn't have made me feel ashamed if it had happened that night," she said fiercely. "You wouldn't have made me feel cheap!"

He seemed about to explode. Then he caught himself and took a calming draw from the cigarette. His dark eyes studied the lean hand holding it. "You hurt me."

It was a shock to hear him admit it. "What?"

"You hurt me." His dark eyes lifted. "I thought we were being totally honest with each other. I trusted you. I let you closer than any other woman ever got. And then out of the blue, you hit me with everything at once. That you were a professional woman, a career woman. Worse," he added quietly, "a city woman, used to city men and city life and city ways. I couldn't take it. I'd been paying you scant wages, and you handed me that check..." He sighed wearily. "My God, I can't even tell you how I felt. My pride took one hell of a blow. I had nothing, and you were showing me graphically that you could outdo me on every front."

"I only wanted to help," she said curtly. "I wanted to buy you the damned bull. Sorry. If I had it to do all over again, I wouldn't offer you a dime."

"Yes, it shows." He sighed. He finished the cigarette and crushed it out. "Who's the redhead?"

"Drew? Sally told you. He's our architect. He has his own firm, of course, but he collaborates with us on big projects."

"Not on mine," he said menacingly, and his eyes darkened. "Not in my house."

She glared back. "That will depend on how much renovation the projects calls for, I imagine."

"I won't have him on my place," he said softly.

"Why?"

"I don't like the way he looks at you," he said coldly. "Must less the way he makes free with his hands."

"I'm twenty-three years old," she reminded him. "And I like Drew, and the way he looks at me! He's a nice man."

"And I'm not," he agreed. "Nice is the last thing I am. If he ever touches you that way again when I'm in the same room, I'll break his fingers for him."

"Everett Donald Culhane!" she burst out.

His eyebrows arched. "Who told you my whole name?"

She looked away. "Never mind," she said, embarrassed.

His hand brushed against her hair, caressing it. "God, your hair is glorious," he said quietly. "It was nothing like this at the ranch."

She tried not to feel his touch. "I'd been ill," she managed.

"And now you aren't. Now you're... fuller and softer-looking. Even your breasts..."

"Stop it!" she cried, red-faced.

He let go of her hair reluctantly, but his eyes didn't leave her. "I'll have you, Jenny," he said quietly, his tone as soft as it had been that night when he was loving her.

"Only if you shoot me in the leg first!" she told him.

"Not a chance," he murmured, studying her. "I'll want you healthy and strong, so that you can keep up with me."

Her face did a slow burn again. She could have kicked him, but they were sitting down. "I don't want you!"

"You did. You will. I've got a whole campaign mapped out, Miss Jenny," he told her with amazing arrogance. "You're under siege. You just haven't realized it yet."

She looked him straight in the eye. "My grandfather held off a whole German company during World War I rather than surrender."

His eyebrows went up. "Is that supposed to impress me?"

"I won't be your mistress," she told him levelly. "No matter how many campaigns you map out or what kind of bribes or threats you try to use. I came with you to save Sally's business. But all this is to me is a job. I am not going to sleep with you."

His dark, quiet eyes searched over her face. "Why?"

Her lips opened and closed, opened again. "Because I can't do it without love," she said finally.

"Love isn't always possible," he said softly. "Sometimes, other things have to come first. Mutual respect, caring, companionship..."

"Can we talk about something else?" she asked tautly. Her fingers twisted the purse out of shape.

He chuckled softly. "Talking about sex won't get you pregnant."

"You've got money now. You can buy women," she ground out. "You said so."

"Honey, would you want a man you had to buy?" he asked quietly, studying her face.

Her lips parted. "Would I..." She searched his eyes. "Well, no."

"I wouldn't want a woman I had to buy," he said simply. "I'm too proud, Jenny. I said and did some harsh things to you," he remarked. "I can understand why you're angry and hurt about it. Someday I'll try to explain why I behaved that way. Right now, I'll settle for regaining even a shadow of the friendship we had. Nothing more. Despite all this wild talk, I'd never deliberately try to seduce you."

"Wouldn't you?" she asked bitterly. "Isn't that the whole point of getting me down here?"

"No." He lit another cigarette.

"You said you were going to..." she faltered.

"I want to," he admitted quietly. "God, I want to! But I can't quite take a virgin in my stride. Once, I thought I might," he confessed, his eyes searching her face. "That night... You were so eager, and I damned near lost my head when I realized that I could have you." He stared at the tip of his cigarette with blank eyes. "Would you have hated me if I hadn't been able to stop?"

Her eyes drilled into her purse. "There's just no point in going over it," she said in a studiously polite tone. "The past is gone."

"Like hell it's gone," he ground out. "I look at you and start aching," he said harshly.

Her lower lip trembled as she glared at him. "Then stop looking. Or take cold showers! Just don't expect me to do anything about it. I'm here to work, period!"

His eyebrows arched, and he was watching her with a faintly amused expression. "Where did you learn about cold showers?"

"From watching movies!"

"Is that how you learned about sex, from the movies?" he taunted.

"No, I learned in school! Sex education," she bit off.

"In my day, we had to learn it the hard way," he murmured. "It wasn't part of the core curriculum."

She glanced at him. "I can see you, doing extracurricular work in somebody's backseat."

He reached out and caught her hair again, tugging on it experimentally. "In a haystall, actually," he said, his voice low and soft and dark. Her head turned and he held her eyes. "She was two years older than I was, and she taught me the difference between sex and making love."

Her face flushed. He affected her in ways nobody else could. She was trembling from the bare touch of his fingers on her hair; her heart was beating wildly. How was she going to survive being in the same house with him?

"Everett..." she began.

"I'm sorry about what I said to you that last day, Jenny," he said quietly. "I'm sorry I made it into something cheap and sordid between us. Because that's the last thing it would have been if you'd given yourself to me."

She pulled away from him with a dry little laugh. "Oh, really?" she said shakenly, turning her eyes to the window. They were out of Houston now, heading south. "The minute you'd finished with me, you'd have kicked me out the door, and you know it, Everett Culhane. I'd have been no different from all the other women you've held in contempt for giving in to you."

"It isn't like that with you."

"And how many times have you told that story?" she asked sadly.

"Once. Just now."

He sounded irritated, probably because she wasn't falling for his practiced line. She closed her eyes and leaned her head against the cool window pane.

"I'd rather stay in a motel," she said, "if you don't mind."

"No way, lady," he said curtly. "The same lock's still on your door, if you can't trust me that far. But staying at Big Spur was part of the deal you and I negotiated."

She turned her head to glance at his hard, set profile. He looked formidable again, all dark, flashing eyes and coldness. He was like the man she'd met that first day at the screen door.

"What would you have done, if I'd given in?" she asked suddenly, watching him closely. "What if I'd gotten pregnant?"

His head turned and his eyes glittered strangely. "I'd have gotten down on my knees and thanked God for it," he said harshly. "What did you think I'd do?"

Her lips parted. "I hadn't really thought about it."

"I want children. A yardfull."

That was surprising. Her eyes dropped to his broad chest, to the muscles that his gray suit barely contained, and she remembered how it was to be held against him in passion.

"Libby said you loved the ranch," he remarked.

"I did. When I was welcome."

"You still are."

"Do tell?" She cocked her head. "I'm a career woman, remember? And I'm a city girl."

His mouth tugged up. "I think city girls are sexy." His dark eyes traveled down to her slender legs encased in pink hose. "I didn't know you had legs, Jenny Wren. You always kept them in jeans."

"I didn't want you leering at me."

"Ha!" he shot back. "You knew that damned blouse was torn, the day you fell off your horse." His eyes dared her to dispute him. "You wanted my eyes on you. I'll never forget the way you looked when you saw me staring at you."

Her chest rose and fell quickly. "I was shocked."

"Shocked, hell. Delighted." He lifted the cigarette to his mouth. "I didn't realize you were a woman until then. I'd seen you as a kid. A little helpless thing I needed to protect." His eyes cut sideways and he smiled mockingly. "And then that blouse came open and I saw a body I'd have killed for. After that, the whole situation started getting impossible."

"So did you."

"I know," he admitted. "My brain was telling me to keep away, but my body wouldn't listen. You didn't help a hell of a lot, lying there on that couch with your mouth begging for mine."

"Well, I'm human!" she burst out furiously. "And I never asked you to start kissing me."

"You didn't fight me."

She turned away. "Can't we get off this subject?"

"Just when it's getting interesting?" he mused. "Why? Don't you like remembering it?"

"No, I don't!"

"Does he kiss you the way I did?" he asked shortly, jerking her around by the arm, his lean hand hurting. "That redhead, have you let him touch you like I did!"

"No!" she whispered, shocking herself with the disgust she put into that one, telling syllable.

His nostrils flared and his dark eyes traveled to the bodice of her dress, to her slender legs, her rounded hips, and all the way back up again to her eyes. "Why not?" he breathed unsteadily.

"Maybe I'm terrified of men now," she muttered.

"Maybe you're just terrified of other men," he whispered. "It was so good, when we touched each other. So good, so sweet...I rocked you under me and felt you swell, here..." His fingers brushed lightly against the bodice of her dress.

Coming to her senses all at once, she caught his fingers and pushed them away.

"No!" she burst out.

His fingers curled around her hand. He brought her fingers to his mouth and nibbled at them softly, staring into her eyes. "I can't even get in the mood with other women," he said quietly. "Three long months and I still can't sleep for thinking how you felt in my arms."

"Don't," she ground out, bending her head. "You won't make me feel guilty."

"That isn't what I want from you. Not guilt."

Her eyes came up. "You just want sex, don't you? You want me because I haven't been with anyone else!"

He caught her face in his warm hands and searched it while the forgotten cigarette between his fingers sent up curls of smoke beside her head.

"Someday, I'll tell you what I really want," he said, his voice quiet and soft and dark. "When you've forgotten, and forgiven what happened. Until then, I'll just go on as I have before." His mouth twisted. "Taking cold showers and working myself into exhaustion."

She wouldn't weaken; she wouldn't! But his hands were warm and rough, and his breath was smoky against her parted lips. And her mouth wanted his.

He bent closer, just close enough to torment her. His eyes closed. His nose touched hers.

She felt reckless and hungry, and all her willpower wasn't proof against him.

"Jenny," he groaned against her lips.

"Isn't . . . fair," she whispered shakily.

"I know." His hands were trembling. They touched her face as if it were some priceless treasure. His mouth trembled, too, while it brushed softly over hers. "Oh, God, I'll die if I don't kiss you . . . !" he whispered achingly.

"No . . ." But it was only a breath, and he took it from her with the cool, moist pressure of his hard lips.

She hadn't dreamed of kisses this tender, this soft. He nudged her mouth with his until it opened. She shuddered with quickly drawn breaths. Her eyes slid open and looked into his slitted ones.

"Oh," she moaned in a sharp whisper.

"Oh," he whispered back. His thumbs brushed her cheeks. "I want you. I want to lie with you and touch you and let you touch me. I want to make love with you and to you."

"Everett . . . you mustn't," she managed in a husky whisper as his mouth tortured hers. "Please, don't do this . . . to me. The driver . . ."

"I closed the curtain, didn't you notice?" he whispered.

She looked past him, her breath jerky and quick, her face flushed, her eyes wild.

"You see?" he asked quietly.

She swallowed, struggling for control. Her eyes closed and she pulled carefully away from his warm hands.

"No," she said then.

"All right." He moved back and finished his cigarette in silence.

She glanced at him warily, tucking back a loose strand of hair.

"There's nothing to be afraid of," he said, as if he sensed all her hidden fears. "I want nothing from you that you don't want to give freely."

She clasped her hands together. Her tongue touched her dry lips, and she could still taste him on them. It was so intimate that she caught her breath.

"I can't go with you," she burst out, all at once.

"Your door has a lock," he reminded her. "And I'll even give you my word that I won't force you."

Her troubled eyes sought his and he smiled reassuringly.

"Let me rephrase that," he said after a minute. "I won't take advantage of any...lapses. Is that better?"

She clutched her purse hard enough to wrinkle the soft leather wallet inside. "I hate being vulnerable!"

"Do you think I don't?" he growled, his eyes flashing. He crushed out his cigarette. "I'm thirty-five, and it's never happened to me before." He glared at her. "And it had to be with a damned virgin!"

"Don't you curse at me!"

"I wasn't cursing," he said harshly. He reached for another cigarette.

"Will you please stop that?" she pleaded. "I'm choking on the smoke as it is."

He made a rough sound and repocketed the cigarette. "You'll be carrying a noose around with you next."

"Not for your neck," she promised him with a sweet smile. "Confirmed bachelors aren't my cup of tea."

"Career women aren't mine."

She turned her eyes out the window. And for the rest of the drive to the ranch she didn't say another word.

The room he gave her was the one she'd had before. But she was surprised to see that the linen hadn't been changed. And the checks he'd written for her were just where she'd left them, on the dresser.

She stared at him as he set her bag down. "It's...you haven't torn them up," she faltered.

He straightened, taking off his hat to run a hand through his thick, dark hair. "So what?" he growled, challenge in his very posture. He towered over her.

"Well, I don't want them!" she burst out.

"Of course not," he replied. "You've got a good paying job now, don't you?"

Her chin lifted. "Yes, I do."

He tossed his hat onto the dresser and moved toward her.

"You promised!" she burst out.

"Sure I did," he replied. He reached out and jerked her up into his arms, staring into her eyes. "What if I lied?" he whispered gruffly. "What if I meant to throw you on that bed, and strip you, and make love to you until dawn?"

He was testing her. So that was how it was going to be. She stared back at him fearlessly. "Try it," she invited.

His mouth curled up. "No hysterics?"

"I stopped having hysterics the day that horse threw me and you got an anatomy lesson," she tossed back. "Go ahead, rape me."

His face darkened. "It wouldn't be rape. Not between you and me."

"If I didn't want you, it would be."

"Honey," he said softly, "you'd want me. Desperately."

She already did. The feel of him, the clean smell of his body, the coiled strength in his powerful muscles were all working on her like drugs. But she was too afraid of the future to slide backwards now. He wanted her. But nothing more. And without love, she wanted nothing he had to offer.

"You promised," she said again.

He sighed. "So I did. Damned fool." He set her down on her feet and moved away with a long sigh to pick up his hat. His eyes studied her from the doorway. "Well, come on down when you're rested, and I'll have Consuelo fix something to eat."

"Consuelo?"

"My housekeeper." His eyes watched the expressions that washed over her face. "She's forty-eight, nicely plump, and happily married to one of my new hands. All right?"

"Did you hope I might be jealous?" she asked.

His broad chest rose and fell swiftly. "I've got a lot of high hopes about you. Care to hear a few of them?"

"Not particularly."

"That's what I was afraid of." He went out and closed the door behind him with an odd laugh.

10

*

Consuelo was a treasure. Small, dark, very quick around the kitchen, and Jennifer liked her on sight.

"It is good that you are here, senorita," the older woman said as she put food on the new and very elegant dining room table. "So nice to see the senor do something besides growl and pace."

Jennifer laughed as she put out the silverware.

"Yes, now he's cursing at the top of his lungs," she mused, cocking her ear toward the window. "Hear him?"

It would have been impossible not to. He was giving somebody hell about an open gate, and Jennifer was glad it wasn't her.

"Such a strange man," Consuelo sighed, shaking her head. "The room he has given you, senorita, he would not let me touch it. Not to dust, not even to change the linen."

"Did he say why?" Jennifer asked with studied carelessness.

"No. But sometimes at night . . ." she hesitated.

"Yes?"

Consuelo shrugged at the penetrating look she got from the younger woman. "Sometimes at night, the senor, he would go up there and just sit. For a long time. I wonder, you see, but the only time I mention this strange habit, he says to mind my own business. So I do not question it."

How illuminating that was. Jennifer pondered on it long and hard. It was almost as if he'd missed her. But then, if he'd missed her, he'd have to care. And he didn't. He just wanted her because she was something different, a virgin. And perhaps because she was the only woman who'd been close to him for a long time. Under the same circumstances, it could very well have been any young, reasonably attractive woman.

He came in from the corral looking dusty and tired and out of humor. Consuelo glanced at him and he glared at her as he removed his wide-brimmed hat and sat down at the table with his chaps still on.

"Any comments?" he growled.

"Not from me, senor," Consuelo assured him. "As far as I am concerned, you can sit there in your overcoat. Lunch is on the table. Call if you need me."

Jennifer put a hand over her mouth to keep from laughing. Everett glared at her.

"My, you're in a nasty mood," she observed as she poured him a cup of coffee from the carafe. She filled her own cup, too.

"Pat yourself on the back," he returned.

She raised her eyebrows. "Me?"

"You." He picked up a roll and buttered it.

"I can leave?" she suggested.

"Go ahead."

She sat back in her chair, watching him. "What's wrong?" she asked quietly. "Something is."

"Bull died."

She caught her breath. "The big Hereford?"

He nodded. "The one I sold and then bought back when I leased the oil rights." He stared at his roll blankly. "The vet's going to do an autopsy. I want to know why. He was healthy."

"I'm sorry," she said gently. "You were very proud of him."

His jaw tautened. "Well, maybe some of those heifers I bred to him will throw a good bull."

She dished up some mashed potatoes and steak and gravy. "I thought heifers were cows that hadn't grown up," she murmured. "Isn't that what you told me?"

"Heifers are heifers until they're two years old and bred for the first time. Which these just were."

"Oh."

He glanced at her. "I'm surprised you'd remember that."

"I remember a lot about the ranch," she murmured as she ate. "Are you selling off stock before winter?"

"Not a lot of it," he said. "Now that I can afford to feed the herd."

"It's an art, isn't it?" she asked, lifting her eyes to his. "Cattle-raising, I mean. It's very methodical."

"Like decorating?" he muttered.

"That reminds me." She got up, fetched her sketch pad, and put it down beside his plate. "I did those before I came down. They're just the living room and kitchen, but I'd like to see what you think."

"You're the decorator," he said without opening it. "Do what you please."

She glared at him and put down her fork. "Everett, it's your house. I'd at least like you to approve the suggestions I'm making."

He sighed and opened the sketch pad. He frowned. His head came up suddenly. "I didn't know you could draw like this."

"It kind of goes with the job," she said, embarrassed.

"Well, you're good. Damned good. Is this what it will look like when you're finished?" he asked.

"Something like it. I'll do more detailed drawings if you like the basic plan."

"Yes, I like it," he said with a slow smile. He ran a finger over her depiction of the sofa and she remembered suddenly that instead of drawing in a new one, she'd sketched the old one. The one they'd lain on that night. . . .

She cleared her throat. "The kitchen sketch is just under that one."

He looked up. "Was that a Freudian slip, drawing that particular sofa?" he asked.

Her face went hot. "I'm human!" she grumbled.

His eyes searched hers. "No need to overheat, Miss King. I was just asking a question. I enjoyed what we did, too. I'm not throwing stones." He turned the page and pursed his lips. "I don't like the breakfast bar."

Probably because it would require the services of an architect, she thought evilly.

"Why?" she asked anyway, trying to sound interested.

He smiled mockingly. "Because, as I told you already, I won't have that redhead in my house."

She sighed angrily. "As you wish." She studied his hard face. "Will you have a few minutes to go over some ideas with me tonight? Or are you still trying to work yourself into an early grave?"

"Would you mind if I did, Jenny?" he mused.

"Yes. I wouldn't get paid," she said venomously.

He chuckled softly. "Hardhearted little thing. Yes, I'll have some free time tonight." He finished his coffee. "But not now." He got up from the table.

"I'm sorry about your bull."

He stopped by her chair and tilted her chin up. "It will all work out," he said enigmatically. His thumb brushed over her soft mouth slowly, with electrifying results. She stared up with an expression that seemed to incite violence in him.

"Jenny," he breathed gruffly, and started to bend.

"Senor," Consuelo called, coming through the door in time to break the spell holding them, "do you want dessert now?"

"I'd have had it but for you, woman," he growled. And with that he stomped out the door, rattling the furniture as he went.

Consuelo stared after him, and Jennifer tried not to look guilty and frustrated all at once.

For the rest of the day, Jennifer went from room to room, making preliminary sketches. It was like a dream come true. For a long time, ever since she'd first seen the big house, she'd wondered what it would be like to redo it. Now she was getting the chance, and she was overjoyed. The only sad part was that Everett wouldn't let her get Drew in to do an appraisal of the place. It would be a shame to redo it if there were basic structural problems.

That evening after a quiet supper she went into the study with him and watched him build a fire in the fireplace. It

as late autumn and getting cold at night. The fire crack-
d and burned in orange and yellow glory and smelled of
ak and pine and the whole outdoors.

"How lovely," she sighed, leaning back in the armchair
cing it with her eyes closed. She was wearing jeans again,
ith a button-down brown patterned shirt, and she felt at
ome.

"Yes," he said.

She opened her eyes lazily to find him standing in front
f her, staring quietly at her face.

"Sorry, I drifted off," she said quickly, and started to
se.

"Don't get up. Here." He handed her the sketch pad and
erched himself on the arm of the chair, just close enough
drive her crazy with the scent and warmth and threat of
is big body. "Show me."

She went through the sketches with him, showing the
hanges she wanted to make. When they came to his big
edroom, her voice faltered as she suggested new Mediter-
anean furnishings and a king-sized bed.

"You're very big," she said, trying not to look at him.
And the room is large enough to accommodate it."

"By all means," he murmured, watching her. "I like a lot
f room."

It was the way he said it. She cleared her throat. "And I
nought a narrow chocolate-and-vanilla-stripe wallpaper
ould be nice. With a thick cream carpet and chocolate-
olored drapes."

"Am I going to live in the room, or eat it?"

"Hush. And you could have a small sitting area if you
ke. A desk and a chair, a lounge chair..."

"All I want in my bedroom is a bed," he grumbled. "I
an work down here."

"All right." She flipped the page, glad to be on to the next
oom, which was a guest bedroom. "This..."

"No."

She glanced up. "What?"

"No. I don't want another guest room there." He looked down into her eyes. "Make it into a nursery."

She felt her body go cold. "A nursery?"

"Well, I've got to have someplace to put the kids," he said reasonably.

"Where are they going to come from?" she asked blankly.

He sighed with exaggerated patience. "First you have a man. Then you have a woman. They sleep together and—"

"I know that!"

"Then why did you ask me?"

"Forgive me if I sound dull, but didn't you swear that you'd rather be dead than married?" she grumbled.

"Sure. But being rich has changed my ideas around. I've decided that I'll need somebody to leave all this to." He pulled out a cigarette and lit it.

She stared at her designs with unseeing eyes. "Do you have a candidate already?" she asked with a forced laugh.

"No, not yet. But there are plenty of women around." His eyes narrowed as he studied her profile. "As a matter of fact, I had a phone call last week. From the woman I used to be engaged to. Seems her marriage didn't work out. She's divorced now."

That hurt. She hadn't expected that it would, but it went through her like a dagger. "Oh?" she said. Her pencil moved restlessly on the page as she darkened a line. "Were you surprised?"

"Not really," he said with cynicism. "Women like that are pretty predictable. I told you how I felt about buying them."

"Yes." She drew in a slow breath. "Well, Houston is full of debutantes. You shouldn't have much trouble picking out one."

"I don't want a child."

She glanced up. "Picky, aren't you?"

His mouth curled. "Yep."

She laughed despite herself, despite the cold that was numbing her heart. "Well, I wish you luck. Now, about the nursery, do you want it done in blue?"

"No. I like girls, too. Make it pink and blue. Or maybe yellow. Something unisex." He got up, stretching lazily, and yawned. "God, I'm tired. Honey, do you mind if we cut this short? I'd dearly love a few extra hours' sleep."

"Of course not. Do you mind if I go ahead with the rooms we've discussed?" she asked. "I could go ahead and order the materials tomorrow. I've already arranged to have the wallpaper in the living room stripped."

"Go right ahead." He glanced at her. "How long do you think it will take, doing the whole house?"

"A few weeks, that's all."

He nodded. "Sleep well, Jenny. Good night."

"Good night."

He went upstairs, and she sat by the fire until it went out, trying to reconcile herself to the fact that Everett was going to get married and have children. It would be to somebody like Libby, she thought. Some nice, sweet country girl who had no ambition to be anything but a wife and mother. Tears dripped down her cheeks and burned her cool flesh. What a pity it wouldn't be Jennifer.

She decided that perhaps Everett had had the right idea in the first place. Exhaustion was the best way in the world to keep one's mind off one's troubles. So she got up at dawn to oversee the workmen who were tearing down wallpaper and repairing plaster. Fortunately the plasterwork was in good condition and wouldn't have to be redone. By the time they were finished with the walls, the carpet people had a free day and invaded the house. She escaped to the corral and watched Eddie saddlebreak one of the new horses Everett had bought.

Perched on the corral fence in her jeans and blue sweatshirt, with her hair in a ponytail, she looked as outdoorsy as he did.

"How about if I yell 'ride 'em, cowboy,' and cheer you on, Eddie?" she drawled.

He lifted a hand. "Go ahead, Miss Jenny!"

"Ride 'em, cowboy!" she hollered.

He chuckled, bouncing around on the horse. She was so busy watching him that she didn't even hear Everett ride up behind her. He reached out a long arm and suddenly jerked her off the fence and into the saddle in front of him.

"Sorry to steal your audience, Eddie," he yelled toward the older man, "but she's needed!"

Eddie waved. Everett's hard arm tightened around her waist, tugging her stiff body back into the curve of his, as he urged the horse into a canter.

"Where am I needed?" she asked, peeking over her shoulder at his hard face.

"I've got a new calf. Thought you might like to pet it."

She laughed. "I'm too busy to pet calves."

"Sure. Sitting around on fences like a rodeo girl." His arm tightened. "Eddie doesn't need an audience to break horses."

"Well, it was interesting."

"So are calves."

She sighed and let her body slump back against his. She felt him stiffen at the contact, felt his breath quicken. She could smell him, and feel him, and her body sang at the contact. It had been such a long time since those things had disturbed her.

"Where are we going?" she murmured contentedly.

"Down to the creek. Tired?"

"Ummm," she murmured. "My arms ache."

"I've got an ache of my own, but it isn't in my arms," he mused.

She cleared her throat and sat up straight. "Uh, what kind of calf is it?"

He laughed softly. "I've got an ache in my back from lifting equipment," he said, watching her face burn. "What did you think I meant?"

"Everett," she groaned, embarrassed.

"You babe in the woods," he murmured. His fingers spread on her waist, so long that they trespassed onto her flat stomach as well. "Hold on."

He put the horse into a gallop and she caught her breath, turning in the saddle to cling to his neck and hide her face in his shoulder.

He laughed softly, coiling his arm around her. "I won't let you fall," he chided.

"Do we have to go so fast?"

"I thought you were in a hurry to get there." He slowed the horse as they reached a stand of trees beside the creek. Beyond it was a barbed-wire fence. Inside it was a cow and a calf, both Herefords.

He dismounted and lifted Jenny down. "She's gentle," he said, taking her hand to pull her along toward the horned cow. "I raised this one myself, from a calf. Her mama died of snakebite and I nursed her with a bottle. She's been a good breeder. This is her sixth calf."

The furry little thing fascinated Jenny. It had pink eyes and a pink nose and pink ears, and the rest of it was reddish-brown and white.

She laughed softly and rubbed it between the eyes. "How pretty," she murmured. "She has pink eyes!"

"He," he corrected. "It will be a steer."

She frowned. "Not a bull?"

He glowered down at her. "Don't you ever listen to me? A steer is a bull that's been converted for beef. A bull has..." He searched for the words. "A bull is still able to father calves."

She grinned up at him. "Not embarrassed, are you?" she taunted.

He cocked an eyebrow. "You're the one who gets embarrassed every time I talk straight," he said curtly.

She remembered then, and her smile faded. She touched the calf gently, concentrating on it instead of him.

His lean hands caught her waist and she gasped, stiffening. His breath came hard and fast at her back.

"There's a party in Victoria tomorrow night. One of the oil men's giving it. He asked me to come." His fingers bit into her soft flesh. "How about going with me and holding my hand? I don't know much about social events."

"You don't really want to go, do you?" she asked, looking over her shoulder at him knowingly.

He shook his head. "But it's expected. One of the penalties of being well-off. Socializing."

"Yes, I'll be very proud to go with you."

"Need a dress? I'll buy you one, since it was my idea."

She lowered her eyes. "No, thank you. I . . . I have one at my apartment, if you'll have someone drive me up there."

"Give Ted the key. He'll pick it up for you," he said, naming his chauffeur, who was also the new yardman.

"All right."

"Is it white?" he asked suddenly.

She glared at him. "No. It's black. Listen here, Everett Culhane, just because I've never . . . !"

He put a finger over her lips, silencing her. "I like you in white," he said simply. "It keeps me in line," he added with a wicked, slow smile.

"You just remember the nice new wife you'll have and the kids running around the house, and that will work very well," she said with a nip in her voice. "Shouldn't we go back? The carpet-layers may have some questions for me."

"Don't you like kids, Jenny?" he asked softly.

"Well, yes."

"Could you manage to have them and a career at the same time?" he asked with apparent indifference.

Her lips pouted softly. "Lots of women do," she said. "It's not the dark ages."

He searched her eyes. "I know that. But there are men who wouldn't want a working wife."

"Cavemen," she agreed.

He chuckled. "A woman like you might make a man nervous in that respect. You're pretty. Suppose some other man snapped you up while you were decorating his house? That would be hell on your husband's nerves."

"I don't want to get married," she informed him.

His eyebrows lifted. "You'd have children out of wedlock?"

"I didn't say that!"

"Yes, you did."

"Everett!" Her hands pushed at his chest. He caught them and lifted them slowly around his neck, tugging so that her body rested against his.

"Ummmm," he murmured on a smile, looking down at the softness of her body. "That feels nice. What were you saying, about children?"

"If... if I wanted them, then I guess I'd get married. But I'd still work. I mean... Everett, don't..." she muttered when he slid his hands down to her waist and urged her closer.

"Okay. You'd still work?"

His hands weren't pushing, but they were doing something crazy to her nerves. They caressed her back lazily, moving up to her hair to untie the ribbon that held it back.

"I'd work when the children started school. That was what I meant... will you stop that?" she grumbled, reaching back to halt his fingers.

He caught her hands, arching her so that he could look down and see the vivid tautness of her breasts against the thin fabric of her blouse.

"No bra?" he murmured, and the smile got bigger. "My, my, another Freudian slip?"

"Will you stop talking about bras and slips and let go of my hands, Mr. Culhane?" she asked curtly.

"I don't think you really want me to do that, Jenny," he murmured dryly.

"Why?"

"Because if I let go of your hands, I have to put mine somewhere else." He looked down pointedly at her blouse. "And there's really only one place I want to put them right now."

Her chest rose and fell quickly, unsteadily. His closeness and the long abstinence and the sun and warmth of the day

were all working on her. Her eyes met his suddenly and th
contact was like an electric jolt. All the memories cam
rushing back, all the old hungers.

"Do you remember that day you fell off the horse?" h
asked in a soft, low tone, while bees buzzed somewher
nearby. "And your blouse came open, and I looked dow
and you arched your back so that I could see you even bet
ter."

Her lips parted and she shook her head nervously.

"Oh, but you did," he breathed. "I'd seen you, watch
ing my mouth, wondering... and that day, it all came to
head. I looked at you and I wanted you. So simply. So hun
grily. I barely came to my senses in time, and before I did,
was hugging the life out of you. And you were letting me."

She remembered that, too. It had been so glorious, bein,
held that way.

He let go of her hands all at once and slid his arms aroun(
her, half lifting her off her feet. "Hard, Jenny," he whis
pered, drawing her slowly to him, so that she could feel he
breasts flattening against his warm chest. It was like bein
naked against him.

She caught her breath and moaned. His cheek slid agains
hers and he buried his face in her throat. His arms tight
ened convulsively. And he rocked her, and rocked her, an
she clung to him while all around them the wind blew an
the sun burned, and the world seemed to disappear.

His breath came roughly and his arms trembled. "I don'
feel this with other women," he said after a while. "Yo
make me hungry."

"As you keep reminding me," she whispered back, "I'n
not on the menu."

"Yes, I know." He brushed his mouth against her throa
and then lifted his head and slowly released her. "No mor
of that," he said on a rueful sigh, "unless you'd like to tr
making love on horseback. I've got a man coming to see m
about a new bull."

Her eyes widened. "Can people really make..." Sh
turned away, shaking her head.

"I don't know," he murmured, chuckling at her shyness. "I've never tried it. But there's always a first time."

"You just keep your hands to yourself," she cautioned as he put her into the saddle and climbed up behind her.

"I'm doing my best, honey," he said dryly. He reached around her to catch the reins and his arm moved lazily across her breasts, feeling the hardened tips. "Oh, Jenny," he breathed shakily, "next time you'd better wear an overcoat."

She wanted to stop him, she really did. But the feel of that muscular forearm was doing terribly exciting things to her. She felt her muscles tauten in a dead giveaway.

She knew it was going to happen even as he let go of the reins and his hands slid around her to lift and cup her breasts. She let him, turning her cheek against his chest with a tiny cry.

"The sweetest torture on earth," he whispered unsteadily. His hands were so tender, so gentle. He made no move to open the blouse, although he must have known that he could, that she would have let him. His lips moved warmly at her temple. "Jenny, you shouldn't let me touch you like this."

"Yes, I know," she whispered huskily. Her hands moved over his to pull them away, but they lingered on his warm brown fingers. Her head moved against his chest weakly.

"Do you want to lie down on the grass with me and make love?" he asked softly. "We could, just for a few minutes. We could kiss and touch each other, and nothing more."

She wanted to. She wanted it more than she wanted to breathe. But it was too soon. She wasn't sure of him. She only knew that he wanted her desperately and that she didn't dare pave the way for him. It was just a game to him. It kept him from getting bored while he found himself a wife. She loved him, but love on one side would never be enough.

"No, Rett," she said, although the words were torn from her. She moved his hands gently down, to her waist, and pressed them there. "No."

He drew away in a long, steady breath. "Levelheaded Jenny," he said finally. "Did you know?"

"Know what?"

"That if I'd gotten you on the grass, nothing would have saved you?"

She smiled ruefully. "It was kind of the other way around." She felt him shudder, and she turned and pressed herself into his arms. "I want you, too. Please don't do this to me. I can't be what you want. Please, let me decorate your house and go away. Don't hurt me any more, Rett."

He lifted and turned her so that she was lying across the saddle in his arms. He held her close and took the reins in his hand. "I'm going to have to rethink my strategy, I'm afraid." He sighed. "It isn't working."

She looked up. "What do you mean?"

He searched her eyes and bent and kissed her forehead softly. "Never mind, kitten. You're safe now. Just relax. I'll take you home."

She snuggled close and closed her eyes. This was a memory she'd keep as long as she lived, of riding across the meadow in Everett's arms on a lovely autumn morning. His wife would have other memories. But this one would always be her own, in the long, lonely years ahead. Her hand touched his chest lightly, and her heart ached for him. If only he could love her back. But love wasn't a word he trusted anymore, and she couldn't really blame him. He'd been hurt too much. Even by her, when she hadn't meant to. She sighed bitterly. It was all too late. If only it had been different. Tears welled up in her eyes. If only.

11

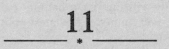

Jennifer wished for the tenth time that she'd refused Everett's invitation to the exclusive party in Victoria. It seemed that every single, beautiful woman in the world had decided to converge on the spot just to cast her eyes at Everett.

He did look good, Jennifer had to admit. There just wasn't anybody around who came close to matching him. Dressed in an elegant dinner jacket, he looked dark and debonair and very sophisticated. Not to mention sexy. The way the jacket and slacks fit, every muscle in that big body was emphasized in the most masculine way. It was anguish just to look at him; it was even worse to remember how it was to be held and touched by him. Jennifer felt her body tingle from head to toe at the memory of the day before, of his hands smoothing over her body, his voice husky and deep in her ear. And now there he stood making eyes at a gorgeous brunette.

She turned away and tossed down the entire contents of her brandy glass. If she hadn't been so tired from overworking herself, the brandy might not have been as potent. But it was her second glass and, despite the filling buffet, she was feeling the alcohol to a frightening degree. She kept telling herself that she didn't look bad herself, with her blond hair hanging long and loose around the shoulders of her low-cut clinging black dress. She was popular enough. So why didn't Everett dance one dance with her?

By the time she was danced around the room a couple of times by left-footed oilmen and dashing middle-aged married men, she felt like leaping over the balcony. How odd that at any party there were never any handsome, available bachelors.

"Sorry to cut in, but I have to take Jenny home," Everett said suddenly, cutting out a balding man in his fifties who was going over and over the latest political crisis with maddening intricacy.

Jennifer almost threw herself on Everett in gratitude. She mumbled something polite and completely untrue to the stranger, smiled, and stumbled into Everett's arms.

"Careful, honey, or we'll both wind up on the floor." He laughed softly. "Are you all right?"

"I'm just fine." She sighed, snuggling close. Her arms slid around him. "Everett, can I go to sleep now?"

He frowned and pulled her head up. "How much have you had to drink?"

"I lost count." She grinned. Her eyes searched his face blearily. "Gosh, Rett, you're so sexy."

A red stain highlighted his cheekbones. "You're drunk, all right. Come on."

"Where are we going?" she protested. "I want to dance."

"We'll dance in the car."

She frowned. "We can't stand up in there," she said reasonably.

He held her hand, tugging her along. They said good night to a couple she vaguely recognized as their hosts; then he got their coats from the maid and hustled her out into the night.

"Cold out here," she muttered. She nudged herself under his arm and pressed against his side with a sigh. "Better."

"For whom?" he ground out. His chest rose and fell heavily. "I wish I'd let Ted drive us."

"Why?" she murmured, giggling. "Are you afraid to be alone with me? You can trust me, honey," she said, nudging him. "I wouldn't seduce you, honest."

A couple passed them going down the steps, and the elderly woman gave Jennifer a curious look.

"He's afraid of me," Jennifer whispered. "He isn't on the pill, you see..."

"Jenny!" he growled, jerking her close.

"Not here, Rett!" she exclaimed. "My goodness, talk about impatience...!"

He was muttering something about a gag as he half-led, half-dragged her to the car.

"You old stick-in-the-mud, you." She laughed after he'd put her inside and climbed in next to her. "Did I embarrass you?"

He only glanced at her as he started the Lincoln. "You're going to hate yourself in the morning when I remind you what you've been saying. And I will," he promised darkly. "Ten times a day."

"You look gorgeous when you're mad," she observed. She moved across the seat and nuzzled close again. "I'll sleep with you tonight, if you like," she said gaily.

He stiffened and muttered something under his breath.

"Well, you've been trying to get me into bed with you, haven't you?" she asked. "Propositioning me that last day at the ranch, and then coming after me, and making all sorts of improper remarks...so now I agree, and what do you do? You get all red in the face and start cussing. Just like a man. The minute you catch a girl, you're already in pursuit of someone else, like that brunette you were dancing with," she added, glaring up at him. "Well, just don't expect that what you see is what you get, because I was in the ladies' room with her, and it's padded! I saw!"

He was wavering between anger and laughter. Laughter won. He started, and couldn't seem to stop.

"You won't think it's very funny if you take her out," she kept on, digging her own grave. Everything was fuzzy and pink and very pleasant. She felt so relaxed! "She's even smaller than I am," she muttered. "And her legs are just awful. She pulled up her skirt to fix her stockings...she hardly has any legs, they're so skinny!"

"Meow," he taunted.

She tossed back her long hair, and leaned her head back against the seat. Her coat had come open, revealing the deep neckline of the black dress. "Why won't you make love to me?"

"Because if I did, you'd scream your head off," he said reasonably. "Here, put your tired little head on my shoulder and close your eyes. You're soaked, honey."

She blinked. "I am not. It isn't raining."

He reached out an arm and pulled her against him. "Close your eyes, sweet," he said in a soft, tender tone. "I'll take good care of you."

"Will you sleep with me?" she murmured, resting her head on his shoulder.

"If you want me to."

She smiled and closed her eyes with a long sigh. "That would be lovely," she whispered. And it was the last thing she said.

Morning came with a blinding light and some confounded bird twittering his feathered head off outside the window.

"Oh, go away!" she whispered, and held her head. "An axe," she groaned. "There's an axe between my eyes. Bird, shut up!"

Soft laughter rustled her hair. She opened her eyes. Laughter?

Her head turned on the pillow and Everett's eyes looked back into her own. She gasped and tried to sit up, then groaned with the pain and fell back down again.

"Head hurt? Poor baby."

"You slept with me?" she burst out. She turned her head slowly to look at him. He was fully dressed, except for his shoes and jacket. He even had his shirt on. He was lying on top of the coverlet, and she was under it.

Slowly, carefully, she lifted the cover and looked. Her face flamed scarlet. She was dressed in nothing but a tiny pair of briefs. The rest of her was pink and tingling.

"Rett!" she burst out, horrified.

"I only undressed you," he said, leaning on an elbow to watch her. "Be reasonable, honey. You couldn't sleep in your evening gown. And," he added with a faint grin, "it wasn't my fault that you didn't have anything on under it. You can't imagine how shocked I was."

"That's right, I can't," she agreed, and her eyes accused him.

"I confess I did stare a little," he murmured. His hand brushed the unruly blond hair out of her eyes. "A lot," he corrected. "My God, Jenny," he said on a slow breath, "you are the most glorious sight undressed that I ever saw in my life. I nearly fainted."

"Shame on you!" she said, trying to feel outraged. It was difficult, because she was still tingling from the compliment.

"For what? For appreciating something beautiful?" He touched her nose with a long, lean finger. "Shame on you, for being embarrassed. I was a perfect gentleman. I didn't even touch you, except to put you under the covers."

"Oh."

"I thought I'd wait until you woke up, and do it then," he added with a grin.

Her fingers grabbed the covers tightly. "Oh, no, you don't!"

He moved closer, his fingers tangling in her blond hair as he loomed above her. "You had a lot to say about that brunette. Or don't you remember?"

She blinked. Brunette? Vaguely she remembered saying something insulting about the woman's body. Then she remembered vividly. Her face flamed.

"Something about how little she was, if I recall," he murmured dryly.

She bit her lower lip and her eyes met his uneasily. "Did I? How strange. Was she short?"

"That wasn't what you meant," he said. One lean hand moved down her shoulder and over the covers below her collarbone. "You meant, here, she was small."

If she looked up, she'd be finished. But she couldn't help it. Her eyes met his and the world seemed to narrow down to the two of them. She loved him so. Would it be wrong to kiss him just once more, to feel that hard, wonderful mouth on her own?

He seemed to read that thought, because his jaw tautened and his breathing became suddenly ragged. "The hell with being patient," he growled, reaching for the covers. "Come here."

He stripped them away and jerked her into his arms, rolling over with her, so that she was lying on him. Where his shirt was undone, her body pressed nakedly into his hairy chest.

His eyes were blazing as they looked up into hers. He deliberately reached down to yank his shirt away, his eyes on the point where her soft breasts were crushed against his body. Dark and light, she thought shakily, looking at the contrast between his dark skin and her pale flesh.

But still he didn't touch her. His hands moved up into her hair, oddly tender, at variance with the tension she could feel in his body.

"Don't you want...to touch me?" she whispered nervously.

"More than my own life," he confessed. "But I'm not going to. Come down here and kiss me."

"Why not?" she whispered, bending to give him her mouth.

"Because Consuelo's on her way up the stairs with coffee and toast," he breathed. "And she never knocks."

She sat up with a gasp. "Why didn't you say so!"

He laughed softly, triumphantly, his eyes eating her soft body as she climbed out of the bed and searched wildly for a robe.

"Here," he murmured, throwing his long legs over the bed. He reached under her pillow and got her nightgown. "Come here and I'll stuff you in it."

She didn't even question the impulse that made her obey him instantly. She lifted her arms as he held the nightgown over her head and gasped as he bent first and kissed her rosy breasts briefly, but with a tangible hunger. While she was getting over the shock, he tugged the long cotton gown over her head, lifted her, tossed her into the bed, and pulled the covers over her with a knowing smile.

And Consuelo opened the door before she could get out a word.

"Good morning!" The older woman laughed, handing the tray to Everett. "Also is hair of the dog, in the glass," she added with a wry glance at Jennifer. "To make the senorita's head a little better."

And she was gone as quickly as she'd come. Everett put the tray down beside Jennifer on the bed and poured cream into her coffee.

"Why did you do that?" she whispered, still shaking from the wild little caress.

"I couldn't help myself," he murmured, smiling at her. "I've wanted to, for a long time."

She took the coffee in trembling hands. He steadied them, watching her shaken features.

"It's part of lovemaking," he said softly. "Nothing sordid or shameful. When we make love, that's how I'll rouse you before I take you."

She shuddered, and the coffee cup began to rock again. Her eyes, meeting his, were wild with mingled fear and hunger.

"Except," he added quietly, "that I won't stop at the waist."

Coffee went everywhere. She cursed and muttered and grumbled and moped. But when she raised her glittering eyes to his the pupils dilated until they were almost black.

He laughed softly, menacingly. "Almost," he said enigmatically. "Almost there." He got up. "I'll get Consuelo to come and help you mop up." He turned with one hand on the doorknob, impossibly attractive, wildly sensuous with his hair ruffled and his shirt open and his bare, muscular chest showing. "The brunette was Jeb Doyle's daughter," he added. "She's looking for a husband. She rides like a man, she loves cattle and kids, she's twenty-eight and she lives about five miles south of here. She may be small, but she's got nice, full hips. Just right for having children. Her name's Sandy."

She was getting madder by the second. He was baiting her! She picked up the coffee cup and, without even thinking, threw it at him.

It shattered against the closed door. He went down the hall laughing like a banshee and she screamed after him. By the time Consuelo got to her, the rest of the coffee and the headache remedy had turned the bedspread a strange shade of tan.

For the next week, she gave Everett the coldest shoulder she could manage. He was gone from the ranch frequently, and she noticed it and remembered what he'd said about the brunette, and wanted desperately to kill him. No, not just kill him. Torture him. Slowly. Over an open fire.

It got worse. He started having supper with Jennifer every night, and the whole time he'd sit there and watch her and make infrequent but agonizing remarks about the brunette.

"Sandy's getting a new colt tomorrow," he mentioned one evening, smiling wistfully. "She asked if I'd come over and look at it for her."

"Can't she see it by herself?" she asked sweetly.

"Conformation is very important in a horse," he said. "I used to breed them years ago, before I got interested in cattle."

"Oh." She concentrated on her food.

"How's the decorating coming?"

"Fine," she said through her teeth. "We're getting the paper up in your bedroom tomorrow. Then there'll only be the other bedrooms to go. You never said how you liked the way the living room and the study came out."

"They're okay," he said. He lifted a forkful of dessert to his mouth and she wanted to jump up and stab him in the lip. Okay! And she'd spent days on the projects, working well into the night alongside the men!

He glanced up at her flushed face. "Wasn't that enthusiastic enough?" He took a sip of coffee. "Damn, Jenny, what a hell of a great job you're doing on the house!" he said with a big, artificial smile. "I'm pleased as punch!"

"I'd like to punch you," she muttered. She slammed down her napkin, slid out of the chair, and stomped out of the room.

Watching her, Everett's eyes narrowed and a faint, predatory smile curved his lips.

The next day, she concentrated on his bedroom. It was difficult to work in there, thinking about whose territory it was. Her eyes kept drifting to the bed where he slept, to the pillow where he laid his dark head. Once she paused beside it and ran her hand lovingly over the cover. Besotted, she told herself curtly. She was besotted, and it was no use. He was going to marry that skinny, flat-chested brunette!

She didn't even stop for lunch, much less supper. The workmen had left long before, and she was working on the last wall, when Everett came into the room and stood watching her with a cup of coffee in his hand.

"Have you given up eating?" he asked.

"Yep."

He cocked an eyebrow. "Want some coffee?"

"Nope."

He chuckled softly. "Bad imitation. You don't even look like Gary Cooper. You're too short."

She glared down at him. Her jeans were covered with glue. So were her fingers, her bare arms, and the front of her white T-shirt. "Did you want something?"

"Yes. To go to bed. I've got to get an early start in the morning. I'm taking Sandy fishing."

She stared into the bucket of glue and wondered how he'd look plastered to the wall. It was tempting, but dangerous.

"I'd like to finish this one wall," she murmured quietly.

"Go ahead. I'm going to have a shower." He stripped off his shirt. She glanced at him, fascinated by the dark perfection of him, by the ripple of muscle, the way the light played on his skin as he started to take off his ... *trousers!*

Her eyes jerked back to the glue and her hands trembled. "Everett?" she said in a squeaky voice.

"Well, don't look," he said reasonably. "I can't very well take a bath in my clothes."

"I could have left the room," she said.

"Why? Aren't you curious?" he taunted.

She gritted her teeth. "No!"

"Coward."

She put glue and more glue on a strip of wallpaper until the glue was three times as thick as the paper it was spread on. Not until she heard the shower running did she relax. She put the wallpaper in place and started scrambling down the ladder.

Unfortunately, just because the shower was running, it didn't mean that Everett was in it. She got down and started for the door, and there he stood, with a towel wrapped around his narrow hips and not another stitch on.

"Going somewhere?" he asked.

"Yes. Out of here!" she exclaimed, starting past him.

She never knew exactly how it happened. One minute she was walking toward the door, and the next she was lying flat on the bed with Everett's hard body crushing her into the mattress.

His chest rose and fell slowly, his eyes burned down into hers. Holding her gaze, he eased the towel away and bent to her mouth.

She trembled with kindling passion. It was so incredibly sweet to let her hands run over his hard, warm body, to feel the muscles of his back and arms and shoulders and hips. To let him kiss her softly, with growing intimacy. To know the crush of his body, the blatant force of his hunger for her. To love him with her hands and her mouth.

He lifted his head a minute later and looked into her awed es. "You're not so squeaky clean yourself," he said softly. Why don't you come and take a bath with me?"

Her hands touched his hard arms gently, lovingly. "Be- use we'd do more than bathe, and you know it," she re- ied on a soft sigh. "All you have to do is touch me, and u can have anything you want. It's always been like that. he only reason I'm still a virgin is that you haven't in- sted."

"Why do you think I haven't?" he prodded.

She shifted. "I don't know. Conscience, maybe?"

He bent and brushed his mouth softly over hers. "Go and ut on something soft and pretty. Have a shower. Then me downstairs to the living room and we'll talk."

She swallowed. "I thought you had to get to bed early. To ke Sandy fishing," she murmured resentfully.

"Did it ever occur to you that you might be formidable mpetition for her, if you cared to make the effort?" he ked, watching her. "Or didn't you know how easy it ould be to seduce me? And once you did that," he mur- ured, touching her soft mouth, "I'd probably feel obliged marry you. Not being on the pill and all," his eyes went ick to her with blazing intensity, "you could get preg- int."

Her breath caught in her throat. She never knew when he as teasing, when he was serious. And now, her mind was hirling.

While she worried over his intentions, he moved away om her and got to his feet, and she stared at him in help- ss fascination.

"You see?" he said, his voice deep and full of secrets, "it n't so shocking, is it?"

She lifted her eyes to his. "You're ... very ..." She tried find words.

"So are you, honey," he said. "Take your bath and I'll e you downstairs."

And he walked off, oblivious to her intent stare.

Minutes later, she went nervously down the staircase in white dress, her hair freshly washed and dried, loose aroun her shoulders. Something that had been brewing betwee them for a long time was coming abruptly to a head, and sh wasn't quite sure how to face it. She had a terrible feelin that he was going to proposition her again, and that she wa going to be stupid enough to accept. She loved him madl wanted him madly. That Sandy person was after him, an Jennifer was afraid. She couldn't quite accept the idea tha he might marry someone else. Despite the pain he'd cause her, she dwelled on the fear of losing him.

He was waiting for her. In beige trousers and a patterne beige shirt, he looked larger than life. All man. Sensual an incredibly attractive, especially when she got close enoug to catch the scent of his big body.

"Here," he said, offering her a small brandy.

"Thank you," she said politely. She took it, touching hi fingers, looking up into dark, quiet eyes. Her lips parte helplessly.

"Now sit down. I want to ask you something."

She sat on the edge of the sofa, but instead of taking th seat beside her, he knelt on the carpet just in front of he Because of his height, that put her on an unnerving leve with his eyes.

"Afraid of me, even now?" he asked softly.

"Especially now," she whispered, trembling. She put th snifter to one side and her trembling fingers reached out an touched the hard lines of his face. "Everett, I'm . . . so ver much in love with you," she said, her voice breaking. "I you want me to be your mistress . . . oh!"

She was on the carpet, in his arms, being kissed so hun grily that she couldn't even respond to him. His mouth de voured hers, hurting, bruising, and he trembled all over a if with a fever. His hands trembled as they touched, wit expert sureness, every line and curve of her body.

"Say it again," he said roughly, lifting his head ju enough to look at her.

Her body ached for his. She leaned toward him help-
sly. "I love you," she whispered, pride gone to ashes. "I
ve you, I love you!"

His head moved down to her bodice, his mouth nudged
the buttons, his hands bit into her back. She reached
wn blindly to get the fabric out of his way, to give him
ything, everything he wanted. There were no more sets. She belonged to him.

His mouth taught her sensations she'd never dreamed her
dy would feel. She breathed in gasps as his lips and teeth
plored her like some precious delicacy. Her hands held
m there, caressed his dark head, loved what he was doing
her.

He raised his head to look at her, smiling faintly at her
pt face, her wide, dark green eyes, her flushed face, the
rious disarray of her hair and her dress.

"I'll remember you like this for the rest of our lives," he
id, "the way you look right now, in the first sweet sec-
ds of passion. Do you want me badly?"

"Yes," she confessed. She brought his hand to her body
d held it against her taut flesh, brushing his knuckles
zily across it. "Feel?"

His nostrils flared and there was something reckless and
bridled in the eyes that held hers. "For a virgin," he
urmured, "you're pretty damned exciting to make love
"

She smiled wild, hotly. "Teach me."

"Not yet."

"Please."

He shook his head. He sat up, leaning back against the
fa with his long legs stretched out, and looked down at her
th a wicked smile. "Fasten your dress. You make me crazy
e that."

"I thought that was the whole point of the thing?" she
ked unsteadily.

"It was, until you started making declarations of love
was going to seduce you on the sofa. But now I suppo
we'd better do it right."

Her eyes widened in confusion. "I don't understand."

He pulled her up and across his lap. "Oh, the hell wi
it," he murmured, and opened the top button of her bodi
again. "God, I love to look at you!"

She swallowed hard. "Don't you want me?"

"Jenny." He laughed. He turned and brought her hi
very gently against his. "See?" he whispered.

She buried her face in his throat and he rocked her softl
tenderly.

"Then, why?" she asked on a moan.

"Because we have to do things in the right order, hone
First we get married, then we have sex, then we ma
babies."

She stiffened. "What?"

"Didn't you hear me?" He eased her head down on h
arm so that he could see her face.

"But, Sandy..." she faltered.

"Sandy is a nice girl," he murmured. "I danced o
dance with her, and she went back to her fiancé. He's a ni
boy. You'll like him."

"Fiancé!"

He jerked her close and held her hard, roughly. "I lo
you," he said in a voice that paralyzed her. His eyes blaz
with it, burned with it. "Oh, God, I love you, Jenny. Lo
you, want you, need you, in every single damned way the
is! If you want me to get on my knees, I'll do it, I'll do an
thing to make you forget what I said and did to you that la
day you were here." He bent and kissed her hungrily, soft
and lifted his head again, breathing hard. "I knew I lov
you then," he said, "when you handed me that check to pa
for my bull, and told me the truth. And all I could think
was that I loved you, and that you were out of my rea
forever. A career woman, a woman with some money of h
own, and I had nothing to offer you, no way to keep yo

And I chased you away, because it was torture to look at you and feel that way and have no hope at all.''

"Rett!" she burst out. Tears welled up in her eyes and she clung to him. "Oh, Rett, why didn't you tell me? I loved you so much!"

"I didn't know that," he said. His voice shook a little. His arms contracted. "I thought you were playing me along. It wasn't until you left that I realized that you must have cared one hell of a lot, to have done what you did for me." He shifted restlessly, and ground her against him. "Don't you know? Haven't you worked it out yet, why I sold the oil rights? I did it so that I'd have enough money to bring you back."

She caught her breath, and the tears overflowed onto his shirt, his throat.

"I didn't even have the price of a bus ticket." He laughed huskily, his voice tormented with memory. "And I knew that without you, the land wouldn't matter, because I couldn't live. I couldn't stay alive. So I sold the oil rights and I bought a car and I called Sally Wade. And then, I parked across the street to watch for you. And you came out," he said roughly, "laughing and looking so beautiful... holding onto that redheaded ass's arm! I could have broken your neck!"

"He was my friend. Nothing more." She nuzzled her face against him. "I thought you wanted revenge. I didn't realize...!"

"I wouldn't let Consuelo touch your room, did she tell you?" he whispered. "I left it the way it was. For the first week or so... I could still catch the scent of you on the pillow..." His voice broke, and she searched blindly for his mouth, and gave him comfort in the only way she could.

Her fingers touched his face, loved it; her lips told him things, secrets, that even words wouldn't. Gently, tenderly, she drew him up onto the sofa with her, and eased down beside him on it. And with her mouth and her hands and her body, she told him in the sweetest possible way that he'd never be alone as long as she lived.

"We can't," he whispered, trembling.

"Why?" she moaned softly.

"Because I want you in church, Jenny Wren," he whispered, easing her onto her side, soothing her with his hands and his mouth. "I want it all to be just right. I want to hear the words and watch your face when you say them, and tell the whole world that you're my woman. And then," he breathed softly, "then we'll make love and celebrate in the sweetest, most complete way there is. But not like this, darling. Not on a sofa, without the rings or the words or the beauty of taking our vows together." He drew back and looked into her damp eyes. "You'll want that, when you look back on our first time. You'll want it when the children are old enough to be told how we met, how we married. You won't want a tarnished memory to put in your scrapbook."

She kissed him softly. "Thank you."

"I love you," he said, smiling. "I can wait. If," he added with a lift of his eyebrow, "you'll put your clothes back on and stop trying to lead me into a life of sin."

"I haven't taken them off," she protested.

"You have." He got up and looked down at her, with the dress around her waist.

"Well, look at you," she grumbled. His shirt was off and out of his trousers, and his belt was unbuckled.

"You did it," he accused.

She burst out laughing as she buttoned buttons. "I suppose I did. Imagine me, actually trying to seduce you. And after all the times I accused you of it!"

"I don't remember complaining," he remarked.

She got to her feet and went into his arms with a warm sigh. "Me, either. How soon can we get married?"

"How about Friday?"

"Three days?" she groaned.

"You can take cold showers," he promised her. "And finish decorating the house. You're not going to have a lot of time for decorating after we're married."

"I'm not, huh?" she murmured. "What will I be doing?"

"I hoped you might ask," he returned with a smile. He bent his head, lifting her gently in his arms. "This is what you'll be doing." And he kissed her with such tenderness that she felt tears running down her warm cheeks. Since it seemed like such a lovely occupation, she didn't even protest. After all, she'd have plenty of time for decorating when the children started school. Meanwhile, Everett showed promise of being a full-time job.

* * * * *

Back by popular demand, some of Diana Palmer's earliest published books are available again!

Several years ago, Diana Palmer began her writing career. Sweet, compelling and totally unforgettable, these are the love stories that enchanted readers everywhere.

This month, six more of these wonderful stories will be available in DIANA PALMER DUETS—Books 4, 5 and 6. Each DUET contains two powerful stories plus an introduction by Diana Palmer. Don't miss:

Book Four	AFTER THE MUSIC DREAM'S END
Book Five	BOUND BY A PROMISE PASSION FLOWER
Book Six	TO HAVE AND TO HOLD THE COWBOY AND THE LADY

Double your reading pleasure this fall with two Award of Excellence titles written by two of your favorite authors.

Available in September

DUNCAN'S BRIDE
by Linda Howard
Silhouette Intimate Moments #349

Mail-order bride Madelyn Patterson was nothing like what Reese Duncan expected—and everything he needed.

Available in October

THE COWBOY'S LADY
by Debbie Macomber
Silhouette Special Edition #626

The Montana cowboy wanted a little lady at his beck and call—the ''lady'' in question saw things differently....

These titles have been selected to receive a special laurel—the Award of Excellence. Look for the distinctive emblem on the cover. It lets you know there's something truly wonderful inside!

Just when you thought all the good men had gotten away, along comes ...

SILHOUETTE® 3 *Desire*™

MAN OF THE MONTH 1990

Twelve magnificent stories by twelve of your favorite authors.

In January, FIRE AND RAIN by Elizabeth Lowell

In February, A LOVING SPIRIT by Annette Broadrick

In March, RULE BREAKER by Barbara Boswell

In April, SCANDAL'S CHILD by Ann Major

In May, KISS ME KATE by Helen R. Myers

In June, SHOWDOWN by Nancy Martin

In July, HOTSHOT by Kathleen Korbel

In August, TWICE IN A BLUE MOON by Dixie Browning

In September, THE LONER by Lass Small

In October, SLOW DANCE by Jennifer Greene

In November, HUNTER by Diana Palmer

In December, HANDSOME DEVIL by Joan Hohl

Every man is someone you'll want to get to know ... and love. So get out there and find your man!

Silhouette Romance®

LONG, TALL TEXANS

Diana Palmer's fortieth story for Silhouette... chosen as an Award of Excellence title!

CONNAL
Diana Palmer

This month, Diana Palmer's bestselling LONG, TALL TEXANS series continues with CONNAL. The skies get cloudy on C. C. Tremayne's home on the range when Penelope Mathews decides to protect him—by marrying him!

One specially selected title receives the Award of Excellence every month. Look for CONNAL this month... only from Silhouette Romance.

FOUR UNIQUE SERIES
FOR EVERY WOMAN YOU ARE...

Silhouette Romance

Love, at its most tender, provocative,
emotional... in stories that will make you laugh and
cry while bringing you the magic of falling in love.

6 titles
per month

Silhouette Special Edition

Sophisticated, substantial and packed with
emotion, these powerful novels of life and love will
capture your imagination and steal your heart.

6 titles
per month

SILHOUETTE Desire

Open the door to romance and passion. Humorous,
emotional, compelling—yet always a believable
and sensuous story—Silhouette Desire never
fails to deliver on the promise of love.

6 titles
per month

Silhouette Intimate Moments

Enter a world of excitement, of romance
heightened by suspense, adventure and the
passions every woman dreams of. Let us
sweep you away.

4 titles
per month